Praise fo

"Here are nine
of ordinary people trying to hold it together when everything is falling apart. I've been a story aficionado for several decades now and I can't think of a more accomplished master of the fantastic short form. Prepare to hunt feral Girl Scouts! Pack your bags for a dinosaur safari! Invite friends to your end of the world party! Dale Bailey is the poet of the apocalypse; his stories are guaranteed to haunt you."

—James Patrick Kelly,
winner of the Hugo, Nebula and Locus awards for short fiction

"Bailey is one of the most powerful voices in contemporary short science fiction, merging the best tools of literary writing with a savvy genre eye, and creating stories that, in their strangeness, are personally, emotionally revelatory."

—Rachel Swirsky,
winner of the Nebula Award

"Dale Bailey has been one of the best kept secrets of the fantasy genre for too many years. A true child of Bradbury, using language as pristine and as robust as his imagination, he writes beautiful, heartbreaking stories for our dark age. It's time everyone knew: Bailey is one of the best writers we've got."

—Nathan Ballingrud,
winner of the Shirley Jackson Award and finalist for the World Fantasy Award

"No stories being written today move me like Dale Bailey's. He always roams farther than most of us dare, and returns bearing something true."

—Andy Duncan,
winner of the World Fantasy Award and the Nebula Award

Also by Dale Bailey

The Subterranean Season
House of Bones
The Fallen
Sleeping Policemen (with Jack Slay, Jr.)

The Resurrection Man's Legacy and Other Stories

THE END OF THE END OF EVERYTHING

THE END OF THE END OF EVERYTHING

STORIES BY
DALE BAILEY

Arche Press

The End of the End of Everything is a collection of fictional works. Names, characters, places, and incidents are the products of the author's imagination or are used in an absolutely fictitious manner. Any resemblance to actual events, locales, or persons—living or dead—is entirely coincidental.

Original publication information about the respective stories is located on page 229.

This is A002, and it has an ISBN of 978-1-63023-007-4.

This book was printed in the United States of America, and it is published by Arche Press, an imprint of Resurrection House (Puyallup, WA).

One by one, the Christmas lights along the coastline blinked out.

Cover Art by Galen Dara
Cover Design by Darin Bradley
Book Design by Aaron Leis

First Arche Press edition: March 2015.

www.resurrectionhouse.com

Patty

Contents

The End of the World As We Know It

Between 1347 and 1450 AD, bubonic plague overran Europe, killing some 75 million people. The plague, dubbed the Black Death because of the black pustules that erupted on the skin of the afflicted, was caused by a bacterium now known as *Yersinia pestis*. The Europeans of the day, lacking access to microscopes or knowledge of disease vectors, attributed their misfortune to an angry God. Flagellants roamed the land, hoping to appease His wrath. "They died by the hundreds, both day and night," Agnolo di Tura tells us. "I buried my five children with my own hands . . . so many died that all believed it was the end of the world."

Today, the population of Europe is about 729 million.

Evenings, Wyndham likes to sit on the porch, drinking. He likes gin, but he'll drink anything. He's not particular. Lately, he's been watching it get dark—really *watching* it, I mean, not just sitting there—and so far he's concluded that the cliché is wrong. Night doesn't fall. It's more complex than that.

Not that he's entirely confident in the accuracy of his observations.

It's high summer just now, and Wyndham often begins drinking at two or three, so by the time the sun sets, around nine, he's usually pretty drunk. Still, it seems to him that, if anything, night *rises*, gathering first in inky pools under the trees, as if it has leached up from underground reservoirs, and then spreading, out toward the borders of the yard and up toward the yet-lighted sky. It's only toward the end that anything falls—the blackness of deep space, he supposes, unscrolling from high above the earth. The two planes of darkness meet somewhere in the middle, and that's night for you.

That's his current theory, anyway.

It isn't his porch, incidentally, but then it isn't his gin either—except in the sense that, insofar as Wyndham can tell anyway, *everything* now belongs to him.

End-of-the-world stories usually come in one of two varieties.

In the first, the world ends with a natural disaster, either unprecedented or on an unprecedented scale. Floods lead all other contenders—God himself, we're told, is fond of that one—though plagues have their advocates. A renewed ice age is also popular. Ditto drought.

In the second variety, irresponsible human beings bring it on themselves. Mad scientists and corrupt bureaucrats, usually. An exchange of ICBMs is the typical route, although the scenario has dated in the present geo-political environment.

Feel free to mix and match:

Genetically engineered flu virus, anyone? Melting polar ice caps?

On the day the world ended, Wyndham didn't even realize it *was* the end of the world—not right away, anyway. For him, at that point in his life, pretty much *every* day seemed like the end of the world. This was not a consequence of a chemical imbalance, either. It was a consequence of working for UPS, where, on the day the world ended Wyndham had been employed for sixteen years, first as a loader, then in sorting, and finally in the coveted position of driver, the brown uniform and everything. By this time the company had gone public and he also owned some shares. The money was good—very good, in fact. Not only that, he liked his job.

Still, the beginning of every goddamn day started off feeling like a cataclysm. *You* try getting up at 4:00 AM every morning and see how you feel.

This was his routine:

At 4:00 AM, the alarm went off—an old-fashioned alarm, he wound it up every night. (He couldn't tolerate the radio before he drank his coffee.) He always turned it off right away, not wanting to wake his wife. He showered in the spare bathroom (again, not wanting to wake his wife; her name was Ann), poured coffee into his thermos, and ate something he probably shouldn't—a bagel, a Pop Tart—while he stood over the sink. By then, it would be 4:20, 4:25 if he was running late.

Then he would do something paradoxical: He would go back to his bedroom and wake up the wife he'd spent the last twenty minutes trying not to disturb.

"Have a good day," Wyndham always said.

His wife always did the same thing, too. She would screw her face into her pillow and smile. "Ummm," she would say, and it was usually such a cozy, loving, early-morning cuddling kind of "ummm" that it almost made getting up at four in the goddamn morning worth it.

Wyndham heard about the World Trade Center—*not* the end of the world, though to Wyndham it sure as hell felt that way—from one of his customers.

The customer—her name was Monica—was one of Wyndham's regulars: a Home Shopping Network fiend, this woman. She was big, too. The kind of woman of whom people say "She has a nice personality" or "She has such a pretty face." She did have a nice personality, too—at least Wyndham thought she did. So he was concerned when she opened the door in tears.

"What's wrong?" he said.

Monica shook her head, at a loss for words. She waved him inside. Wyndham, in violation of about fifty UPS regulations, stepped in after her. The house smelled of sausage and floral air freshener. There was Home Shopping Network shit everywhere. I mean, *everywhere*.

Wyndham hardly noticed.

His gaze was fixed on the television. It was showing an airliner flying into the World Trade Center. He stood there and watched it from three or four different angles before he noticed the Home Shopping Network logo in the lower right-hand corner of the screen.

That was when he concluded that it must be the end of the world. He couldn't imagine the Home Shopping Network preempting regularly scheduled programming for anything less.

The Muslim extremists who flew airplanes into the World Trade Center, into the Pentagon, and into the unyielding earth of an otherwise unremarkable field in Pennsylvania, were secure, we are told, in the knowledge of their imminent translation into paradise.

There were nineteen of them.

Every one of them had a name.

Wyndham's wife was something of a reader. She liked to read in bed. Before she went to sleep she always marked her spot using a bookmark Wyndham had given her for her birthday one year: it was a cardboard bookmark with a yarn ribbon at the top, and a picture of a rainbow arching high over white-capped mountains. *Smile*, the bookmark said. *God loves you*.

Wyndham wasn't much of a reader, but if he'd picked up his wife's book the day the world ended he would have found the first few pages interesting. In the opening chapter, God raptures all true Christians to Heaven. This includes true Christians who are driving cars and trains and airplanes, resulting in uncounted lost lives as well as significant damages to personal property. If Wyndham *had* read the book, he'd have thought of a bumper sticker he sometimes saw from high in his UPS truck. *Warning*, the bumper sticker read, *In case of Rapture, this car will be unmanned*. Whenever he saw that bumper sticker, Wyndham imagined cars crashing, planes falling from the sky, patients abandoned on the operating table—pretty much the scenario of his wife's book, in fact.

Wyndham went to church every Sunday, but he couldn't help wondering what would happen to the untold millions of people who *weren't* true Christians—whether by choice or by the geographical fluke of having been born in some place like Indonesia. What if they were crossing the street in front of one of those cars, he wondered, or watering lawns those planes would soon plow into?

∞

But I was saying:

On the day the world ended Wyndham didn't understand right away what had happened. His alarm clock went off the way it always did and he went through his normal routine. Shower in the spare bath, coffee in the thermos, breakfast over the sink (a chocolate donut, this time, and gone a little stale). Then he went back to the bedroom to say good-bye to his wife.

"Have a good day," he said, as he always said, and, leaning over, he shook her a little: not enough to really wake her, just enough to get her stirring. In sixteen years of performing this ritual, minus federal holidays and two weeks of paid vacation in the summer, Wyndham had pretty much mastered it. He could cause her to stir without quite waking her up just about every time.

So to say he was surprised when his wife didn't screw her face into her pillow and smile is something of an understatement. He was shocked, actually. And there was an additional consideration: she hadn't said, "Ummm," either. Not the usual luxurious, warm-morning-bed kind of "ummm," and not the infrequent but still familiar stuffy, I-have-a-cold-and-my-head-aches kind of "ummm," either.

No "ummm" at all.

The air-conditioning cycled off. For the first time Wyndham noticed a strange smell—a faint, organic funk, like spoiled milk, or unwashed feet.

Standing there in the dark, Wyndham began to have a very bad feeling. It was a different kind of bad feeling than the one he'd had in Monica's living room watching airliners plunge again and again into the World Trade Center. That had been a powerful but largely impersonal bad feeling—I say "largely impersonal" because Wyndham had a third cousin who worked at Cantor Fitzgerald. (The cousin's name was Chris; Wyndham had to look it up in his address book every year when he sent out cards celebrating the birth of his personal savior.) The bad feeling he began to have when his wife failed to say "ummm," on the other hand, was powerful and *personal*.

Concerned, Wyndham reached down and touched his wife's face. It was like touching a woman made of wax, lifeless and cool, and it was at that moment—that moment precisely—that Wyndham realized the world had come to an end.

Everything after that was just details.

Beyond the mad scientists and corrupt bureaucrats, characters in end-of-the-world stories typically come in one of three varieties.

The first is the rugged individualist. You know the type: self-reliant, iconoclastic loners who know how to use firearms and deliver babies. By story's end, they're well on their way to Re-Establishing Western Civilization—though they're usually smart enough not to return to the Bad Old Ways.

The second variety is the post-apocalyptic bandit. These characters often come in gangs, and they face off against the rugged survivor types. If you happen to prefer cinematic incarnations of the end-of-the-world tale, you can usually recognize them by their penchant for bondage gear, punked-out haircuts, and customized vehicles. Unlike the rugged survivors, the post-apocalyptic bandits embrace the Bad Old Ways—though they're not displeased by the expanded opportunities to rape and pillage.

The third type of character—also pretty common, though a good deal less so than the other two—is the world-weary sophisticate. Like Wyndham, such characters drink too much; unlike Wyndham, they suffer badly from *ennui*. Wyndham suffers too, of course, but whatever he suffers from, you can bet it's not *ennui*.

We were discussing details, though:

Wyndham did the things people do when they discover a loved one dead. He picked up the phone and dialed 9-1-1. There seemed to be something wrong with the line, however; no one picked up on the other end. Wyndham took a deep breath, went into the kitchen, and tried the extension. Once again he had no success.

The reason, of course, was that, this being the end of the world, all the people who were supposed to answer the phones were dead. Imagine them being swept away by a tidal wave if that helps—which is exactly what happened to more than 3000 people during a storm in Pakistan in 1960. (Not that this is *literally* what happened to the operators who would have taken Wyndham's 9-1-1 call, you understand; but more about what *really* happened to them later—the important thing is that one moment they had been alive; the next they were dead. Like Wyndham's wife.)

Wyndham gave up on the phone.

He went back into the bedroom. He performed a fumbling version of mouth-to-mouth resuscitation on his wife for fifteen minutes or so, and then he gave that up, too. He walked into his daughter's bedroom (she was twelve and her name was Ellen). He found her lying on her back, her mouth slightly agape. He reached down to shake her—he was going to tell her that something terrible had happened, that her mother had died—but he found that something terrible had happened to her as well. The same terrible thing, in fact.

Wyndham panicked.

He raced outside, where the first hint of red had begun to bleed up over the horizon. His neighbor's automatic irrigation system was on, the heads whickering in the silence, and as he sprinted across the lawn, Wyndham felt the spray, like a cool hand against his face. Then, chilled, he was standing on his neighbor's stoop. Hammering the door with both fists. Screaming.

After a time—he didn't know how long—a dreadful calm settled over him. There was no sound but the sound of the sprinklers, throwing glittering arcs of spray into the halo of the street light on the corner.

He had a vision, then. It was as close as he had ever come to a moment of genuine prescience. In the vision, he saw the suburban houses stretching away in silence before him. He saw the silent bedrooms. In them, curled beneath the sheets, he saw a legion of sleepers, also silent, who would never again wake up.

Wyndham swallowed.

Then he did something he could not have imagined doing even twenty minutes ago. He bent over, fished the key from its hiding place between the bricks, and let himself inside his neighbor's house.

The neighbor's cat slipped past him, mewing querulously. Wyndham had already reached down to retrieve it when he noticed the smell—that unpleasant, faintly organic funk. Not spoiled milk, either. And not feet. Something worse: soiled diapers, or a clogged toilet.

Wyndham straightened, the cat forgotten.

"Herm?" he called. "Robin?"

No answer.

Inside, Wyndham picked up the phone, and dialed 9-1-1. He listened to it ring for a long time; then, without bothering to turn it off, Wyndham dropped the phone to the floor. He made his way through the silent house, snapping on lights. At the door to the master bedroom, he hesitated. The odor—it was unmistakable now, a mingled stench of urine and feces, of all the body's muscles relaxing at once—was stronger here. When he spoke again, whispering really—

"Herm? Robin?"

—he no longer expected an answer.

Wyndham turned on the light. Robin and Herm were shapes in the bed, unmoving. Stepping closer, Wyndham stared down at them. A fleeting series of images cascaded through his mind, images of Herm and Robin working the grill at the neighborhood block party or puttering in their vegetable garden. They'd had a knack for tomatoes, Robin and Herm. Wyndham's wife had always loved their tomatoes.

Something caught in Wyndham's throat.

He went away for a while then.

The world just grayed out on him.

When he came back, Wyndham found himself in the living room, standing in front of Robin and Herm's television. He turned it on and cycled through the channels, but there was nothing on. Literally nothing. Snow, that's all. Seventy-five channels of snow. The end of the world had always been televised in Wyndham's experience. The fact that it wasn't being televised now suggested that it really *was* the end of the world.

∞

This is not to suggest that television validates human experience—of the end of the world or indeed of anything else, for that matter.

You could ask the people of Pompeii, if most of them hadn't died in a volcano eruption in 79 AD, nearly two millennia before television. When Vesuvius erupted, sending lava thundering down the mountainside at four miles a minute, some 16,000 people perished. By some freakish geological quirk, some of them—their shells, anyway—were preserved, frozen inside casts of volcanic ash. Their arms are outstretched in pleas for mercy, their faces frozen in horror.

For a fee, you can visit them today.

∞

Here's one of my favorite end-of-the-world scenarios by the way:

Carnivorous plants.

∞

Wyndham got in his car and went looking for assistance—a functioning telephone or television, a helpful passer-by. He found instead more non-functioning telephones and televisions. And, of course, more non-functioning people: lots of those, though he had to look harder for them than you might have expected. They weren't scattered in the streets, or dead at the wheels of their cars in a massive traffic jam—though Wyndham supposed that might have been the case elsewhere in the world, where the catastrophe—whatever it was—had fallen square in the middle of the morning rush.

Here, however, it seemed to have caught most folks at home in bed; as a result, the roads were more than usually passable.

At a loss—numb, really—Wyndham drove to work. He might have been in shock by then. He'd gotten accustomed to the smell, anyway, and the corpses of the night shift—men and women he'd known for sixteen years, in some cases—didn't shake him as much. What *did* shake him was the sight of all the packages in the sorting area: he was struck suddenly by the fact that none of them would ever be delivered. So Wyndham loaded his truck and went out on his route. He wasn't sure why he did it—maybe because he'd rented a movie once in which a post-apocalyptic drifter scavenges a US Postal uniform and manages to Re-Establish Western Civilization (but not the Bad Old Ways) by assuming the postman's appointed rounds. The futility of Wyndham's own efforts quickly became evident, however.

He gave it up when he found that even Monica—or, as he more often thought of her, the Home Shopping Network Lady—was no longer in the business of receiving packages. Wyndham found her face down on the kitchen floor, clutching a shattered coffee mug in one hand. In death she had neither a pretty face nor a nice personality. She did have that same ripe unpleasant odor, however. In spite of it, Wyndham stood looking down at her for the longest time. He couldn't seem to look away.

When he finally *did* look away, Wyndham went back to the living room where he had once watched nearly 3000 people die, and opened her package himself. When it came to UPS rules, the Home Shopping Network Lady's living room was turning out to be something of a post-apocalyptic zone in its own right.

Wyndham tore the mailing tape off and dropped it on the floor. He opened the box. Inside, wrapped safely in three layers of bubble wrap, he found a porcelain statue of Elvis Presley.

Elvis Presley, the King of Rock 'N' Roll, died August 16, 1977, while sitting on the toilet. An autopsy revealed that he had ingested an impressive cocktail of prescription drugs—including codeine, ethinimate, methaqualone, and various barbiturates. Doctors also found trace elements of Valium, Demerol, and other pharmaceuticals in his veins.

For a time, Wyndham comforted himself with the illusion that the end of the world had been a local phenomenon. He sat in his truck outside the Home Shopping Network Lady's house and awaited rescue—the sound of sirens or approaching choppers, whatever. He fell asleep cradling the porcelain statue of Elvis. He woke up at dawn, stiff from sleeping in the truck, to find a stray dog nosing around outside.

Clearly rescue would not be forthcoming.

Wyndham chased off the dog and placed Elvis gently on the sidewalk. Then he drove off, heading out of the city. Periodically, he stopped, each time confirming what he had already known the minute he touched his dead wife's face: the end of the world was upon him. He found nothing but non-functioning telephones, non-functioning televisions, and non-functioning people. Along the way he listened to a lot of non-functioning radio stations.

ꝏ

You, like Wyndham, may be curious about the catastrophe that has befallen everyone in the world around him. You may even be wondering why Wyndham has survived.

End-of-the-world tales typically make a big deal about such things, but Wyndham's curiosity will never be satisfied. Unfortunately, neither will yours.

Shit happens.

It's the end of the world after all.

ꝏ

The dinosaurs never discovered what caused *their* extinction, either.

At this writing, however, most scientists agree that the dinosaurs met their fate when an asteroid nine miles wide plowed into the Earth just south of the Yucatan Peninsula, triggering gigantic tsunamis, hurricane-force winds, worldwide forest fires, and a flurry of volcanic activity. The crater is still there—it's 120 miles wide and more than a mile deep—but the dinosaurs, along with 75% of the other species then alive, are gone. Many of them died in the impact, vaporized in the explosion. Those that survived the initial cataclysm would have perished soon after as acid rain poisoned the world's water and dust obscured the sun, plunging the planet into a years-long winter.

For what it's worth, this impact was merely the most dramatic in a long series of mass extinctions; they occur in the fossil record at roughly 30 million-year intervals. Some scientists have linked these intervals to the solar system's periodic journey through the galactic plane, which dislodges millions of comets from the Oort cloud beyond Pluto, raining them down on Earth. This theory, still contested, is called the Shiva Hypothesis in honor of the Hindu god of destruction.

∞

The inhabitants of Lisbon would have appreciated the allusion on November 1, 1755, when the city was struck by an earthquake measuring 8.5 on the Richter Scale. The tremor leveled more than 12,000 homes and ignited a fire that burned for six days.

More than 60,000 people perished.

This event inspired Voltaire to write *Candide*, in which Dr. Pangloss advises us that this is the best of all possible worlds.

∞

Wyndham could have filled the gas tank in his truck. There were gas stations at just about every exit along the highway, and *they* seemed to be functioning well enough. He didn't bother, though.

When the truck ran out of gas, he just pulled to the side of the road, hopped down, and struck off across the fields. When it started getting dark—this was before he had launched himself on the study of just how it is night falls—he took shelter in the nearest house.

It was a nice place, a two-story brick house set well back from the country road he was by then walking on. It had some big trees in the front yard. In the back, a shaded lawn sloped down to the kind of woods you see in movies, but not often in real life: enormous, old trees with generous, leaf-carpeted avenues. It was the kind of place his wife would have loved, and he regretted having to break a window to get inside. But there it was: it was the end of the world and he had to have a place to sleep. What else could he do?

∞

Wyndham hadn't planned to stay there, but when he woke up the next morning he couldn't think of anywhere to go. He found two non-functional old people in one upstairs bedroom and he tried to do for them what he had not been able to do for his wife and daughter: using a spade from the garage, he started digging a grave in the front yard. After an hour or so, his hands began to blister and crack. His muscles—soft from sitting behind the wheel of a UPS truck for all those years—rebelled.

He rested for a while, and then he loaded the old people into the car he found parked in the garage—a slate-blue Volvo station wagon with 37,312 miles on the odometer. He drove them a mile or two down the road, pulled over, and laid them out, side-by-side in a grove of beech trees. He tried to say some words over them before he left—his wife would have wanted him to—but he couldn't think of anything appropriate so he finally gave it up and went back to the house.

It wouldn't have made much difference: though Wyndham didn't know it, the old people were lapsed Jews. According to the faith Wyndham shared with his wife, they were doomed to burn in hell for all eternity anyway. Both of them were first-generation immigrants; most of their families had already been burned up in ovens at Dachau and Buchenwald.

Burning wouldn't have been anything new for them.

Speaking of fires, the Triangle Shirt Waist Factory in New York City burned on March 25, 1911. One hundred and forty-six people died. Many of them might have survived, but the factory's owners had locked the exits to prevent theft.

Rome burned, too. It is said that Nero fiddled.

Back at the house, Wyndham washed up and made himself a drink from the liquor cabinet he found in the kitchen. He'd never been much of a drinker before the world ended, but he didn't see any reason not to give it a try now. His experiment proved such a success that he began sitting out on the porch nights, drinking gin and watching the sky. One night he thought he saw a plane, lights blinking as it arced high overhead. Later, sober, he concluded that it must have been a satellite, still whipping around the planet, beaming down telemetry to empty listening stations and abandoned command posts.

A day or two later the power went out. And a few days after that, Wyndham ran out of liquor. Using the Volvo, he set off in search of a town. Characters in end-of-the-world stories commonly drive vehicles of two types: the jaded sophisticates tend to drive souped-up sports cars, often racing them along the Australian coastline because what else do they have to live for; everyone else drives rugged SUVs. Since the 1991 Persian Gulf War—in which some 23,000 people died, most of them Iraqi conscripts killed by American smart bombs—military-style Humvees have been especially coveted. Wyndham, however, found the Volvo entirely adequate to his needs.

No one shot at him.

He was not assaulted by a roving pack of feral dogs.

He found a town after only fifteen minutes on the road. He didn't see any evidence of looting. Everybody was too dead to loot; that's the way it is at the end of the world.

On the way, Wyndham passed a sporting goods store where he did not stop to stock up on weapons or survival equipment. He passed numerous abandoned vehicles, but he did not stop to siphon off some gas. He *did* stop at the liquor store, where he smashed a window with a rock and helped himself to several cases of gin, whiskey, and vodka. He also stopped at the grocery store, where he found the reeking bodies of the night crew sprawled out beside carts of supplies that would never make it onto the shelves. Holding a handkerchief over his nose, Wyndham loaded up on tonic water and a variety of other mixers. He also got some canned goods, though he didn't feel any imperative to stock up beyond his immediate needs. He ignored the bottled water.

In the book section, he *did* pick up a bartender's guide.

Some end-of-the-world stories present us with two post-apocalypse survivors, one male and one female. These two survivors take it upon themselves to Re-Populate the Earth, part of their larger effort to Re-Establish Western Civilization without the Bad Old Ways. Their names are always artfully withheld until the end of the story, at which point they are invariably revealed to be Adam and Eve.

The truth is, almost all end-of-the-world stories are at some level Adam-and-Eve stories. That may be why they enjoy such popularity. In the interests of total disclosure, I will admit that in fallow periods of my own sexual life—and, alas, these periods have been more frequent than I'd care to admit—I've often found Adam-and-Eve post-holocaust fantasies strangely comforting. Being the only man alive significantly reduces the potential for rejection in my view. And it cuts performance anxiety practically to nothing.

There's a woman in this story, too.

Don't get your hopes up.

By this time, Wyndham has been living in the brick house for almost two weeks. He sleeps in the old couple's bedroom, and he sleeps pretty well, but maybe that's the gin. Some mornings he wakes up disoriented, wondering where his wife is and how he came to be in a strange place. Other mornings he wakes up feeling like he dreamed everything else and this has always been his bedroom.

One day, though, he wakes up early, to gray pre-dawn light. Someone is moving around downstairs. Wyndham's curious, but he's not afraid. He doesn't wish he'd stopped at the sporting goods store and gotten a gun. Wyndham has never shot a gun in his life. If he did shoot someone—even a post-apocalyptic punk with cannibalism on his mind—he'd probably have a breakdown.

Wyndham doesn't try to disguise his presence as he goes downstairs. There's a woman in the living room. She's not bad looking, this woman—blonde in a washed-out kind of way, trim, and young, twenty-five, thirty at the most. She doesn't look extremely clean, and she doesn't smell much better, but hygiene hasn't been uppermost on Wyndham's mind lately, either. Who is he to judge?

"I was looking for a place to sleep," the woman says.

"There's a spare bedroom upstairs," Wyndham tells her.

ꝏ

The next morning—it's really almost noon, but Wyndham has gotten into the habit of sleeping late—they eat breakfast together: a Pop Tart for the woman, a bowl of dry Cheerios for Wyndham.

They compare notes, but we don't need to get into that. It's the end of the world and the woman doesn't know how it happened any more than Wyndham does or you do or anybody ever does. She does most of the talking, though. Wyndham's never been much of a talker, even at the best of times.

He doesn't ask her to stay. He doesn't ask her to leave.

He doesn't ask her much of anything.

That's how it goes all day.

ꝏ

Sometimes the whole sex thing *causes* the end of the world.

In fact, if you'll permit me to reference Adam and Eve just one more time, sex and death have been connected to the end of the world ever since—well, the beginning of the world. Eve, despite warnings to the contrary, eats of the fruit of the Tree of Knowledge of Good and Evil and realizes she's naked—that is, a sexual being. Then she introduces Adam to the idea by giving him a bite of the fruit.

God punishes Adam and Eve for their transgression by kicking them out of Paradise and introducing death into the world. And there you have it: the first apocalypse, *eros* and *thanatos* all tied up in one neat little bundle, and it's all Eve's fault.

No wonder feminists don't like that story. It's a pretty corrosive view of female sexuality when you think about it.

Coincidentally, perhaps, one of my favorite end-of-the-world stories involves some astronauts who fall into a time warp; when they get out they learn that all the men are dead. The women have done pretty well for themselves in the meantime. They no longer need men to reproduce and they've set up a society that seems to work okay without men—better in fact than our messy two-sex societies ever have.

But do the men stay out of it?

They do not. They're men, after all, and they're driven by their need for sexual dominance. It's genetically encoded so to speak, and it's not long before they're trying to turn this Eden into another fallen world. It's sex that does it, violent male sex—rape, actually. In other words, sex that's more about the violence than the sex.

And certainly nothing to do with love.

Which, when you think about it, is a pretty corrosive view of male sexuality.

The more things change the more they stay the same, I guess.

Wyndham, though.

Wyndham heads out on the porch around three. He's got some tonic. He's got some gin. It's what he does now. He doesn't know where the woman is, doesn't have strong feelings on the issue either way.

He's been sitting there for hours when she joins him. Wyndham doesn't know what time it is, but the air has that hazy underwater quality that comes around twilight. Darkness is starting to pool under the trees, the crickets are tuning up, and it's so peaceful that for a moment Wyndham can almost forget that it's the end of the world.

Then the screen door claps shut behind the woman. Wyndham can tell right away that she's done something to herself, though he couldn't tell you for sure what it is: that magic women do, he guesses. His wife used to do it, too. She always looked good to him, but sometimes she looked just flat-out amazing. Some powder, a little blush. Lipstick. You know.

And he appreciates the effort. He does. He's flattered even. She's an attractive woman. Intelligent, too.

The truth is, though, he's just not interested.

She sits beside him, and all the time she's talking. And though she doesn't say it in so many words, what she's talking about is Re-Populating the World and Re-Establishing Western Civilization. She's talking about Duty. She's talking about it because that's what you're supposed to talk about at times like this. But underneath that is sex. And underneath that, way down, is loneliness—and he has some sympathy for that, Wyndham does. After a while, she touches Wyndham, but he's got nothing. He might as well be dead down there.

"What's wrong with you?" she says.

Wyndham doesn't know how to answer her. He doesn't know how to tell her that the end of the world isn't about any of that stuff. The end of the world is about something else, he doesn't have a word for it.

&

So, anyway, Wyndham's wife.

She has another book on her nightstand, too. She doesn't read it every night, only on Sundays. But the week before the end of the world the story she was reading was the story of Job.

You know the story, right?

It goes like this: God and Satan—the Adversary, anyway; that's probably the better translation—make a wager. They want to see just how much shit God's most faithful servant will eat before he renounces his faith. The servant's name is Job. So they make the wager, and God starts feeding Job shit. Takes his riches, takes his cattle, takes his health. Deprives him of his friends. On and on. Finally—and this is the part that always got to Wyndham—God takes Job's children.

Let me clarify: in this context "takes" should be read as "kills."

You with me on this? Like Krakatoa, a volcanic island that used to exist between Java and Sumatra. On August 27, 1883, Krakatoa exploded, spewing ash 50 miles into the sky and vomiting up five cubic miles of rock. The concussion was heard 3000 miles away. It created tsunamis towering 120 feet in the air. Imagine all that water crashing down on the flimsy villages that lined the shores of Java and Sumatra.

Thirty thousand people died.

Every single one of them had a name.

Job's kids. Dead. Just like 30,000 nameless Javanese.

As for Job? He keeps shoveling down the shit. He will not renounce God. He keeps the faith. And he's rewarded: God gives him back his riches, his cattle. God restores his health, and sends him friends.

God replaces his kids. Pay attention: word choice is important in an end-of-the-world story.

I said "replaces," not "restores."

The other kids? They stay dead, gone, non-functioning, erased forever from the Earth, just like the dinosaurs and the 12 million undesirables incinerated by the Nazis and the 500,000 slaughtered in Rwanda and the 1.7 million murdered in Cambodia and the 60 million immolated in the Middle Passage.

That merry prankster God.

That jokester.

That's what the end of the world is about, Wyndham wants to say. The rest is just details.

By this point the woman (You want her to have a name? She deserves one, don't you think?) has started to weep softly. Wyndham gets to his feet and goes into the dark kitchen for another glass. Then he comes back out to the porch and makes a gin and tonic. He sits beside her and presses the cool glass upon her. It's all he knows to do.

"Here," he says. "Drink this. It'll help."

The Bluehole

That was the summer of '82, a bastard hot summer if there ever was one. Sauls Run sweltered in the crucible of the Reagan recession. "Hungry Like the Wolf" blasted down the airwaves from WROK, in Princeton, a county of unemployed coal miners away. *E.T.* flickered in the dark at the Lavon Theater on Main Street. Lines stretched around the block well into June. I must have seen that movie half a dozen times.

Mom had been dead just a little over six months by then. Thirty-eight years old, and a stroke dropped her in her tracks while she was wrapping Christmas presents in the spare bedroom. A bleeder, the doctors called it, the worst kind, like you even needed to know that when you'd found your mother laid out on the rug, a square of Christmas paper crumpled across her chest and a rope of saliva leaking out of the corner of her mouth. A bleeder. Like you didn't know that was the worst kind of all. Like you couldn't fucking see.

We buried her the day after Christmas and went home to a houseful of presents. I remember Dad shoving them unopened into plastic garbage bags and dragging them down to the curb while Chris and I watched from the door. A Mom-shaped black hole had opened in the center of our lives and it sucked everything we'd ever known down into it. "Don't cry, faggot," Chris said, knuckling my head, and after that we subsisted on week-old milk, cold cereal, and silence.

The silence lasted into the spring. Dad spent even off-duty hours in his squad car, patrolling the streets of the Run. Chris took to the pavement as well, skipping school to cruise around in Joey Stratton's beater of a Camaro, drinking Thunderbird and smoking weed. Me? I trudged along the way I always had, keeping my head down at school and pounding out my homework at the kitchen table, the way Mom would have wanted me to. Things got a little better in May. The seventh graders took a field trip to the World's Fair in Knoxville the last week of school. My class shared a bus with some kids from Broadview Junior High, across town, and I kissed a girl on the bus the night we came back. I forgot her name a long time ago, but I still recall the bump in the bridge of her nose and the way her hard little tongue probed at the closed fence of my teeth.

The seventeen-year cicadas emerged in force a month after that, mammoth green insects an inch long or longer, with red eyes and enormous translucent wings. Some mornings I woke to find the yard littered with their husks. They sounded like helicopters when they took flight; their din reached colossal proportions in the heat of the afternoon.

That was the summer I turned thirteen, the summer I smoked pot for the first time, the summer I fell in love with movies and science fiction and rock 'n' roll. That was the summer of the Bluehole, and whatever it was that plied its opaque, fathomless depths. That was the summer Jimmy moved into the house across the street. I think I was half in love with him from the start.

I dreamed of him last night, him and the Bluehole both. I do sometimes. Not as often as you'd think, two or three times most years, I guess. Maybe four. But every cicada summer, twice seventeen years ago now, the visitations grow more frequent, especially as July tips over into August.

In the dreams, the vast expanse of the Bluehole opens like a gray eye before me, the far shore a humid blur, reeds upright in the windless afternoon. The flat drone of the cicadas booms out of the trees. We are swimming—as we did that day. Jimmy slices the water before me, his arms knifing through the chop. I struggle along behind him as I always do, gasping for breath, doomed by foreknowledge, jaws locked, tongue swollen in my mouth. Then, ahead, the water froths and begins to boil. And something comes. By morning, only the faintest impressions linger: a long shadow arrowing through the depths beneath me, a glimpse of slick black skin, rolling for a heartbeat above the waves. Three nights running, that dream, and I knew it was time to go back. To scramble down through the underbrush to the steaming, mosquito-infested rim of the lake, and there to take a reckoning.

Oddly, what came back to me in that moment of decision is something my second wife said, in the weeks just before our marriage finally came apart. I recall her leaning over the sink, scrubbing her hands raw, her face streaked with tears. "When are you going to accept yourself for what you are, Jeremy?" she said.

But Jimmy came before all that, in a yellow Ryder moving van that pulled up one day late in June at the house across the street. They were all company houses in that neighborhood, built in the twenties when Holland Coal still owned Sauls Run. By '82 Holland was long gone, Woolworths had replaced the company store, and work in the deep holes was dwindling in the face of mountaintop removal. But the company houses remained, scabrous and gray in the sunlight, grimly uniform: two narrow dormers, a concrete stoop, a front yard the size of a fingernail paring. That was where I saw Jimmy for the first time, a few days after the van departed. He was sitting on the stoop in the shade of a towering oak: a lean, smooth-limbed boy, reading a paperback and smoking Marlboro Reds, methodically snapping off the filters and flipping them into the sparse grass.

I'd been staring at him through a gap in my mother's curtains for half an hour or so when he set aside the book and came striding purposefully toward my house. He knocked on the door. Sometimes I think everything would have been different, my whole life up to now, if I hadn't answered that knock. Sometimes I dream about that, too: just turning away and wandering back through the house into the living room, snapping on the television, and letting the bilge of daytime programming wash over me: *Wheel of Fortune* and *The*

Price is Right. Sometimes I think everything would have been better. Sometimes I know it.

The truth is, I almost did turn away. I felt a faintly voyeuristic embarrassment for one thing. For another he was everything I was not: tall, tan, blond, handesome. The confidence that had propelled him across the cracked, weedy pavement of Maple Street was breathtaking.

But then he knocked again, and this time his voice came through the door as well.

"If you're going to sit there and stare all day, you might as well come outside."

Trapped, I opened the door.

He stood on the stoop, smoking, clad in cut-off blue jeans and black Converse high tops, blond hair tousled over a perfectly symmetrical face. *L.A.M.F.*, his tee shirt read, pink dripping letters scrawled across a field of black, and I remember wondering what the letters stood for.

It was ten o'clock in the morning, the sunlight almost blinding. The heat settled over my shoulders like a sodden blanket. The cicadas were tuning up for the afternoon show. Jimmy took a final drag on his cigarette, pinched the cherry between his fingers, and flipped it into the street. He blew the smoke out through his nostrils. The smell of it brought tears to my eyes. It reminded me of my mom's Virginia Slims—she used to smoke them right there on the stoop, squinting into the fumes as she snapped beans—and a torrent of grief so powerful that I thought I might drown thundered through me.

"You okay?"

"Yeah, sun got in my eyes."

Jimmy had drifted back toward his own house. We sat side-by-side on his stoop. Music blared through the open window, something raucous and loud and totally alien to me in that month when "Ebony and Ivory" ruled the charts.

"What're you listening to?"

"Dead Boys," he said. He picked up his paperback, creased the spine, and started to read. I crossed my arms over my knees, rested my chin upon them, and gazed out over the yard, letting the raw power of "Sonic Reducer" wash over me. The music's barreling sense of chaos barely under control—not to mention the lyrics, which declared that they didn't need no "mom and dad"—spoke to me strongly in that summer of rage and loss. I leaned back, letting the fury wash over me. When I finally opened my eyes, a cicada, involute and green, clung to a stalky weed nearby, its abdomen pulsing. The heat summoned shimmering pools out of the pavement. The day smelled of dry grass and smoldering slag. Dad was long gone. Chris would crawl out of his sheets like a troll sometime in the next hour or so; he'd scarf down a bowl of dry Fruit Loops and hit the road with Joey Stratton for another day of sucking down Budweiser—Because U Deserve What Everyone Should Enjoy Regularly—behind the abandoned mill on Mount Horeb Road. The long day stretched before me. I might wander down to the Woolworths and look for a new Robert B. Parker on the spinner rack. Not that I could afford it if I found one. I'd long since exhausted the library's paltry collection—and I could do little more than steal a few paragraphs at the Woolworths before Mr. Kowalski ran me off, jabbing his finger at the sign that said *This Is Not a Library. Please Buy Before You Read.* At four, I'd watch a rerun of *Batman*, and after that an episode of *Battle of the Planets*. Most days I masturbated—with a certainty of impending doom—and then I napped away the restless afternoon.

Jimmy shook two more Marlboros out of the pack and snapped off the filters. He lit up and handed me a cigarette. I took a deep drag and vomited over the side of the stoop.

"Nice," he said without looking up from his book.

What can I tell you of that summer, thirty-four years later? What can anyone say about the past? Memory is the kingdom of deceit, self-serving, colored by desire. I'm forty-seven now, almost half a century of life behind me: two wives and three children, two of whom no longer speak to me; six cars, though I've never owned a new one; three novels that sank like stones; more jobs than I care to count, framing houses, tending bar, you name it, whatever it took to make a living while I banged out stories on a Remington manual typewriter, a secondhand IBM Selectra, and almost as many reconditioned Macs as cars. How do you disinter the past and see it for what it is? The summer of 1982 was the golden moment of my life, even if it culminated in a horror that has never quite ended—but what can I really see, or say, beyond the haze of nostalgia?

The soundtrack of that summer still thunders in my ears—Television, the Jam, the Undertones, Jimmy's long row of vinyl. Summer days we used to lay roasting in his bedroom listening to *Blank Generation* and talking about girls. Jimmy was infinitely more knowledgeable than I was. I had my kiss. He had a hand job in the back seat of a '77 Caprice while *Darkness on the Edge of Town* played on the 8-track mounted under the dash.

And I remember the day out on the stoop when he changed the course of my life forever. He handed me a Marlboro with the butt snapped off and a battered paperback copy of *The Hitchhiker's Guide to the Galaxy*. The smokes will probably kill me—I still snap the filters off and flip them into the street—but the books saved my life. It started with Arthur Dent and Ford Prefect and the Vogon Constructor Fleet, and it went on from there—Silverberg and Bradbury, Simak and Lovecraft, the lights that would illuminate my miserable high school years. A whole new well of call numbers opened up before me down at the public library; when that went dry, Jimmy taught me the fine art of shoplifting down at the Woolworths. That's how I sustained my addiction in the years that followed, when Jimmy was gone—*The Three Stigmata of Palmer Eldritch*, *Sandkings*, *The Day of the Triffids*, two dozen others. I still have them on my shelf at home.

What else?

Summer days down at the pool, where I sat on a towel, my heart clenched with anxiety, while Jimmy disported himself in the water with an expert's abandon. I didn't swim well, and hadn't been in the pool since an incident involving the high dive last summer. Overwhelmed with terror—of the height and of the water below—I'd had to climb back down from the board. Yes, that, plus banging stones off the pitted stop sign at the end of Maple Street. Shooting bottle rockets at eighteen-wheelers on the turnpike. Stealing cigarettes from the gas station vending machines they used to have back then: two quick blows from the flat of Jimmy's hand and a deck of Winstons or Marlboros would rattle down into the tray. He must have shown me how to do that trick a thousand times, but I never mastered it.

And there was the booze, of course. The bottle of MD 20/20 we snagged out of Rodger Dillon's glove box while he and Chris were behind the high school getting high. The six-pack of Schlitz we lifted from the 7-Eleven. The fifth of vermouth we filched from Jimmy's mom's liquor cabinet. We sucked it down in the patch of scrub behind Loudon's Hardware. Jimmy held it together, but I staggered out of the woods to vomit on the battered dumpster. All fun and games until Old Man Loudon himself put in an appearance. Reeling or not, we scooted. He must have chased us fifty yards down High Street, his face brick-red and his gut swaying, before he turned back, cursing between gasps.

Later that afternoon, Jimmy sprawled sweating across his bed. I sat cross-legged—Indian-style we called it those days—on the floor, still buzzing as we listened to the cicadas and the LP spinning on the stereo just then—*Germfree Adolescents,* by the X-Ray Spex.

I wondered aloud where he'd buy records in Sauls Run—knowing that the limited selection at the Woolworths would not cater either to his taste or my developing one (on the other hand, if you wanted "Ebony and Ivory," you were in luck).

"Beats the hell out of me," Jimmy said bitterly.

I'd heard the story by then, of course. Jimmy had been dragged back to his mother's home in West Virginia from southern California when his parents divorced. His mother had found work pulling the day shift at the Maidenform plant over in Princeton.

So much for the Pacific, bye-bye to the Buzzcocks, sayonara to the Slits.

The last chords of "Identity" faded. The needle bumped the center of the record; the looming wall of cicada song filled the room. I picked up a copy of *Starlog*: Kurt Russell and *The Thing* were on the cover. We didn't actually see the film until early August, but our anticipation had been thoroughly whetted by mid-July. Between the two of us we'd thumbed that magazine slick. *Fuck that fifties Gunsmoke guy,* Jimmy had said, *this is going to be the real deal.* We'd hunted up a copy of "Who Goes There?" in *The Best of John W. Campbell* in the library. One sentence still sticks with me: MacReady was a bronze man.

So there were a lot of firsts that summer. A lot of beginnings.

But this story's really about endings. I think most stories are. What I really remember about Sauls Run in the summer of '82 is that mom-shaped hole, which occluded everything that had come before it. What I really remember is the stultifying heat, the din and hum of the cicadas.

What I remember most is the Bluehole.

It looms large in my memory—another turning of the way—but at the time it was just another late-July morning. Jimmy had pinched ten bucks from his mother's wallet and we blew it playing *Galaga* at Dewey's Arcade on Main Street. Afterward, we scrambled down the overgrown embankment under the great arc of the Stone Bridge. We lounged in the shadow of the bridge, smoking Marlboros as cars rumbled by overhead. The tangle of railroad tracks before us stretched a hundred yards to the other side of the declivity. Every once in a while a freight train, cars loaded with glittering mounds of coal, would rumble by. In between, we talked about music, girls, or the murderous heat. The sun boiled in a flat gray sky, and the underbrush was parched and brown. Jimmy wiped sweat from his forehead with the back of one hand.

Finally, he said, "The hell with this," and climbed to his feet. He struck off west, his sneakers scuffing the gravel. We hiked down the tracks in the blistering noon sun, jumping from crosstie to crosstie, or walking the curving rails side-by-side like tight-rope artists, placing one foot carefully in front of the other, our arms outstretched like wings. Everything was a contest. Who could leap the most crossties? Who could balance the farthest walking the rail?

When we discovered the abandoned caboose on a spur of track that ran down into the tangled woods, I shrank from what we found inside—a cache of damp-swollen men's magazines, a handful of wrinkled condoms, a graying bra draped over the back of a vinyl seat. Jimmy crowed in delight. I wondered what kind of woman left her underclothes behind when she was done. Hell, I wonder that still.

He looked up at me, grinning as he peeled apart the pages of a moldy *Gallery ("Home of the Girl Next Door")* and dangled a mossy centerfold before me. "How'd you like a piece of that, Jeremy?"

"Who knows where that thing has been? C'mon, let's go."

"Don't be a faggot all the time," he said.

But he cast aside the magazine, pushed his way the length of the caboose—I still remember that way he passed through the bars of shadow and light slanting down through the high louvered windows—and out onto the platform at the other end. There, far below us, sparkling like a toxic sapphire through the trees, lay the Bluehole.

The name is misleading, I guess—it suggests an abandoned quarry, something deep and narrow. It was actually a lake, a mile or so wide and three times or more as long, winding through the hollows with great forested massifs climbing to either side. In another time—in a place less stricken by poverty and despair—it might have been developed; instead, trees and brush, a mix of evergreen and stunted oak, bramble and thorn, ran untouched down its steep, rocky shingles. Its waters glimmered an opaque blue; I suppose it must have been irretrievably polluted by run-off from the Holland mines.

But none of that would stop Jimmy.

"Hey, wait up!" I called, but he was already swinging over the platform's railing. He landed with characteristic grace. I climbed over the railing and set off in pursuit. By the time I'd blundered up behind him, he'd already stripped off his shirt. His upper body was lean and tan, well muscled.

"Care for a swim?" he said, grinning as he unzipped his shorts.

"You can't," I gasped, head down, hands on my knees. "You can't."

"Sure I can."

"No, really, you can't—"

"Why not?"

He slid down the shorts and stood before me. I swallowed hard. "There are stories."

I guess there must be stories about any large lake, particularly one as deep and cold as the Bluehole. My father told me the first story, or at least the first one I recall. I was probably four or five years old then, and I suppose he intended it to warn me away from the potential hazards the lake posed. But in later years I would learn that his story of the Bluehole—in some variation or other—was common currency around town. The gist of the tale was that back in the early days of the railroad—this would have been sometime in the 19th Century, I guess—the C&W line had run a track down into the water, loaded up obsolete freight cars, and disposed of scrap iron in the hole. How long this went on (or indeed if it went on at all) I cannot say. But when the war came—the sources disagree on which war—the battle on the home front called for civil engineers to salvage any scrap metal they could lay hands on. So a team of divers deployed to locate the abandoned cars. Anyway, the story goes that the divers never found the cars, of course; worse yet, they never found the bottom. Nor did the divers themselves escape unscathed. One never came back at all. Another spent the rest of his life in the Weston State Hospital for the Insane, raving about monsters. The rest of the divers never spoke of what they had seen in the shadowy depths.

As a kid, this story held me mesmerized with terror. I could imagine the divers flipping backwards off the boats, the lake growing calm as the algae-thick water took them in. Kicking deeper then, the water growing colder, the pressure tremendous, the darkness ever more impenetrable. How puny their flickering cones of hand-held light must have seemed—I could see the glittering sparks of sediment in the murk, the flash of schooling fish wheeling away into the gloom, the rails themselves plunging ever deeper into the midnight depths, red and scaly with rust and strung with veils of greenish-blue weed, until the earth gave out beneath them and they twisted away into the abyss at last, torn asunder, as if by some unimaginable geological cataclysm.

"Bullshit," Jimmy said. "Bullshit on the divers and bullshit on the monster, too. Especially the monster." Shaking his head in disgust, he waded naked into the water. A moment later, he began dancing from foot to foot. "Cold, jeez it's cold."

"I told you."

"No, you didn't. You told me some crap about railroad cars disappearing into the bottomless depths." He hugged himself, shivering. "And lake monsters."

"Screw you."

He didn't bother acknowledging this riposte, just waded farther out, still shaking his head in disbelief. And then he disappeared. For a moment of heart-stopping panic, I feared that the bottom had cut away beneath him, but then he surfaced, flinging water out of his hair. The spray glittered in the sun. "Cold's always better once you get your head wet," he called back to me; then he swam away from the shore, five yards, ten—

I sat down by his scattered clothing, pulled my knees to my chin, and wrapped my arms around my shins. The incessant clatter of the cicadas rang from the trees around us. Jimmy swam with natural grace, his body slicing the murk. At twenty yards, anxiety began to build in my chest. At twenty-five it felt like someone had jammed a hand grenade between my lungs. At thirty they pulled the pin.

I stood, cupping my hands around my mouth. "Far enough, you idiot."

Jimmy executed a perfect flip, like a seal, and dove. White legs flashed in the sunlight. Water frothed around his kicking feet. A moment later the surface settled into a placid, unnatural blue.

He was gone.

I don't know how long it was before I started counting seconds, but I was at sixty-five when he breeched the surface. Treading water, he laughed out loud, a laugh so full of joy that I couldn't hold on to my resentment at the scare. "You touch bottom?" I shouted.

"Too deep," he gasped as he began the swim back to shore. A minute later he walked out of the lake and flopped down beside me. He leaned on his elbows and turned his face to the sun. He was as unconscious about his body as any human being I have ever known, and I count myself lucky, even now, to have had the opportunity, if only for the space of a single summer, to have known him.

Did I envy him, then? I don't think I did. Not yet. What I felt was a kind of worshipful adoration: he was everything I wanted, everything I could never be. His ease in his own skin, his casual disdain of authority, his physical grace: I admired them all. I wanted to be Jimmy, I guess. And if I couldn't be him, I wanted to bask in his charisma, to look at him, to love him from afar.

Kids had drowned there.

Three that I knew of for sure, and others that the high-school mythology I'd overhead only dimly hinted at. The three were easy to confirm: they had died together nine years ago in a Senior Skip Day challenge gone very bad indeed. I don't suppose the tradition of Senior Skip Day varies much from town to town. If you were shooting for the perfect attendance badge come Awards Day, it placed you in a tight spot; otherwise it was a day free of the stultifying boredom of Sauls Run High School. By ten that morning a two-keg bash had gotten underway down at the Bluehole. By noon, a third keg had been procured and the Bluehole was rocking: kids splashed in the shallows, made out along the shoreline, thronged the keg. Somebody in the scrum—it could never later be determined who—issued an alcohol-emboldened challenge, and five young men set off to swim to the far shore, over a mile away as the subsequent investigation would confirm.

Three of them never made it back.

What exactly happened was never quite clear. The small audience on shore lost interest and drifted away as the figures disappeared into the distance. The two strongest swimmers pulled ahead; by the time they threw themselves panting on the far shore, the tragedy must have already occurred. The other three must have drowned, of course: one can imagine the onset of beery exhaustion; the panicky cries for help skipping unheard across the sun-shot surface; the final thrashing resistance as the waters closed overhead. A last desperate splash. Then, nothing: just water, opaque, icy, indifferent.

Two of the bodies were never recovered. The third, what was left of it, washed up on shore months later—long after the official investigation had issued its conclusion. But by then, whispers had already gotten started: some of the students out there that day, working the deep edge where the bottom sheared away into the abyss, had seen and heard things that their friends on shore had missed: a clap as of distant thunder, a brief animal stench, a thin shriek, like the screech of torn metal. Then, far out in the blue haze at the horizon, a great silver plume shot up and pinned itself glittering to the wind. A heartbeat later, it collapsed into spray; and a heartbeat after that, the kids floating out there in the deep water felt the shockwave pass, a gentle rocking in the deep, like the sway of ocean currents.

ꝏ

The Lavon Theater debuted *The Thing* near the end of July and then only as a late-show special. It was rated R, and Hazel Pinsky, who sold tickets most nights, sternly policed admission. Getting in required some ingenuity: Jimmy's idea was to stand outside waiting for the late showing of *E.T.* to end, then slip through the exiting crowd murmuring—*lost my wallet, excuse me, ma'am, lost my wallet*—and hey presto, magic. Usually, the mere threat of a hiding would have precluded such a stunt. But three *Starlog* articles on *The Thing*—including one about special effects, accompanied by appropriately gruesome photos—had whetted our appetites to a razor edge.

Besides, Jimmy shamed me into it.

"Come on, Jeremy, do you want to be a pussy forever?" he would say, tousling my hair to show it was friendly. Or, abruptly, spinning down the volume on Black Flag, he would chant, "Jeremy is a pussy," his voice lilting over the syllables.

By the time we slipped outside that evening, the summer sky had deepened to indigo and the first stars were starting to wink through. The windows of the neighboring houses printed buttery trapezoids on the scorched grass. The constant buzz saw of the cicadas cut the air. "*The Thing*, baby," Jimmy crowed, throwing an arm around my shoulder as we loped across the lawn. And soon after we'd managed the not-so-difficult trick of free admission—Jimmy's idea worked like a charm—we were settling into front-row seats.

The theater went dark. The previews began and the lingering dread of Hazel Pinsky faded. I barely remember the sticky floor underneath my feet or the teenagers hooting at the screen in faux terror. What I do remember—the last thing I remember before the film swept me into its spell—is an image of Jimmy staring rapt at the screen. He was handsome in profile, a vision of the man he'd never live to become.

Then the movie took me. Despite the Antarctic setting, despite the film's surgical dissection of posturing male heroics, what I saw on that screen—what I see to this day—was a reflection of myself. Campbell's story of an alien that could take the form of any living thing spoke to someone who felt so much like an imposter in his own skin. And the paranoid premise of the film—that you couldn't trust anyone, not even your closest friends—hit me with unexpected urgency. Maybe that's simply the existential condition of adolescence, but to me it felt—it still feels—stunningly real.

But that intellectual understanding of why the film spoke to me came later—much later. What came that night was sheer exhilarating terror. From the opening frames to the final shot, what I recall is a series of stark flashbulb images, so sharply limned that even to think of them now is to plunge me back into the lacerating dark of the Lavon Theater. Can a movie haunt you? Those images haunt me still—a dog gnawing in terror at its chain link enclosure, the sheer magnitude of the spaceship buried in the ice, a man's severed head growing spider legs and scurrying toward an open door, before the white-hot flare of a flamethrower consumes it. What I remember most of all is a single eidetic image of a man only partially transformed, standing alone in a sea of churned-up snow, his face transfixed with terror and loss, great alien talons where his hands should be. What I remember is his cry of desolation and despair, his echoing and alien lament at being stranded forever in a body—in a world—that is not his own. That alien wail still haunts my imagination, all these years later.

∞

I couldn't sleep that night, of course.

The walk home in darkness had been dreadful enough.

But the darkness of my room was, in the short run, anyway, infinitely worse. The streetlight outside my window swathed the room in shadows. A basketball in the corner might any moment grow legs and scurry across the room toward my bed. And when I closed my eyes, I could see that pitiful man in the snow and hear his awful alien scream. How long I endured it, I cannot say. But the true measure of my fear came somewhere in the small hours of the night, when, exhausted by terror, I clambered from my bed and stole down the hall to Chris's room. He lay snoring on his back, arms out flung, sleeping the sleep of the drugged or the drunk or both. I crept into his bed and snuggled into his heat, thinking of my mother, the way she used to crawl into my bed and wrap me in her arms when I was afraid.

Chris's snoring hitched—I could smell the ripe stench of beer on his breath—and he turned his back to me. "Don't touch me, faggot," he groaned, and then he resumed snoring. I lay awake for a long time after that, until somewhere toward dawn I fell into a restless, tossing sleep.

I dreamed of Jimmy that night—maybe for the first time, though I can't say for sure. But I remember standing naked before a mirror, staring at my reflection in wonder, for the boy staring back at me wasn't me at all. It was Jimmy, lean and tan, his penis tumescent in its nest of golden hair. I reached out to touch him and the boy on the other side of the mirror reached out as well. Our fingers met, sending concentric ripples expanding across the surface of the glass—

Then I was awake, clutching at the corona of pain that had burst just above the small of my back. "What the fuck are you doing in here?" my brother was saying. I curled fetal to protect myself from the next kick—it exploded in a bright flare of agony square above my kidney—all too aware of the morning erection tenting my undershorts.

My brother must have been aware of it, too—I had a nightmarish image of him stirring to wakefulness with it pressing stiff against his back—for as he aimed another kick at me he snapped, "Go play with yourself in your own room." Which would have been fine, except he didn't seem inclined to let me go. I scrambled across the bed, dragging the sheets over my crotch. Chris, shirtless, advanced on me, his thick hands—he had my father's hands—curled into fists. I think he might have beaten me badly—very badly—if the horn of Joey Stratton's Camaro hadn't split the morning air.

"Shit," Chris said, turning away. "You got off lucky this time, faggot."

He shoved his feet into a pair of beat-up Adidas and snatched an Iron Maiden tee shirt from atop a pile of dirty clothes. "You better be gone like the fucking wind when I get back," he said. He slammed out of the room and clattered down the stairs. A moment later, the Camaro screeched away and I was alone.

I took a deep breath and tipped my head against the wall, panting.

I must have sat like that for fifteen minutes, breathing through the pain, before I heaved myself off the bed. That's when I noticed that

Chris's bureau drawer was ajar—and glimpsed the yellow box shoved in among the rat's nest of unmatched socks. I should have left the room, of course.

All I can say is that I found myself pulling open the drawer instead. I pushed the socks back, pulled out the box—it was a cardboard cigar box—and put it down on the bureau. And then—remember that scene in *Pulp Fiction* where John Travolta opens the briefcase and golden light comes pouring out?—I lifted the lid.

A wad of bills as thick as my fist had been shoved in on one side. A heap of neatly rolled joints lay upon the other. It didn't take long to put two and two together. Chris was dealing—at the very lowest rung of the ladder, true, selling individual joints in the halls of Sauls Run High School for three dollars a pop—but dealing all the same. Once upon a time—when my mother was alive—I would have closed that box and turned away. But Mom was gone now. I think sometimes that her death was the catalyst for everything that followed. I don't know. All I could say for sure was that I had nothing left other than the kid across the street. So I took another step down that fatal path. I palmed two joints and counted ten bucks out of the unruly wad of cash.

The ten dollars sustained us through the morning in the arcade on Main Street.

It's just empty storefront now—I drove by it yesterday—but all I have to do is close my eyes and the years peel away to disclose the place to me in all its shabby reality: the astringent stink of the urinal cake in the boy's room, the cacophony of beeps and explosions, most of all the rattle of quarters in the change tray. For a single cultural heartbeat, a lot of people made a lot of money. But it's all gone now, of course; you can get better games on your phone—though your reception in the Run, deep in its cleft of mountains, is basically for shit. It doesn't matter anyway. Who have I got to call?

It's the past that lies before me now, if that makes any sense—the summer when Minor Threat and X banged out of Jimmy's speakers, and the sticky days of July spilled over into the still stickier ones of early August, bringing us ever closer to our fatal rendezvous with the Bluehole. But our doom—and I use the term deliberately, *our* doom—had yet to fall upon us, and if I hadn't nicked those joints from Chris's cigar box, if I'd taken only the money that we blew at the arcade that morning—it might never have fallen upon us at all.

But I did take the joints, and the money only lasted so long.

Ten or fifteen minutes after we ran dry of quarters, Dewey showed us the door. "You're loiterers," he said from behind the array of novelty prizes under the counter. He squinted at us through smoke from the butt jammed between his teeth. "You're fucking loitering, aren't you? So scram." He waved his hand dismissively and turned back to his paper.

"Screw you, Dewey, you old fuck," Jimmy said outside, kicking at a Miller Lite can that someone had thrown out in front of the pool hall. It rattled into the street and rolled into the mouth of a sewer grate. The pavement baked in flat, oppressive heat. Sunlight flashed off chrome in dazzling silver bursts as cars whipped past. Jimmy hopped the guardrail by the Stone Bridge. I followed reluctantly. We scrambled down the slope and hunkered in the shadow of the overpass. A dry breeze chased dust devils across the tracks. The air smelled of spent oil and shale. "Jesus," Jimmy said, leaning on his elbows, legs extended. He laced his hands behind his head and stared up into the shadows. I reclined beside him. A crumpled can of Tab leached white in the sunlit weeds beyond the bridge. Ants marched across the open lip and disappeared into the dark. The undergrowth rang with cicada song.

"I'm so bored," Jimmy announced, and in that moment I made the worst decision of the summer: I dug in my pocket, extracted the two joints I'd stolen from Chris's cigar box, and straightened them between my fingers.

"Holy shit," Jimmy said, and suddenly I felt like the coolest kid who had ever walked the streets of the Run. "Where'd you get those?"

"I have my sources," I said, feeling even cooler—feeling in fact almost as cool as Jimmy. "Wanna?"

Jimmy dug out his lighter and passed it my way. I sat up and got the joint going. Holding it between my thumb and forefinger like the seasoned pothead I would soon become, I took a long coughless drag: the apprenticeship with the Marlboros had served me well. I passed the joint to Jimmy. "Chris," he said, holding it to his lips. And then, exhaling: "Chris's gonna kill you."

I dropped back on my elbows beside him, feeling the pressure of the smoke in my lungs. I let it stream through my nostrils. "Chris's never going to say a word, not unless he wants Dad to know he's dealing," I said, and Jimmy, shaking his head in something like admiration—I felt the pleasure of it all through my body—passed the joint back to me. As it burned down, the cars overhead seemed to *woosh* by. The bridge's shadow sharpened; the light beyond grew brighter. The cicada song deepened. Complex rhythms now textured the blank drone. I suppose the pot must have been absolute skunk weed compared to the stuff I buy today, but I still nurse a kind of reverence for that first buzz: arms out flung, buoyed weightless by the earth, watching the smoke eddy in the dim under the bridge. A cicada blurred to rest on a blade of sunshot heather, and I remember watching its jeweled belly throb, pushing out song. Harmony pervaded everything. I've never been able to get back that sense of primal unity, no matter how much I smoke.

Jimmy flipped the roach out on the tracks and we lay there for a while—I don't know how long—marinating in heat. I might have dozed—I would have—if Jimmy hadn't nudged me.

"Leave me alone."

"C'mon. Let's jet. It's fucking hot out here."

"Where?"

"That lake. You know, the Bluehole."

"Screw you."

"C'mon," he said. He got to his feet and extended his hand to me.

"I'm not swimming."

"So don't swim."

A train rumbled past, kicking up dust. I closed my eyes. Jimmy prodded me with his foot.

"Get up."

"Fine. Okay."

"C'mon, man," he said, "It'll be fun."

I opened my eyes, and let him heave me to my feet. Seduced again. What I think about that summer now is how often Jimmy used some variation of those words—

—*it'll be fun*—

—to entice me into doing things I would never have considered when Mom had been alive: smoking Marlboros on his front stoop, lifting a six of Schlitz at the 7-Eleven, sneaking into the Lavon Theater. I could name half a dozen other cases. And the Bluehole, of course, that most of all. I told my first wife about it once, the way he lured me down there, the way I was helpless to resist him. "Sounds like you were in love," she told me, and I suppose I was. So I tagged along. I could name the boys who had drowned there—Milton Childs, Sam Procter, and Loyal Brown—and though I had said that I would not swim, I knew that Jimmy would coax me into the water. It was the water that I thought of most of all: the Bluehole itself, how cold and dark it was, how deep.

"People have drowned there, you know."

"People have drowned in their bathtubs. You gotta go in."

"No, I don't."

"Sure you do. This hot? You gotta be kidding me."

"I'm not kidding."

We turned aside from the tracks, slipping down through the undergrowth, past the derelict caboose, and into the jungle of brush and stunted pine beyond. Jimmy bushwhacked through the bracken ahead of me, skidding now and then. The lake glimmered through the foliage, a flat, poisonous blue, flashing diamonds of light when the sun caught it. I could smell it, a rich organic funk of rot and regeneration, and when we emerged panting on the shore, the stench grew stronger, almost overpowering. The Bluehole lay before us, still, opaque, the far shore lost in a haze of humidity. Dragonflies darned the air, setting off concentric ripples whenever they settled to the dark water. Cattails stood in the shallows, unmoving in the windless afternoon. Down here in the woods, the racket of the cicadas was louder still, shot through with those complex polyrhythms. It sounded beautiful to me then, God's music raining down upon the planet, and maybe that was the last turning point in that summer of turning points, maybe everything would have been different if I hadn't been overwhelmed with the stoned beauty of the place, the lake and the cloudless sky, and Jimmy beside me in the grass, his knees pulled up to his chest. We could have stripped down and splashed around in the shallows. Instead I pulled out the second joint.

"Now you're talking," Jimmy said, and we sat in the grass, looking out over the lake, and smoked it. Occasionally, I stole glances at Jimmy. He too had taken on an ethereal beauty: his blue eyes, and his blond hair, and the way the light fired the tiny beads of perspiration along his jaw, so that his whole face glowed with that particular quality of light you see in impressionist paintings. I thought then—I still think—that he was the most beautiful person I had ever seen. When I leaned toward him to flip the roach into the water our faces were maybe six inches apart, and what I thought of then was the girl on the bus from the World's Fair—Nina, her name was Nina, it comes back to me after all these years. What I thought of was Nina, her determined little tongue probing at the closed rank of my teeth. I don't believe I thought at all about what I did next. It seemed to happen of its own accord. My hand came up and I brushed Jimmy's face with the tips of my fingers. He didn't say anything. He just looked at me out of those pale blue eyes, and then my face moved closer and my lips grazed his. They were chapped and peeling from the sun, I remember that, and I remember that he neither moved toward me nor pulled away. Everything was very still: the lake and the air and the tiny rustlings in the weeds. Even the cicadas seemed to have gone silent.

Then the moment was over.

I pulled away, I could feel the heat rising in my face. But Jimmy only stared at me. We sat like that for a long time, just staring at one another. There was no apprehension in those blue eyes of his, no judgment, no shock, no welcome. Just a flat blankness. The world resumed turning once again. Something splashed at the verge of the lake. The cicada song sprang suddenly into the air, a flat featureless drone. Somewhere in the thirty seconds between the kiss and the heartbeat that followed, all that beauty had drained out of the world. I was my old self again, stunted, dark, and unlovely, riven with desires I could neither name nor fulfill. Doomed.

"Jimmy—" I said.

"Let's swim the lake," he said.

Milton Childs. Sam Procter. Loyal Brown.

The names rang in my head as I waded into the waters of the Bluehole. The ground underfoot was weedy and slick. Icy hands climbed my legs—ankles, calves, thighs. I gasped when they seized my crotch and I felt my nuts retract into the heat of my body—what remained of it—like hard little stones.

Laughing, Jimmy ducked his head. "C'mon," he said, "You'll feel better."

But when I lowered myself into the water, I felt only another icy shock—and then, abruptly, he was right. The water was still cold—painfully cold—but no longer intolerable. I waded deeper. The water rose chest high, then shoulder, until finally it lapped at my chin—and the old terror reasserted itself: the divers, the three boys, the rumors of something out there in the deep waters.

"Jimmy," I said, "people have died swimming the lake. Seriously. Three kids I know of for sure—"

"We're not going to die."

"I just think—"

"Don't think," he said

And he dove. He surfaced ten feet farther out.

"C'mon," he said, and I came.

One step, two steps, three—and the bottom dropped out beneath me. I went down, flailing, water filling my nose. I kicked toward the sun, a dim blur through the greenish water. Exhilaration seized me when I broke the surface, and I thought even at the time that this was what it must be like to be Jimmy, this constant surge of reckless confidence. A sliver of envy pierced my heart in that moment, a shard of hatred so bright and hard that it might have killed me. I recalled the feel of his flesh, the touch of his lips, peeling and chapped from the heat, tasting slightly of salt.

"C'mon, pussy," he called from twenty feet farther out, and with that shard sawing at my heart, I struck out after him. He waited for me, flinging water from his hair as I drew near.

"C'mon," he said again, and with that he struck off into the deep water.

I followed. Dear God, I followed.

He drew slowly away from me—five feet, then ten, swimming smoothly, his hands slicing the water. My own arms hacked at the surface. My breath burned in my lungs. My legs already felt leaden. I could feel the terrible gravity of the abyss dragging me down.

And then—the near shore was but a distant line at our back, our destination still lost in haze before us—then it happened. There in the sweltering heat of an early August afternoon, with the sun beating down on the iridescent blue water and the song of the cicadas ringing in my ears, I watched my best friend die.

It happened fast.

Jimmy was maybe thirty yards ahead of me, gliding through the water, when something came out of the icy depths below. I glimpsed it in a single strobic flash—ten seconds or so, that's all—a deeper shadow against the dark as it streaked below me, twenty feet long or longer. There and gone again, passing bullet-like thirty or forty feet down, trailing a violent churning wake that swayed me in the water, so alien that I might have imagined it, that I thought I *had* imagined it, and then, for the space of a breath, a heartbeat, nothing more, it was gone.

The water was still.

You have to understand how quickly it all happened. I screamed at Jimmy—I don't remember the words to this day—and he turned, treading water, as I hurled myself thrashing through the water toward him. I reached out to him, and he shrugged me away.

"I want to swim the lake."

"Jimmy—"

"What?" And then: "Did you want to kiss me again?"

It was like a blade sliding between my ribs.

And then the thing took him. I smelled it, a deep animal reek, like the reek of the lake itself, but I barely saw it—a black tentacle, rolling languidly above the surface to encircle Jimmy's chest. Nothing more.

The sound of the cicadas boomed across the lake.

"Jeremy—" Jimmy cried. He reached out for me, grasping, tearing at my flesh, and, God help me, I clawed at him like an animal, gouging furrows of blood down his cheeks. I drove my feet deep into his belly—I heard the plosive gasp as air exploded from his lungs—and I saw him go down. I remember it like it was yesterday—his arms outstretched to me, his mouth frozen in a silent scream, bubbles trailing up as he went under. I dove then, and swam as deep and far as I could, until my breath screamed in my lungs, and when I burst through the water at last, I looked back, helpless not to, Lot's wife. The lake was placid and still.

All my life I've been a pillar of salt.

In the years since, I've given those moments a lot of thought. Sometimes it seems like I've thought of little else. The thing that took Jimmy was too big—no lake the size of the Bluehole could sustain a breeding population for long. Not enough food. Not enough water. And if it did, sooner or later one of the things would wash up dead on shore.

But the countervailing evidence speaks for itself: that animal reek, that glimpse of black flesh rolling up through the water. Milton Childs, Sam Procter, Loyal Brown. Most of all maybe, the diver who died in Weston State Hospital, raving about monsters—if he even existed at all.

Maybe I've read too much science fiction. Maybe I've written too much.

But I wonder.

Maybe there really are thousands of realities, pressed close against each other like bubbles. Maybe there are thin places in the membranes between. Maybe something sometimes breaks through.

Speculation, of course, but speculation is my trade.

Maybe.

I told them nothing of the sort, of course. I told them he drowned.

I pulled on my clothes and pelted back toward the tracks, yanking myself up-hill by the weeds and the stunted saplings and the sticky, sickly looking pines. I remember the way the brush seemed to come alive around me. The way it seized at me and dragged me back, the way it clutched at my ankles and drew stinging lines across my face.

And then I was free, still pulling on my shirt as I raced toward the Stone Bridge.

I leapt in front of the first car I saw, waving my arms, and when the man inside yanked open the door—

"What the hell, kid?"

—I fell upon him, weeping.

After that I don't remember much. Just fragments. The first of the police to arrive, old Charlie Bevins, who used to drink beer with my dad in those days, and then Dad himself, thin lipped and grim. He embraced me; I'll always remember that, the scent of cigarettes on his clothes and the flash of the wedding ring upon his hand. He walked beside me as I led them back down the tracks, past the abandoned caboose, to the shore of the Bluehole. Jimmy's clothes were still piled in the weeds. One of his sneakers lay turned on its side, a black high-top Chuck Taylor, the laces dangling. I remember that. It's funny the things you remember.

The men just stood there, looking out over the water.

There was nothing they could do. He was gone. There was nothing anyone could do.

They didn't drag the lake. I didn't like to think about it anyway, those curved hooks scraping the bottom until they dislodged a body; I didn't like to think of Jimmy bobbing to the surface and peering out at me from his death-glazed eyes. I didn't want to see the accusation reflected there.

So here I am, thirty-four years gone, camped in a dingy motel with threadbare sheets, writing out the past in a composition book that I purchased at Finnaker's Drug, or what is left of it. The lunch counter is gone, most of the newsstand, the spinner rack of paperbacks near the checkout counter. It's just a drugstore now; the Run is just another dying town.

Time slips away from you. The world changes. These days, looking at the Run is like looking at a palimpsest, the town I knew as a kid just barely visible beyond the shell it has become. Woolworths is gone. So is Loudon's Hardware. And the company houses on Maple Street have been cleared away for trailers and prefabs.

But the Stone Bridge is still there. Yesterday, I hiked out the railroad tracks that run beneath it. The cicadas sang me on my way, and time slipped its sprocket, the way it does sometimes. For the space of a breath or two, I was a boy, my best friend tramping along beside me;

the past erased itself, and it all lay before me once again, the whole world. Then the moment collapsed. History will have its way: I was pushing fifty, paunchy, panting in the heat. Three or four miles later, I glimpsed a spangle of sunlight far down among the trees. I pushed through the brush and stood on an embankment two hundred steep, overgrown yards above the water. It was still there, all right, poison blue and depthless, stretching its length alongside the tracks for miles. The far shore was invisible in the haze.

I stood there for a long time, just looking at it.

The Creature Recants

During breaks in shooting, the Creature from the Black Lagoon usually rests in a pond on the studio back lot and dreams of home. The pond isn't much even as ponds go. It's maybe four feet deep at its deepest point and a hundred yards or so around, an abandoned set carved out of the scorched southern California earth for some forgotten film or other: cattails and reeds and occasionally a little arrow of ripples when a dry breeze skates across the surface. Not even a fish if he's feeling peckish. Which he often is. The catering is suspect at the best of times, and it's even more so when you're accustomed to a diet of raw fish and turtle flesh prized living from the shell.

This is Hollywood.

"Don't expect too much," Karloff had advised him over sushi not long after he'd arrived, full of ambition and optimism, and Lugosi, strung out on morphine and methadone by the time the Creature made the scene, had been even more blunt. "They vill fuck you every time," he'd said in that thick Hungarian accent. The both of them typecast by their most famous roles. The Creature had assumed he could beat the odds, but on those blazing afternoons in the pond, now and again scooping up handfuls of water to moisten his gills, he'd begun to reconsider. The water was unkind, perpetually casting his reflection back at him: the bald, barnacle-encrusted skull, the eyes sunk beneath shelves of armored bone, the frills of tissue encasing the gills around his neck. Not what you would call leading-man material.

To think, he'd once been the king of his little world—the vast, dark Lagoon, overhung with the boughs of enormous trees, and the mighty Amazon itself, where anacondas slithered through the algae-clotted water, caiman slid into the flood without a splash, their tails lashing, and catfish the size of Chevrolets trolled the mossy bottom. Not to mention the jungle, humid, rank, and festering, clamorous with the chitinous roar of millions of insects. And here he was in southern California instead, spending his days in waist-deep water and sleeping his nights in an oversized bathtub in a crummy apartment.

Such are the Creature's thoughts when a member of the crew—it's Bill, a gopher who's trying to break into the biz as a lighting tech—walks down to the pond to tell him that Jack's finished setting up the next shot. It's time for the Creature to come back up to the set and stagger around the deck of the *Rita*—not even a real boat, just a cheap mock-up in one of the soundstages on the Universal lot—and menace Julie Adams for another hour or so. She's a real scream queen, Julie, the genuine article, but she's nice enough in real life; she even walks down to the pond to chat once in a while between set-ups.

They're all nice enough. Even Jack's okay, though he's always badgering the Creature to focus on his motivation when the Creature has enough trouble just hitting his marks. To tell the truth, the Creature's heart isn't in it anymore, but he's signed a deal with Universal, and his agent—who rarely returns his calls anyway—tells him there's no way to break the contract.

So the Creature hauls himself out of the pond, and tramps back up to the soundstage, trying not to think about the fact that he could decapitate Bill with a single stroke of his taloned hand. Trying not to think that at some level he wants to.

It wasn't supposed to turn out this way.

You never know happiness until it's gone, that's the way the Creature figures it. The present always seems like a mess. It was only once he left the Lagoon that he realized how good he'd had it there. In Hollywood, he recalls its dark waters with longing. Sometimes at night, his head pillowed on the bottom of his brimming bathtub and his webbed feet slung over either side to brush the peeling vinyl floor, he even dreams of it. How perfect it seems now, the murky bottom where he'd nested for hours among the drifting fronds of plants he cannot name and the hidden channel that led to his rocky underground lair. Armored with scales and impervious to jaguar and piranha alike, the Creature had hunted both the overgrown shores and the black fathoms, snatching spider monkeys screaming from their roosts and feasting on the great fish that slipped through the Lagoon's sulfurous depths. He recalls even his isolation with melancholy regret. What had seemed like loneliness—he'd never known another of his kind—now seemed like autonomy, and when the boat that spelled his expulsion from paradise had first steamed into the lagoon he had approached it with a curiosity that now seemed like folly.

He hadn't planned to leave the Black Lagoon, but life always takes the unexpected turn: caiman poachers in this case, though he hadn't known that then. It had been the boat, anchored in a sun-dappled inlet, that fascinated him. He'd taken it for some kind of novel creature, and because no denizen of the Amazon posed a threat to him—because he pined for novelty in those days—he hadn't given a second thought to approaching the thing. He'd been backstroking along, his face turned to the sun, when it came chugging into the Lagoon, stinking of gasoline. When he saw it, the Creature dove into the sun-spangled water, surfaced in the shadow of the boat, and dragged a talon along its rusting keel. He hadn't seen the net until it was too late. He found himself entangled. Panicked, he began to claw at it. He'd have freed himself had the poachers not reacted so quickly, winching him out of the water even as his talons tore long rents in the ropy mesh.

"My God," one of the poachers screamed, staggering back.

"Jesus, what the hell is that thing?" his companion cried, reaching for a spear gun. (The Creature reconstructed this dialogue only later.) The Creature was thinking the same thing. What could these soft, distorted reflections of his scaly self be, he wondered—

Then the harpoon punctured his shoulder and he stumbled flailing into the water. He'd never felt such agony. By the time he bobbed to the surface, he was unconscious. When he woke he found himself imprisoned behind steel bars.

The poachers weren't dumb—grimy, stubbled, and foul-mouthed—but not dumb. Three times a day, they tossed a fish, still flopping, between the bars of his cage. When they saw him pour his bucket of drinking water over his head, they realized that he needed to moisten his gills regularly. Using a spare gaff, they poked fresh buckets into his pen on the hour. The rest of the time he spent curled in a corner, whimpering. His terror of the boat at first overwhelmed him: the roar of the engine, the stench of his own waste, the curious faces (if you could call such doughy parodies of his own batrachian features faces) staring at him jaws agape from outside his cage. But you can get used to anything. By the time they anchored in the headwaters of Peru, his terror had dwindled to a dull simmer of anxiety.

What next?

He had no concept of the worst possibilities—not then, anyway. He could have been sold to a marine biology institute, where sooner or later scientists would have gotten around to dissecting him to see what made him tick (the Creature's rudimentary knowledge of scientists derives mostly from horror movies; scientists were all mad, as far as he is concerned). He could have been sold to a zoo, and spent the rest of his life paddling around in a wading pool, while small children gawped at him and tossed half-eaten ice cream cones through the bars. These would no doubt have been more profitable avenues. But the caiman poachers weren't anxious to disclose their reasons for cruising the Amazon. So he was sold instead to a carny scout combing the region for freak-show specimens, shipped north, and sold yet again, this time to Southeby & Sons Travelling Carnival, a fly-by-night operation that worked the south-western circuit through the spring and fall, wintering in Gibsonton, Florida, along with most of the other carnies in North America.

And here was happiness again—sort of, anyway—though he didn't recognize it at the time. By then, he'd pretty well been tamed. After he'd raked the shoulder of one of the poachers with his claws, a cattle prod had been brought into play, and three or four applications of *that* had been sufficient to cool his heels. So when he came to Southeby & Sons he'd been pliable enough. Besides, he fit right in with the freaks. They too were unique: the Living Skeleton, the Fat Lady (fat hardly did her justice), Daisy and Violet, the Siamese Twins, and half a dozen others, midgets and bearded ladies and the Monkey Boy: a community of sorts, a family that assuaged the loneliness that had been his lot back home in the Black Lagoon.

What's more, he had a vertical glass aquarium he could call his own, smaller than he might have wished, true, but brimful of water. Southeby billed him as the Gill Man and his sideshow performances were no hardship. He could bob in the green water, or kick to the surface for a breath of rank air (the Monkey Boy wasn't particular in matters of personal hygiene), or even doze if so inclined. Something of a romance—unconsummated, for the Creature's sexual organs, if he had any, were incompatible with those of human beings—blossomed between him and Daisy, much to Violet's dismay, who for unknown reasons took an immediate and abiding dislike of him. It was Daisy who taught him to talk, though his vocal cords, unfit for human speech, rendered his voice guttural and unintelligible to the untutored ear. And there was a kind of freedom during the winters in Gibsonton, this perhaps most precious of all. A simple walk of a mile or so brought him to the beach, and he sometimes lazed for hours in the warm, briny waters of the Gulf.

So he might have passed his life, or at least a longer portion of it, for who could say how long he might yet exist? The Creature had no memory of his birth and growth. He was then as he always had been and might always be. But restlessness possessed him. Violet's inescapable abhorrence was a constant blight on the affection he shared with Daisy, his tank grew cramped, and even his sojourns in the waters of the Gulf too brief, restricted by nine months on the road, burning the lot in one town to set up the next day in another. The midway—the flashing lights of the rides, the alluring chants of the barkers, the sugary reek of cotton candy and funnel cake—grew oppressive.

So when the chance to escape presented itself, in the person of a low-rent Hollywood agent who paused before his tank, the Creature was quick to take it. The agent took the time to decipher his rasping tones, sensed his discontent, and persuaded him to give the silver screen a try. L.A. was close to the beach year round, after all, and the Creature was already in show biz. If stardom didn't suit him, he could always return to the carny circuit. So it was the Creature signed up to be a contract player for Universal. He didn't count on being typecast as, well, the Creature, forever flapping about on his great rubbery feet after one nubile beauty or another, his scaly green arms outstretched. Didn't count on being mistaken for a stunt man in a rubber suit. Didn't count on the bathtub or the crummy apartment.

Most of all he didn't count on Julie Adams.

This is Hollywood.

As Bela Lugosi put it, "They vill fuck you every time."

The Creature has begun to believe that he might be in love with Julie Adams.

"Are you lonely?" she asks him one day down by the pond.

He floats on his back in a stand of cattails, keeping an eye on her through a screen of gently bending stalks. He understands all too well what it's like to be stared at. Every time he strolls outside his apartment, people stare. He's learned to ignore the occasional cries of "Hey, fish man," and no longer stops to explain that he's not a fish, but an amphibian. Yet the mockery has had its effect. The Creature has begun to wonder if there's something cannibalistic about him every time he chomps into a fish taco or spears a sushi roll on a single curved claw—with his webbed fingers, chopsticks and silverware are out of the question. The truth is, that's another reason the Creature has given up on the set's catering: he senses that people would just as soon not see him eat. He's never quite overcome the gastronomic habits of the jungle. He wolfs down his meals, smacks his oversized red lips, chews with his mouth open, gets gobs of food caught in his fangs. The whole thing is unsightly. The studio has ignored his requests to stock the pond with bluegills and catfish so that he can eat in privacy, and rather than protest—the negligent agent again—the Creature elects to spend his days hungry. He figures it sharpens his hostile motivations in the film; he's become a student of Stanislavski.

The Creature has, in short, begun to accept the norms of Hollywood. He no longer sees any beauty in his fellow denizens of the freak show (the mere thought of Daisy now repulses him)—but he has very much come to see the beauty in Julie Adams, a tall busty brunette who spends most of her days in their scenes together wearing a white one-piece bathing suit that accentuates her considerable curves. He's not sure that what he feels is love—love is a relatively new concept to him—but he knows that he eagerly anticipates her occasional visits to the pond, that the sound of her voice sets his heart racing, that sometimes he has trouble sleeping nights, and not merely because the bathtub provides no comfortable accommodation for his dorsal ridge. No, he has trouble sleeping because he can't stop thinking of Julie Adams.

Is he lonely? In a word, yes.

But the question begs closer examination. He glides out of the bed of cattails and gives Julie his full attention. Perhaps she's come to suspect his amorous intentions, for she has taken to wrapping herself in a thick white bathrobe before she walks down to the pond. Perhaps she's merely cold. It's hard to know.

"Lonely?" he says, hating his inhuman rasp. He cannot help comparing it to the rich, clear timbre of Richard Carlson, the (let's face it) star of the movie, despite the Creature's eponymous billing. With a languid kick he turns to face Julie. She sits at the edge of the shore, with her knees drawn up and her hands clasped around her legs. The Creature can't help staring at her bare ankles. Lonely? He muses on the question.

"That's right."

"I suppose I haven't really thought about it."

"Well, there are no other Creatures, are there?"

"None that I know of," he says, recalling the splendid isolation of the Lagoon.

"It must be very lonely, then. I wouldn't like to be all alone."

"I'm not alone anymore."

Implying that he has become a companion to the human race in general, and perhaps, hopefully, to Julie in particular.

She doesn't take his meaning. "Sometimes I think we're all alone, every one of us. Do you ever think that?"

The Creature composes his largely immobile features into an expression of tragic acceptance. "I suppose we are," he says. "But if you can find someone to love—"

She interrupts him. "I guess that's true. But it must be especially difficult for you. You're not human, but you're not . . . not human, either, if you see what I mean." She sighs, resting her chin on her knees. "Dick says you're the Missing Link." She seems to be blind to the cruelty of this statement, but the Creature has become as accustomed to this appellation as he is to "Fish Man." If he really thinks about it, he supposes he does stand somewhere between the modern human and his piscine ancestry, but he doesn't much like what this implies about his place on the evolutionary spectrum.

Annoyed, he backstrokes off in a snit, arcs his body gracefully backward, and dives, dragging his armored belly on the muddy bottom of the shallow pond (oh, how he longs for the fathomless depths of the Black Lagoon!) He surfaces to face Julie across the stretch of sun-shot water—only to find her striding back to the soundstage. Bill is waving him in from the water's edge. It must be time to resume shooting. Sighing, the Creature breaststrokes toward shore. Once the scourge of the Amazon, he has been reduced to a bit player in his own story.

∞

For it *is* his story. Or was supposed to be.

History will record it differently—attributing the film's origins to Maurice Zimm, but Zimm did little more than transcribe the Creature's narrative during a series of interviews conducted while the Creature lounged in producer William Alland's swimming pool. That's how the Creature remembers it anyway. He would have pounded out the screenplay himself if he could have. That task fell instead to two inveterate Hollywood journeymen, Harry Essex and Arthur Ross. When the final draft fell into the Creature's hands, he recoiled in disbelief. The caiman poachers had been transformed into intrepid paleontologists, the Black Lagoon into an arena of horrors, the Creature himself—an innocent victim!—into a vicious monster. About the only thing the trio of scribes had managed to do right was add a love interest—otherwise, the Creature thinks, he might never have met Julie Adams.

"I won't do it," the Creature protested. "I'll go back to the carnival. Hell, I'll go back to the Amazon!"

His agent—a balding, mousy little man named Henry Duvall—shook his head dolefully. "You've signed a contract."

"I didn't sign anything," the Creature growled. "I can't even hold a pen."

"I signed *for* you in the presence of two witnesses and a notary public," Duvall replied. "Same difference."

Cue Bela Lugosi.

So the Creature reported to the set as ordered, climbed aboard the *Rita* to terrorize Julie as required, shrank before the virile posturings of Richard Carlson (as required)—and fell in love.

"Love," he tells Karloff, pacing the actor's capacious study. By this time, Karloff has long since settled into stardom. He lives comfortably in L.A. and has steady work, though he's still typecast as a horror icon. Smaller than the Creature expected—the Creature towers a good two feet above him—Karloff in his late sixties remains handsome and slim, his dark hair silvering. Five times married, he is perhaps not the best person to approach for romantic advice, but the Creature's options are limited. His film, the first of a projected trilogy, is not yet completed, much less released, and he is beginning to see that he has been played for a fool. If Boris Karloff can't escape his defining role—if this charming, gentle man still clumps around in the American zeitgeist wearing elevator boots and bolts in his neck—then what hope has the Creature, who cannot even shuck his costume? There are no Oscars in his future, just endless sequels to this initial pack of lies. *Revenge of the Creature. The Creature Walks Among Us.* Even *Abbot and Costello Meet the Creature,* if things go badly enough (or well enough, from Universal's perspective).

"Love?" Karloff says. He leans back in his armchair and steeples his fingers. "Love is always a delicate matter."

"Tell me about it," says the Creature.

"If your love is unrequited"—Karloff retains a trace of his native British accent, a genteel formality—"then there is little you can do."

This is not the advice the Creature sought. This is not advice at all. This is a statement of fact. The Creature has come to suspect that Julie's visits to his pond are little more than kindnesses. After all, he sees the way she looks at Richard Carlson, the way she moistens her lips and gazes up at him in adoration. Carlson is nice enough to him, but nice won't do. While the Creature occasionally daydreams of raking Bill's head off in annoyance, his fantasies of violence toward Carlson burn icy and pure. He would like to kill him slowly, to spear each eyeball upon a talon and pop them into his mouth like jellybeans, to unseam his belly and feed upon the steaming offal, to wrench off his limbs one by one. For a start. The Creature does what he can to repress these unsavory flights of imagination, but they retain a vividness he cannot deny. He may work in a black-and-white 3D horror flick, but his fantasies are projected in widescreen Technicolor. Perhaps this is his true nature, savage and immutable, antediluvian and, yes, appropriate to the Missing Link. You can take the Creature out of the jungle, but you can't take the jungle out of the Creature.

He senses that this is not the way to Julie's heart.

Karloff clears his throat. "You face many obstacles, of course. You are not handsome. You are not human. You have, insofar as you have been able to detect, no potential for procreation. Yet there might be a way."

A way? The Creature pauses. He takes a seat across from Karloff. He'd like to lean back, but his goddamn dorsal ridge is, as always, in the way. Another reminder of his inhumanity. Yet there might be a way past even that.

He is all attention.

"Beauty comes in many forms," Karloff says. "It is, as the expression goes, in the eye of the beholder. But that eye is often best attuned when its object is set against its natural environment."

"What are you saying?"

Now Karloff leans forward. He smiles. "Underwater, my friend. Water is your natural milieu."

True enough. In his pond on the Universal lot, submerged to the waist and ladling up clear freshets with one spade-like hand, the Creature looks ridiculous. In the Black Lagoon, however, he glides through the water with a grace and beauty no man can hope to match. Human beings are no more suited to thrive underwater than he is suited to a purely land-bound existence. Clumsy and ill equipped for a submarine life, they don wet suits that are but sad reflections of his own glistening hide. They have rubber flippers where he has feet, heavy oxygen tanks and re-breathers where he has gills. If he shambles gasping across the Universal lot, his adversary in love will shamble—or anyway flail—beneath the surface. In the water, Carlson's beauty will be but a paltry thing. And while a return to the Black Lagoon is cost prohibitive, the underwater scenes are scheduled to be filmed in Wakulla Springs, Florida, a return to his beloved Gulf and (yes, he has researched the location shoots) the largest freshwater cave system in the world—if not his beloved Lagoon, the next best thing. Flush with renewed optimism, the Creature thanks Karloff and takes his leave.

The same optimism carries him across the continent, canted awkwardly in his seat—his dorsal ridge; again—and staring out at the blur of the propellers. Halfway through the flight, Julie walks down the aisle to take the seat beside him. She leans past him to look out the window, so close that he can smell the faint lavender scent of her perfume. "Isn't it beautiful?" she says, gazing down at the green hills unscrolling below the streaming scud. "It makes me think of the film."

"How?" says the Creature, who can see no clear connection.

"Well, it seems so deep, you know, so . . . dimensional . . . looking down from up here like this. I imagine the way the audience will experience it when they see us swimming out of the screen like that."

Ah. 3D. If he's been told once he's been told a thousand times. Alland's ambitions for the film hinge upon two factors: the realistic creature effects (which certainly *should* look realistic, the Creature ruminates) and the use of 3D, only the second Universal film to be released in the innovative format. But then he realizes that Julie has dozed off against his shoulder, and he wonders if he too can have a three-dimensioned life.

Wakulla Springs is everything the Creature had hoped it would be. There are shortcomings, to be sure. He could have wished for a more tropical setting—strangler figs, lianas, and buttress-rooted trees—but there is much to be thankful for as well. The alligators slipping into the murky water recall the caiman of the Black Lagoon; the bulky manatees the nine-foot piracuru and catfish that call his native waters home; the boom of insects the constant roar of the jungle. And the springs themselves are fathoms deep and riddled with caverns. Against his better judgment—Julie will think him hardly human at all, he fears—the Creature dispenses with the pretense of his trailer and abandons the on-set catering altogether. Halfway abandons the film, in fact. More often than not, when Jack dispatches Bill to summon the Creature to the set, he's off touring the depths. He explores the cave system in search of a rocky grotto like the one he had in the Amazon. He dozes in deep, cold currents where no human being can follow. He gluts himself on the abundance of prey, devouring fish raw in clouds of ichthyic blood. Life is good, or better anyway, but he is not happy (or if he is, he does not recognize it). Thoughts of Julie torture him like an inflamed scale under a ridge of his armored breast.

Finally, Jack calls him in for a meeting. Like Karloff, Jack is a kind man. Anger is not his natural métier, yet the Creature is forced to stand dripping on the carpet in the director's trailer, listening to his gentle rebuke. Somehow that makes it worse, Jack's generosity of spirit. "I have no choice, you see," the director admonishes him. "We're on a tight schedule. We're not making *Gone With the Wind*, you know."

"It's going to be a good picture," the Creature says.

"I didn't say it wasn't going to be a good picture. I said that we have to make our release date or both our careers are on the line."

"Your career," the Creature rasps. "What kind of career am I likely to have, Jack?"

"You're unique. After people see this picture, offers are going to come rolling in."

"Don't patronize me, Jack. We both know there's only one role I can play."

Jack sighs. "I guess you're right. But still, this is going to be a good film. You'll get to play *this* role again."

The Creature laughs humorlessly, snared in a dilemma even his human colleagues must share, forever trapped in the prison house of self. That's the appeal of acting, he supposes: the chance to be someone else, if only for a little while. And isn't that what he's doing here, playing at being something he's not? He's not a monster. He never has been. If his range of roles is limited—if he is doomed to be the Creature from the Black Lagoon—well that's Hollywood. He thinks of Karloff and Lugosi. Who does he want to become? Does he wish to accept his fate with grace or does he wish to rail perpetually against it, strung out on drugs and bitterness? Is being the Creature any different than being a carnival freak? Yet still he longs for his lost home. How he hates the poachers who have done this to him. He'd like to poke *their* eyeballs out, too. And eat them.

So maybe he's a monster, after all.

"I need you on the set on time," Jack is saying while these thoughts run through the Creature's head. "It's expensive to shoot underwater, especially with the 3D rig. Every time you don't show up when you're supposed to, you cost us money."

"I'm sorry, Jack," the Creature says.

"Look, I know this is hard for you. Nobody ever said acting was easy. Look at Brando. Channel your anger into the role. I need you to be the Creature I know you can be."

The Creature doesn't know quite what Jack means by this. He doesn't even know who—or what—he is anymore. Yet he vows to himself that he will try for something more complex than a B-movie monster—to draw not only upon his fury and resentment, but upon his passion for Julie. He vows to do better.

He does, too.

The Creature shows up promptly as requested. He lingers between shots. He tries to make small talk with the crew. But what is there to say, really? He's an eight-foot amphibian, finned and armored in plates of bone. He could eviscerate any one of them with the twitch of a talon. Monster or not, he is a monster to them.

Not Julie, though, or so he tells himself. Perhaps Karloff is right: set against his natural environment, she seems to recognize his grace. Indeed she seems to share it. Unburdened by the clunky scuba tanks the men's roles demand, she glides through the water. And between shots she dispenses with the bathrobe she'd taken to draping herself in on the Universal lot, as if swimming together has drawn them closer. Of all the actors on the set, she alone seems entirely at ease with him. They spend more and more time talking. As he lolls in the shallows, she tells him about her recent divorce and about growing up in Arkansas; she tells him about her first days in Hollywood, working as a secretary and taking voice lessons on the side. Yet she is still capable of blind cruelty.

"You're lucky," she says. "You never had to fight for your dreams."

The Creature hardly knows how to respond. So what if Universal picked him up the minute William Alland laid eyes on him? Unlike Julie, he'll never play another role in his life; all the elocution lessons in the world won't change his inhuman growl. He's not even sure what he aspires to anymore. Stardom? Freedom? A return to the Black Lagoon? In his dreams, he sweeps Julie into his embrace, carries her off to the Amazon, unveils to her the wonders of his vanished life: the splendid isolation of the Lagoon, the sluggish currents of the great river, the mystery of the crepuscular forest.

Maybe this newfound intimacy accounts for the otherworldly beauty of the Wakulla scenes. In the dailies, Julie cuts the surface, her white bathing suit shining down through the gloom like god light. The Creature stalks her from below, half-hidden among drifting fronds of thalassic flora, rapt by her ethereal beauty. His webbed hands cleave the water. Bubbles erupt skyward with his every kick. As she swims, he glides toward her from below, up, up, up, until he is swimming on his back beneath her and closing fast: a dozen feet, half a dozen, less, his immovable face frozen in an expression of impossible longing. He reaches out a tentative hand to brush her ankle as she treads water—and pulls it away at the last moment, as terrified of her rejection on celluloid as he is terrified of her rejection in life. What one does not risk, one cannot lose; worse yet, he thinks, what one does not risk, one cannot gain. A sense of inconsolable despair seizes him. In the images projected on the screen, he sees now how little their worlds can connect. She is a creature of the daylit skin of the planet, he of the shadowy submarine depths.

Jack praises the silent yearning in the Creature's performance.

Yet the whole thing drives the director crazy nonetheless. Frustrated by the task of stitching the haunting underwater scenes together with the mundane L.A footage, he asks the studio for reshoots and is denied. For the first time—the only time—the Creature sees Jack angry, his face a mask of fury. "This could be so much more than another goddamn monster flick," he says in the dim projection trailer, flinging away the 3D glasses perched on his nose. Even this angry gesture drives home the Creature's inhumanity. Alone in the back row, he must pinch his glasses between two delicate claws. His flattened nose provides no bridge to support them. He has no external ears to hook them over. Everything about him is streamlined for his underwater existence.

The Creature grinds his cardboard glasses under one webbed foot. He slams out of the trailer, the door crumpling with a screech of tortured metal as he hurtles into the moonlit night. He is halfway to the water when Julie catches up with him. "Wait," she says, "Wait—"

Her voice hitches in the place where his name ought to be—for of course he has no name, does he? He is the Creature, the Gill Man, nothing more. There has been no one to name him—even the freaks did not name him—and he has never thought to name himself. He would not know how to begin. Fred? John? Earl? Such human names fall leaden on the tongue, inadequate to describe a . . . a creature, a fiend, an inhuman monster. How will they credit him in the film? *The Creature as the Creature*?

"Wait," Julie says again. "Creature, wa—"

The Creature whirls to face her, one massive hand drawn back to strike.

"Don't," she whispers, and the Creature checks the blow. For an instant, everything hangs balanced on a breath. Then the Creature lowers his hand, turns away, and shambles toward the water, his great feet flapping. Something feels broken inside him. Jack's words—

—*another goddamn monster flick*—

—echo inside his head. That's all he is, isn't he? A monster. A monster who in a moment of fury, would have with a single swipe of his claws torn from her shoulders the head of the woman he loved. A monster who would in the grip of his rage, feed upon her blood. The Creature would cry, but even that simple human solace is denied him. The dark waters beckon.

"Wait," Julie says. "Please."

Almost against his will, the Creature turns to face her. She stands maybe a dozen feet away. In the moonlight, tears glint upon her cheeks. Beyond her, the men—Jack and Dick and Richard Denning, the third lead—stand silhouetted against the beacon of golden light pouring through the trailer's shattered door.

"Why?" the Creature says, knowing the doom that will come upon him if he stays.

"Because," Julie says, "because I love you."

So Karloff was right. For a heartbeat, happiness—a great and abiding contentment that no mere human being can plumb—settles over the Creature like a benediction. But what is the depth of love, he wonders, its strange currents and dimensions? What is its price, and is he willing to pay it? And a line from another monster movie comes to him, one that Jack showed him in pre-production: *It was beauty killed the beast*.

This is Hollywood.

It vill fuck you every time.

"I love you, too," he says in his inhuman rasp, and in the same instant, in his heart, he recants that love, refuses and renounces it. For Julie. For himself. He will not be the monster that loves. He will not be the monster that dies. He will not be their freak, their creature. He will not haunt their dreams. They can finish their fucking film with a man in a rubber suit.

The Creature puts his back to Julie and wades into the water, glimmering with moonlight. It welcomes him home, rising to his shins and thighs before the bottom drops away beneath him, and he dives. He has studied the locations, he has explored the Springs' network of caverns: from here the Wakulla River to the St. Marks and Apalachee Bay, and thence to the Gulf. The Black Lagoon calls out to him across the endless miles, and so the Creature strikes off for home, knowing now how fleeting are the heart's desires, knowing that Julie too would ebb into memory, this perfect moment lost, this happiness receding forever into the past.

Mating Habits of the Late Cretaceous

They'd come to the Cretaceous to save their marriage.

"Why not the Paleogene," said Peter, who had resolutely refused to look at any of the material Gwyneth had sent him. "Or the Little Ice Age for that matter? Some place without carnivores."

"There are only two resorts," Gwyneth said, waving a brochure at him. "Jurassic and Cretaceous. People want to see dinosaurs."

She wanted to see dinosaurs.

"And I'm afraid travel to inhabited eras is no longer permitted, Mr. Braunmiller," the agent put in. "Ever since the Eckels Incident. So the Little Ice Age is out."

"Besides," Gwyneth said. "I wouldn't mind a few carnivores."

Peter sighed.

Cool air misted down from unseen vents. The agent's desk, a curved wedge of gleaming mahogany, floated in emptiness. Surround screens immersed them in sensory-enhanced three-dimensional renderings from the available eras. One moment the hot siroccos of some time-vanished desert stung their skin. The next, the damp, shrieking hothouse of a Jurassic jungle sprang sweat from their brows.

"Why not a sim?" Peter asked.

"I've had enough of simulations, Peter," Gwyneth said, thinking of the expense. Over Peter's protests, she had mortgaged the house they'd bought three years ago, cashed in retirement and savings accounts, taken on loans they couldn't afford.

All for this.

"You're certain, then?" the agent asked.

Peter opened his mouth and closed it again.

Twilight waters washed the barren shingles of some ancient inland sea.

"We're certain," Gwyneth said.

Tablets materialized in front of them.

"Just a few releases to sign," the agent said. "Warranties, indemnities against personal injury—"

"I thought the yoke—" Peter said, and a fresh draft of whispering air blew down upon them.

"The lawyers insist," the agent said, smiling.

An hour later, forms signed in triplicate, notarized, and filed away, the agent ushered them into an airlock. When they stripped, Gwyneth could feel Peter's gaze upon her; she didn't so much as glance at him, though he was lean and fit, as well muscled at thirty-five as he had been at their wedding seven years before. Stinging jets of anti-bacterial spray enveloped them. Industrial-strength compressors blasted them dry. They dressed in tailored, featherweight safari gear, and cycled through another airlock, their luggage hovering behind them. The adjoining chamber was bereft of luxury—no surround screens or polished mahogany, no calming mists of murmuring air. Their boots rang on polished concrete. Fluorescent globes floated high in the latticed spaces above them, leaching color from their faces. White-clad technicians looked up from their tablets as the airlock dilated. Behind them crackled the time machine, more impressive than Gwyneth had thought it would be, a miracle of sizzling yellow-green energy, the raw stuff of creation itself, harnessed by human ingenuity and bound screaming into colossal spider arms of curving steel and iron.

The technicians took charge of them. The hiss of hypodermic injections followed, then diaphanous bands of black that melted closed around their wrists like wax. The technician touched Gwyneth's; far down in its polished depths a series of lights—orange and red and green—flashed once and was gone.

Her yoke.

The other technician, finishing up with Peter, smiled. "Your guide will meet you on the other side," he said. "Ready to go?"

The time machine spat fire, throwing off scorching arcs of green and yellow.

They stepped into the light.

And were gone.

A sheet of green flame blinded them. Time blurred—a day, a week, a year, then more, the centuries peeling away like leaves, so that Gwyneth, who was barely thirty-four, felt young and alive as she had not felt in this last year. The time machine stank of history, of the sun beating down upon the tiered pyramids of new-built Aztec temples; of wheat flourishing for the first time under the hands of men; and further yet, of a dark age where shrewd monkeys huddled in terror around their lightning-struck fires. But Eckels had closed all that to them, and just as well, Gwyneth supposed, for he had bestowed upon them in its lieu the immense panorama of geologic time. And how she longed to step out of her life into a world fresh made, where great Triceratops lifted his three-pronged head and the sky-flung demon of the age, titanic Quetzalcoatlus, still spread his leathery wings; where the greatest of the thunder lizards, the tyrant king of all that he surveyed, Tyrannosaurus Rex, yet bestrode the terrified earth. Where, most of all, none of it had happened yet, and she could pretend that maybe it never would.

Then there was an enormous jolt, and Gwyneth cried aloud in terror or delight. Peter reached for her hand, and a lean, leathery man whose smile never reached his eyes stood before them.

They were there.

It was a resort, all right—a rugged dream carved out of the primeval wilderness. Below and to the west, a long savannah sloped away to a distant glimmer of sea. Above and to the east a jagged mountain range knifed through the earth's crust, so that morning came late there and afternoons lingered into a blue twilight that seemed to stretch out forever. To the south and to the north, encircling arms of forest fell in ranks toward the distant plain. And in the heart of it all, like a precious stone set in swirls of green and brown, gleamed Cretacia, a maze of sandy paths and hidden glades where clear fountains tumbled and stone benches grew black with lichen. Private cabanas perched on tiers cut into the wooded ridges, and jeweled swimming pools glinted among the trees. Below the whitewashed sprawl of the hotel itself wound a quaint commercial district. Restaurants staffed by murmuring servers crowded up against narrow shops that sold books—actual books—and bath salts and summer dresses at such exorbitant rates that Gwyneth laughed in disbelief.

Yet her heart quickened in delight when the tall man with fine crinkles around his eyes—Wilson, Robert Wilson, he'd introduced himself—thumbed open their door for the first time and she saw the sheer decadence of the place: a bower of eggshell white and blue with a bed veiled in gauzy shadow, a vase of tropical flowers, and a south-facing floor-to-ceiling window (no sim screen, but glass, thick, reinforced glass) that gave upon a forested ravine, where something small and dappled scurried through the shadows, and if you stood on tip-toe and craned your neck, you could catch a glimpse of diamonds glittering upon the sea.

"I'll leave you to unpack," Wilson said, and turning from the window Gwyneth saw him—really saw him—for the first time: a hard, sun-baked man with sandy hair and an unhandsome face like a promontory of granite. His khakis were worn and stained, his boots scuffed. For a moment she was ashamed of their own gear, so new that it rustled when they walked.

"The concierge can take care of all your needs here on the grounds," Wilson said. "If you want to go outside—when you want to go outside—I'll be your guide."

Turning from the window, Peter extended his hand. Gwyneth saw to her horror the folded fifty inside it.

Wilson stiffened. "No thank you, sir. That's very kind of you."

The door closed softly behind him.

"Peter," Gywneth said. "You've insulted him now. He's a wilderness guide, not a bellhop."

"Just as well, I suppose. God knows we can't afford to spend another dime."

Then:

"Well, how was I to know?"

"Perhaps if you'd bothered to read some of the material I sent you—"

"This was your idea, not mine, Gwyneth."

"But it's *our* vacation," she snapped. "And you ought to remember why and start acting like it."

She crossed her arms and turned back to the windows.

It was still and peaceful out there.

A moment passed. They waited to see if what had been so long unsaid would break through the stillness. She knew that it would sometime soon, or that it had better. The wound had festered. It needed to be lanced and drained.

Peter came up and stood behind her, so close she could feel his breath, warm upon the back of her neck. "I'm sorry." His hand came up to her lower back.

Did she flinch? And did he feel it?

She wanted this to work, yet her body betrayed her.

"I'm sorry," he said.

When he leaned in to kiss her, she turned her face away.

They breakfasted on a long shaded terrace overlooking a pool. Fans stirred the air overhead. Just outside the compound, bright tiny dinosaurs strutted, pecking at the earth like chickens. Far below, beyond a stunning vista of tree-studded cliffs, huge sauropods feasted on towering groves of conifer. Something else had spooked a dinosaur herd. A cloud of dust obscured them, but their cries—a mournful lowing like the faraway lament of a foghorn—rose up to the terrace. Gwyneth wondered what had set them running.

"The coffee is fine," Peter said, the meal done.

A server took their plates. He came back and used a long blade to scrape the linen cloth of crumbs.

Gwyneth took her coffee black; to please Peter she took a sip. "It is fine," she said. Insipid banalities—that was all they could find to say. They'd forgotten the language of their own marriage, so they skated along the surface, stripping away any hint of ugliness as efficiently as the hotel staff spirited away a stained pillow. Last night, in a darkness rich with the strange music of the Cretaceous woods, he had reached out to touch her, and her body had gone rigid of its own accord. They had lain like that, so stiff and silent and distant that they might have been on separate continents, lying wakeful under foreign skies. Now, when he reached out to rest a hand upon her own where it lay brown against the white tablecloth, her fingers twitched and were still.

She felt tears well up, and choked them back, determined not to cry.

She said, "Peter—"

Then Robert Wilson was leaning over them, his own hand closing about the back rail of her chair and brushing her shoulder blade. He smelled of earth and dusty leather and the dry plain below. Gwyneth looked up through a sheen of unshed tears. When he returned her smile, his eyes remained as watchful and cold as marbles under the bony ridge of his brow. They were the color of agates, washed out and narrow from squinting across the blazing savannah. Something quickened inside her. She leaned forward and he wasn't touching her shoulder anymore.

"Something spooked down there," she said.

"Hydrosaurs," he said. "Bloody cows startle easily enough. Could have been anything. A pack of raptors, maybe, but mostly they lie up under the trees until dusk."

"But the big ones—" Peter said.

"The Alamosaurs. Go right on munching at the treetops, don't they? Not much spooks an Alamosaur. A T-Rex maybe. Too big to worry about the raptors, and tails like whips. It's an ecosystem, right? Like the African veldt. An elephant doesn't worry much about a lion, does he?"

"Will we see a T-Rex?" Gwyneth asked.

"You'll hear them cough at night if one's around," he said. "Last night was silent as a grave. Snorkeling today. Plesiosaurs, maybe a Kronosaur—T-Rex of the sea—if we're lucky."

"Sounds dangerous," Gwyneth said.

"Feels dangerous," Wilson said. "Safe as houses, though. Your yoke will see a Kronosaur turning aggressive before we even know it's there," he added, and for the first time Gwyneth noticed that his wrist was bare.

"You're not yoked."

He laughed. "I'm too ornery too eat."

"Let's take a pass," Peter said. "I think we'll spend the day settling in."

"Your call. You'll have plenty of time."

Wilson nodded and strode away into the shadows.

They sat in silence for a moment, listening to the subdued babble of conversation around them.

"I think I'd like to be consulted about any future decisions, if you don't mind," she said quietly.

"Gwyneth—"

"It's *my* vacation, right?"

"He's talking about swimming with dinosaurs, for Christ's sake."

"Well, what did you think we were here to do, Peter?"

"To—"

"To what?"

"To try and fix things." He shook his head. "To try and fix things, that's all."

"Well, we're not going to fix them sitting on the terrace drinking coffee, are we? We might as well get our money's worth." She set her cup down and stood. "I think I'll go change into something more appropriate for settling in."

Gwyneth was halfway across the room, weaving her way between the tables, when someone reached out and touched her elbow. A woman—blonde and handsome, with a strong jaw line and narrow lips—smiled up at her. Her companion looked up from his breakfast.

"I'm Angela," she said. "And this mannerless brute"—

—said brute swiped his face with a linen napkin—

—"is Frank—"

"Stafford," the brute said, clambering to his feet. "Frank Stafford. But just Frank'll do." He took Gwyneth's fingertips, and bowed slightly, lifting his eyebrows. Crockery rattled.

"Careful, Frank—" the woman—Angela—cried.

But by this time Peter had appeared at Gwyneth's shoulder, and the brute—he really was something of a brute, Gwyneth thought, barrel chested and broad shouldered as an ox—was reaching past her to shake Peter's hand.

"Just Frank," Peter said—Stafford acknowledged this tepid witticism with a deep belly laugh—"Peter Braunmiller."

"Here, have a sit." Stafford shoved a chair in their direction, and when they were seated over fresh cups of coffee, he said, "That guy, Wilson, he's your guide, too? What a piece of work, huh?"

"Fearless as a bandersnatch," Angela said. "We did a trail with him the other day, and got within twenty feet of this awful thing called an anklysaur—"

"Armored bastard. Club on its tail the size of a fucking Volkswagen. He started to swing that thing when he saw us, and I swear to God I felt the wind on my face, we were that close." Stafford laughed. "Felt my yoke give a good tug, I swear I did."

"Anyway," Angela said. "We overheard—really we weren't eavesdropping—that you weren't going on the excursion today, and since we aren't either—"

"Can't swim a lick," Stafford said. "Afraid of the water my whole life. Sink like a stone, and if I didn't a dinosaur'd eat me for sure."

"— we were hoping you might play tennis. Please say you do or we'll just sit on the terrace and drink Bloody Marys all morning."

"Terrible for the health, Bloody Marys."

"I suppose we could play tennis," Peter said, and then—was he mocking her? Gwyneth wondered—"You up for tennis, Gwen?"

And Gwyneth, thinking of the Kronosaur—the T-Rex of the sea—forced a smile. "Tennis it is," she said.

Gwyneth and Peter lost in straight sets.

The Staffords were formidable opponents. Peter, a finesse player who relied on superior endurance, couldn't handle Stafford's powerful serves. Angela's shots had a wicked backspin that Gwyneth never quite mastered.

"Luck, that's all," Stafford assured them, clapping Peter on the back, but as they headed back to the room to clean up, Peter whispered, "All the same to you, Gwen, I think I'd rather have gone snorkeling with the Karnosaurs."

"Kronosaurs," she said.

"Right. Except Frank Stafford is the damned carnivore," he said. "Seriously. I think my yoke must be malfunctioning. I was getting the life beat out of me, and it didn't so much as twitch."

Against her will, Gwyneth laughed. Peter flung an arm across her shoulder, and for a moment the effortless camaraderie of their first years together—that playful, irreverent sense of humor, the easy way their bodies seemed to fit together—came back to her. For a moment she even thought of Peter's hand upon her in the night, of how it might have been if she had turned to face him—

And then, of its own accord, her mind swerved away.

They showered and met the Staffords for lunch, where they learned that their tennis partner had been a subcontractor on the Museum of Post-Modern Art in D.C., among other things.

"Just a little piece of it," Stafford said, holding up pinched fingers. "The duct work. Keep people cool in all that heat."

"That's a lot of duct work," Peter said.

"You bet it is," Stafford said, and Gwyneth suddenly had a sense of just how much she and Peter had sacrificed for this trip—of how much she had forced him to sacrifice. Stafford could buy and sell them a hundred times over, and she had nearly impoverished them.

"Angela's idea, this trip," Stafford was saying. "I told her I'd already found my niche. A lot of money in duct bills." He dropped them a wink. "My little evolution joke," he said.

"His only joke," Angela said drily. And then: "What do you do, Peter?"

"I'm an assets manager."

"Gambling," Stafford said, thrusting his plate away. "Pushing money around, that's all that is. End of the day, I like to put my hands on something solid. Like to say, I did that."

Peter flinched, but if Stafford noticed, he didn't let on.

Afterward, the men strolled off in search of cigars, though Gwyneth had never known Peter to smoke a cigar in her life. The two women found themselves in a secluded bar overlooking the cliffs.

"Sorry about that last bit," Angela said over gin and tonics.

"Peter's too sensitive."

Gwyneth sipped her drink. She was beginning to feel the alcohol. The world had taken on a lush beauty. The edges of everything had sharpened. Each discrete bead of condensation glistened on her glass; every needle of the nearby conifers stood articulate against the azure sky. The full heat of the day had come on, and the plain below stretched empty toward the blue horizon. Gwyneth supposed the raptors must be lying up under the trees, and that made her think of Robert Wilson. She wondered if he had found his Kronosaurs, and if he was back from the sea yet.

"It's very quiet in the Cretaceous," Angela said. "There's something missing, I can't figure out what."

Gwyneth listened.

But for them, the bar was empty. The barman stood polishing glasses. The stillness was pervasive. "Birds," she said suddenly. "There were no birds"—and then, laughing, corrected herself. "There *are* no birds. Or hardly any. They haven't evolved yet. Birds are dinosaurs. Or dinosaurs are birds. Or will be. I remember reading that somewhere."

"You're very amusing, Gwyneth Braunmiller."

The barman came and freshened their drinks. When he was gone, Angela said, "What do you do?"

"I'm a technical writer. I mostly write instruction manuals," Gwyneth said. "Or rewrite them, anyway." She laughed. "You've probably read some of my stuff."

Angela absorbed this in silence.

"Do you have children?"

Gwyneth laughed ruefully.

"I'm awfully nosy," Angela said. "You needn't answer."

"No, I don't mind. It's just—" She broke off.

"You haven't reached an agreement on that issue."

"No, I guess we haven't."

The truth was they'd never really talked about it much. Neither of them felt strongly either way, she supposed. The problems were deeper than that, harder to pin down—the way minor disagreements had of settling into arguments and arguments into something worse, a cool distance, like planets orbiting different stars. And then, not wanting to be rude, she said, "What do you do, Angela?"

"I sit on charity boards. I spend Frank's money. You'd be surprised how taxing it can be—no pun intended." She raised her eyebrows and smiled.

"Children?"

"None. Frank has a grown son from a previous marriage. Musn't threaten the heir to the empire."

The alcohol made Gwyneth incautious. "And what brings you here?"

"Our twentieth anniversary."

She sipped her drink.

"I still remember the wedding. Predictions for longevity were dire." Angela laughed and touched Gwyneth's hand. "What a pleasure to have proven them wrong."

"To love," Gwyneth said, lifting her glass.

They were quiet then, listening to the birdless afternoon.

The next day they went hiking—fifteen of them, Wilson's entire excursion group. Despite the novelty of the towering conifers and angiosperms, a bleak melancholy fell over Gwyneth. The medication prescribed by her psychiatrist—"just to get you through this rough patch," she'd said—hadn't helped, nor had the trouble with Peter, the—what, exactly? The silence where there had been voices, the blind staring into the dark, their bodies separate and apart. And underneath that, turning its immense body in the fretful depths of sleep that finally claimed them, that unspoken sense of despair that eluded words. Malaise? Ennui? She didn't know. Day after day after day it had worsened, for months, for a year and more, until one listless afternoon, Gwyneth happened across a documentary on Time Safaris, Ltd. Not since college paleontology had she seen live footage of dinosaurs. A desire to see them for herself, to plant her feet on the soil of another age, had seized her. And something else, as well: the conviction that two weeks away from the world—*really* away from the world—might fix the broken things between them.

"Jesus, Gwyneth, do you want to break us?" Peter had asked when he'd seen the cost.

She didn't quite have the nerve to respond as she had wanted to: *We're already broken.*

Her foot slipped on an outcropping of stone, and she would have fallen but for Angela's steadying hand at her elbow. Gwyneth swiped perspiration from her eyes with the back of one hand.

"Drinks, darling. The moment we return," Angela whispered—quiet being a condition imposed upon them at the beginning of the excursion—and Gwyneth laughed, and said, "By all means, yes," feeling closer to this virtual stranger than her own husband of almost a decade.

That morning the two women had gravitated toward one another like old friends. They tramped side-by-side, midway in the group strung out along the trail like pearls. Their husbands forged along behind Wilson, who took the rocky path without effort, a canteen at his belt and a rifle slung across one shoulder. Late afternoon and the Cretaceous alive with sound, the hooting complaint of the striped, knee-high theropods that scattered into the underbrush before them, the steady hush of insects, the arboreal rustle of mammals the size of squirrels—"Our forbears," Wilson had said. "The meek shall inherit the earth."

From on high the alien shriek of some sky-borne pteranodon drifted down.

They stopped in a clearing of tall, flowering grass to search the thing out.

It was Stafford who spotted it, his arm out-stretched. They gathered around him to stare at the creature circling high above them in a sky of sun-shot blue.

"Quetzalcoatlus?" someone asked.

"Nothing so large, I should think." Wilson unclipped his binoculars. "Looks to have a wingspan of maybe fifteen feet, about half that of Queztalcoatlus. Could be a juvenile, I suppose, but it's hard to tell at this distance. Anyone want to see?"

The binoculars made the rounds. When her turn came, Gwyneth lifted them to her eyes, but she could never hold the image in frame long enough to get anything more than a glimpse of the creature, a fleeting impression of beak and bony crest, the vast leathery wings taut as a wind-blown kite.

They moved on then, deeper into the woods. The familiar smell of pine needles and dry loam enveloped her, the scent of unfamiliar flowers. Stafford had acquired the aura of a minor hero. Wilson had clapped him on the shoulder. "Sharp eyes," he'd said, and the big man seemed to have expanded still more under the praise. Despite his size, he moved through the woods with a confidence Peter lacked, surefooted, a creature of the physical world, his bearish frame poised over his center of gravity.

The terrain grew more forgiving, dropping away into a broad vale. The pace slowed, as Wilson paused to point out the flowering angiosperms and broad-leaved deciduous trees that had only recently—geologically speaking—evolved to compete with the pervasive conifers. They paused for water. Wilson moved among them, spare and purposeful, no gesture wasted.

"Okay, then?" he said to Gwyneth.

"I'm fine."

He nodded, and moved on.

They got moving again fifteen minutes later.

Not long after that the woods thinned. Another glade opened ahead of them. Moted beams of sunlight slanted through the treetops, firing the bracken with a yellow-green glow. The boles of trees climbed the heavens in dark silhouette, dwarfing Wilson where he stood black against the green effulgence, the back of his hand upraised in universal semaphore. He waved the straggling line to either side. Something snorted, blew out breath in a long waning note. It called out—a kind of groan, long and deep-pitched, like a rusty nail being wrenched from an ancient board. Then it took a step. Weeds thrashed. Gwyneth slipped with Peter through the ferny undergrowth to the right.

The trees fell away and the glade unveiled itself.

Gwyneth gasped for the beauty of it, the shining clearing and the creatures that grazed there: majestic, ponderous beasts—three horned, twenty-five or thirty feet long, ten feet at the shoulder—cropping peacefully at the waist-high grass. Triceratops, Gwyneth thought, gazing in wonder at the massive bony frill that curved up behind their heads, flushed bright with pink and red. The breeze combing the grass smelled of the creatures in the glade, a scent of old leather and manure and fresh-mown grass.

She caught snatches of Wilson murmuring—

". . . a bull, two cows—the smaller ones—and a yearling. See it?"

He broke off as the largest of the dinosaurs—the bull—swung its elongated head in their direction. It regarded them with a single beady eye. In three quarter profile, the beast was more impressive still, battle scarred and ancient, the horns above its eyes razor-sharp spears of bone, jutting out three feet or more. It lumbered toward them, a single step, then two and three—

"Steady, now," Wilson whispered. "Steady—"

—chuffed, and paused, as if assessing the danger they posed; a moment later, it lowered its beaked snout and began to tear at the weeds once again. This close Gwyneth could see parasites—insects maybe—crawling across its mottled green and brown hide. She was about to ask about them, when her eye caught a rustle in the tall grass—

The underbrush erupted, shrieking.

For a moment, Gwyneth didn't see them, they were so well camouflaged. Then she did, three, four—was it five, or more?—green- and yellow-striped raptors the size of men or larger, hurtling across the clearing from half a dozen woody blinds, so fast that the eye could barely track them. Three of them corralled the yearling and herded it, toward the trees. More than half the pack—there were seven of them, she saw—no, eight—wheeled away to face the charge of the bull Triceratops. Just as it lowered its head to impale them, they gave ground, hurling themselves at the monster's unprotected haunches, their razor-clawed feet digging for purchase in its hide. The animal's belly split, spilling a bulge of glistening viscera—

Peter clutched at her, trying to drag her deeper under the trees. The bull Triceratops wheeled around, lunging at its tormentors. Its tail whipped the air, flinging a raptor screeching into the undergrowth, and somewhere at the edge of the clearing the yearling screamed and screamed and screamed, until, abruptly, it fell silent. Dear God, she could see the raptors tearing it limb from limb. Grass thrashed. Geysers of blood erupted. Her heart pounding, Gwyneth wrenched free of Peter's hand. She stepped into the clearing, she didn't know why. The yearling's companions, the bleeding bull among them, broke for the trees. As the remaining raptors swung around to their kill, they saw her—

—they *saw* her—

—and for a heartbeat—she felt a single nightmarish pulse at her temple—the moment hung in equipoise. Fathomless silence enveloped her. Then, shrieking, the nearest raptor flung itself toward her, its taloned feet clawing the earth. Gwyneth felt the tug of the yoke, like gravity seizing her as she careened through the loop of a roller coaster—

Then Robert Wilson stepped up beside her, leveling the rifle. The thing was almost upon them—the scene going watery around her as the yoke began to draw her home—when he pulled the trigger. There was a sound of thunder. The raptor's skull dissolved into a spray of blood and bone. Its body spun convulsing to the ground. The next moment her vision cleared.

The glade was silent and empty.

"Quickly, now," Wilson said, touching her shoulder. "They'll be back soon."

He spun her around and they retreated under the trees. The rest of the group awaited them there. She saw Peter, his long face pale with fury, and she reached out an entreating hand to him.

"Peter—" she said.

But he turned away.

Then Angela was there, catching an arm around her waist and cooing, "It's okay now, it's all over." And then, half-supporting her as they trudged homeward through the suddenly menacing woods: "We'll get a drink into you first thing," she whispered. "A drink is what it wants."

A drink, thought Gwyneth, with a mounting hilarity she did not recognize as her own. A drink would be just the thing.

Yes, a drink.

Maybe two, Gwyneth thought—definitely two, as it turned out, and she sensed a third one coming on. Fire pits threw up sparks and music swirled in the night air. She leaned against the railing, lifted her face to the breeze, sipped her martini. The gin smelled of pine trees, of the vast conifer forest, unsullied by human hands, that sprawled across the continent.

The scent triggered a flash of memory: the raptor hurling itself across the clearing at her, Wilson leveling the gun—

And here he was, speak of the devil.

Elbows on the railing, he leaned beside her. The party was in full swing now. Dancers twirled under muted lights. Wisps of conversation drifted through the air. She spied Peter, talking to Stafford by the buffet, and glanced away.

Wilson set her empty glass on the tray of a passing server and handed her a fresh martini. "Cheers," he said.

They touched glasses. She held the gin in her mouth, savoring it.

They turned their backs to the party. For a long time, they leaned on their elbows, staring out into the dark. Before them ran the long blue savannah.

"Something else, isn't it?" he said.

She gazed up at the sky, bereft of the old constellations. Or was it new? She laughed, and a small voice inside her said, *You must be careful. He'll think you're drunk.* Which she was. Why it should matter, she could not say.

"The stars look strange."

"The skies change in sixty-five million years. Or seventy."

"You don't know, then?"

"No one knows."

"But Eckels—"

"The recent past they're pretty good at. The further back you go—" He shrugged. "Slippage."

"And why is that, Mr. Wilson?"

"You're talking to the wrong man, Mrs.—"

"Gwyneth."

"—Braunmiller. You'd need a physicist to answer that."

"Yet you were waiting the moment we arrived."

"Once they have a focal point to lock in on—once some brave soul plants a flag, so to speak—then you're fine."

"But you don't know when that focal point is?"

"Never will. Rough calculations can pin it down some—we're toward the end of the era, we know that. But dinosaurs don't keep calendars, I'm afraid."

She could feel the alcohol buzzing through her veins. Her face was not unpleasantly numb.

"Dance?" he said.

"If you insist."

Leaving their drinks on a nearby table, they stepped on to the dance floor.

"I haven't thanked you for saving my life today."

"I didn't save your life."

"Didn't you?"

"Your yoke would have saved you if it came to that. You could feel it, couldn't you?"

"Like gravity moving through me. A roller coaster. That's what I thought."

Her mind replayed that snippet of memory once again—the raptor lunging at her, Wilson lifting the gun—

"Why did you wait so long to shoot?"

"Wouldn't do to miss, would it? We're not all yoked."

"You've been yoked before, Mr. Wilson?"

"Yes."

"And had to use it."

"Oh sure."

"What happened?"

"Female tyrannosaur cornered me in a ravine. They're the bad ones. The females."

He raised his eyebrows. She wasn't sure if he was joking.

"What's it feel like?"

"The yoke?"

"Yes."

"Like being turned inside out."

"So why aren't you wearing one now?"

"Because it feels like being turned inside out."

"Seriously."

"It would hardly do if your guide disappeared, would it? If I'd been yoked today, we both might have gone home. Who'd have led your intrepid hikers back to the hotel?"

She glimpsed Peter, watching them from the buffet, and had a momentary image of him trying to find his way back through the woods alone—Peter, who lived almost entirely in a world of complex financial transactions, a world where meaning was not innate, but created by the universal assent of billions. What had Stafford called it the other day? Pushing money around. He'd said something else, too: *I like to put my hands on something solid. Like to say, I did that.*

Yet—

"You risk your life for that?"

"There's money, of course. And more."

"More?"

"It doesn't bear talking to death."

She fell silent. They revolved to the music.

Wilson said: "What the devil possessed you to do that, anyway?"

The sound of the yearling screaming echoed in her memory.

"I don't know," she said. She said, "I can't stand to see things in pain."

"This is no good for you, then."

"I'm not sure what's good for me, anymore."

"Who is?"

"You seem to be pretty certain."

"I've stripped my life to certain basics, that's all."

"There's no Mrs. Wilson?"

"Not for many years now."

"Are you lonely?"

"You're very curious, aren't you? Let's collect our drinks."

They stood at the railing again. Gwyneth sipped her martini. She was being careful now.

"I thought perhaps some great heartache in your past—"

"Nothing so romantic, I'm afraid. She wasn't willing to live with the risks I take. I wasn't willing to live without them."

"Why not?"

"Do you know Wallace Stevens? Death is the mother of beauty?"

"Poetry, too?"

"You know it then."

"I've read it, I think. In college once."

"You should read it again."

She laughed. "What would I find there, Robert Wilson. Truth or beauty?"

"A bit of both, maybe."

"You must feel great disdain for your charges."

He shrugged.

"You must feel great disdain for me."

"If I felt disdain, I wouldn't be talking to you, would I?"

"What do you feel?"

"Are you flirting with me, Mrs. Braunmiller?"

"I'm curious, that's all."

"What you did was very brave. Also very stupid. I admire the courage."

"And the stupidity?"

Wilson didn't answer. He lifted his glass and finished his whiskey. He held it in his mouth for a long moment. He set the glass on the railing. "Laphroaig," he said. "Nectar of the gods."

"Mr. Wilson—"

He squared up to face her. "I don't admire stupidity in anyone, Mrs. Braunmiller. But I admire courage very much. Courage compensates for many failings." Then, after a moment: "It was the yearling, was it?"

"I suppose."

"It won't do to anthropomorphize them. You're likely to get me killed that way."

When she didn't answer, he said, "What have you come here for? Nobody comes here without a reason."

"To see the dinosaurs, what else?"

But he wouldn't take that as an answer. She could see it in the set of his shoulders, in the observing blue eyes that held hers to account.

"I'm not sure," she said.

"No one ever is," he said.

The party settled into the languid rhythm that dying parties acquire. The band swung into something soft and jazzy. There was no more dancing. The guests who lingered clustered around the fire pits and talked quietly, occasional bursts of laughter lifting into the air like larks.

Gwyneth stood at the edge of the terrace with a glass of wine, watching as someone threw a log onto a dying fire. A shower of sparks swirled up to print themselves against the swollen moon that had lately cleared the mountains. She felt a surge of gladness, a kind of nostalgia in reverse, that at least that had not changed. The old familiar moon still gazed down upon her from the alien wash of stars.

A hand touched her elbow.

She turned, half expecting to see Wilson—she wasn't sure where he had gone, or when—and found herself staring into Peter's face instead.

"It's late," he said.

She didn't know the time.

They leaned their elbows on the railing and stared into the night.

"I waited up."

"I thought you might." Her wine caught a spark of firelight and held it. "I didn't mean to worry you."

"You didn't worry me."

She saw the lie in the set of his jaw, the muscle twitching there.

"I just wondered where you were."

"I've been right here."

"I know." That twitch of muscle. "I just wondered, that's all."

They were silent for a time.

"We didn't dance," he said.

"You didn't ask."

Gwyneth turned to look at him. In the moonlight, Peter's face looked older, gaunt, his eyes deeply shadowed. How strange he had become to her.

What had happened to them?

Peter laughed quietly. "No, I suppose I didn't."

Then: "Was he scolding you?"

"Mr. Wilson?"

She hadn't thought so at the time, but—

"Not scolding exactly," she said. "Reminding me, maybe."

"Reminding you?"

"That he wasn't yoked. That he was putting himself at risk in ways the rest of us are not."

And now, for the second time that evening: "What possessed you, Gwen?"

"Something came over me. I don't know."

The whole thing—the entire trip from the moment she'd seen that footage on her screen back home—had been something she'd had to do, a mute imperative that she could not resist. *Why did you come here?* Wilson had asked her.

I don't know.

Something came over me, she thought.

"You could have gotten the man killed."

Wind rustled the conifer needles. The cries of unknown creatures rose up to her. Gwyneth thought about the thousand battles for survival unfolding in the darkness below, marveling that someday millions of years hence, that eternal struggle would give rise to men, and that not long after that as the earth measured its days, men too would reach their apogee and subside into the muck.

Sighing, Peter said, "Come on, it's late, Gwen."

And this time, with a wistful glance back at the glowing fire pits and the looming globe of the enormous moon, she consented. As they climbed the plush stairs to their room, Peter put his hand to the small of her back and drew her to him. Their lips brushed in a cool, dry kiss. Gwyneth turned away. A veil of dark hair fell between them. When Gwyneth hooked it over her ear, she could not bear to look him in the face.

"Gwen—"

"Not here," she whispered.

Yet later still, in the moon-splashed room, as they lay together in their gauzy eggshell bower, Gwyneth drew away once more. Peter turned his back to her. She watched the rigid line of his shoulders. When at last he spoke, Peter's voice was tense with fury.

"The hell with it then."

"Peter," she said. "I'm sorry. I'm sorry," she said.

But it wasn't enough.

Gwyneth turned away, tears welling in her eyes. They lay still then, back to back, like slow continents adrift. After a time, Peter's breathing deepened into sleep, but Gwyneth lay awake for hours, staring out the moonlit square of window into the shadowy forest beyond. As she hovered at the edge of sleep, there came a faraway cough in the darkness. She tossed restlessly.

Something ponderous moved in her dreams.

She woke at seven to find Peter staring across the bed at her.

"What?" she said.

"Nothing."

But his voice was cool and he didn't seem to be in any hurry to get up. He lounged in a nest of sheets and watched her dress, scratching his chest and tossing out an occasional desultory comment like a bomb. And when he finally joined her for breakfast, he sprawled unshaven in his chair, ordered pancakes, and leveled his gaze over the table at her. "So what's on the agenda for today, Gwen?"

She sipped her coffee. "Yet to be seen."

"A Stegosaurus? A Brontosaurus? A fucking woolly mammoth?"

"Not tennis, you can be sure of that."

"Tennis might do us good. At least we'd be spending some time together."

She threw her napkin to the table. "Jesus, Peter! Why can't you be reasona—"

"Why can't you, Gwen? Why can't you—"

Robert Wilson pulled out a chair and sat between them.

"You've got your eras confused, Mr. Braunmiller."

Gwen slumped in embarrassment. How much had he overhead?

When Wilson spoke again, he leaned forward. "Today it's the biggest game of all, my friends. The one animal everyone comes here to see, the one most of them never do—"

"A T-Rex," Gwen breathed, embarrassment forgotten.

"Did you hear it in the night?"

"I thought I dreamed it."

"It was no dream. I woke at five. It was far away, but moving closer."

Peter kicked out the fourth chair and propped up his feet.

"And how would you know this?"

"I'm a professional, Mr. Braunmiller. I'm very good at what I do. I forget what it is you do exactly—"

"I'm a financial analyst."

"That's right. And I'm betting you would spot a trend in the markets long before I would, wouldn't you?" He didn't wait for Peter to answer. "Look, I've been hunting these animals for the last twenty-five years, and I've only seen fourteen of them—one of them nearly killed me, I was telling Mrs. Braunmiller about it last night. These creatures are the apex predators of their era. They're rare as hell and they can pick up the scent of blood thirty miles away or more."

"The triceratops," Gwyneth said.

"You're a natural, Mrs. Braunmiller." He propped his elbows on the table. "The way I figure it, this bastard got upwind of that wounded triceratops, and has been following the scent down out of the mountains all night. We'll be hard-pressed to catch up to it—but if we do—" He shook his head. "Six-and-a half-tons of pure carnivorous aggression. Forty-two feet, nose to tail. Thirteen feet at the hip. Olfactory bulbs the size of grapefruit. A fucking monster is what I'm saying—and I apologize for the language, but there's really no other way I can say it. You'll never forget it."

He put his hands flat on the table and pushed himself to his feet. "West gate in fifteen minutes. See you there."

"Along with all the other excursion groups, I'd imagine," Peter said.

"You underestimate my expertise, Mr. Braunmiller," Wilson said without rancor. "And overestimate that of my colleagues. Besides, we know something they don't: we'll be tracking the bloody triceratops."

He didn't wait for a response.

Peter's pancakes arrived. He buttered them in silence.

Gwyneth finished her coffee and stood. "I'll go to the room and get our things together."

"You needn't bother with mine."

She turned in disbelief.

"What did you say?"

He cut a bite of pancake, taking his time about it. When he was done, he said, "I said, you needn't bother about mine."

"You have to be kidding me."

"No."

"Don't sulk, Peter. It's not attractive."

"You don't seem to find me attractive, anyway."

People at surrounding tables had begun to sneak glances at them.

Gwyneth sat down, pushing her plate away. She leaned forward. "Look," she said quietly. "The only way we're going to solve anything is if we spend time together."

"But we're not, are we?"

He speared another deliberate forkful of pancake.

"We're spending time with a dozen other people—not to mention your friend Wilson—chasing down giant lizards—"

"Jesus, Peter, did you read anything I sent you? They're not lizards. They're—"

"Warm blooded. I know. That's not the point. The point is that you care more about that than you do about trying to fix things. They've been dead sixty-five million years or more. And staring in awe at them isn't working on our marriage. Isn't that what we spent all this money to do? Isn't that what we both wanted?"

"Yes, but—"

"But what? We could have had gone to the Caymans for a twentieth of the expense and actually spent some time together—"

"We've been to the Caymans. We've been to Paris, for God's sake. None of it helped, Peter. None of it—"

And then he said something that stopped her cold in her tracks. "The problem isn't in Paris, Gwen. The problem isn't in the goddamn Cretaceous. The problem is in us."

"Then come with me and help me fix it, Peter. Please."

"Help *me*," he said. "For God's sake, help me."

She stared at him for a long moment, and then, like Wilson, she put her hands flat against the table and pushed herself to her feet.

"I'm going to get my things," she said.

Peter was right: when the west gate swung open, a mass of excursion groups was sorting themselves out. Most of them chose the more difficult route, clambering up the steep ridge in fifteen-minute intervals. Wilson's alone struck out in the direction of the clearing where the raptors had taken down the yearling.

Later, two memories from the journey stuck in Gwyneth's mind:

Robert Wilson's cool competence.

And the beast.

The rest was but hazy recollection. The march triple time through the looming woodland. The sweat that poured down her face till it stung her eyes. The tiny theropods that scattered before them. Even the charnel house stench of the clearing itself.

The yearling's carcass lay on its side in a bed of thrashed and flattened grass, the great ribcage nearly stripped of flesh. Its horns lanced from a face that had been gashed and half devoured. Scavengers had descended upon what remained: opalescent maggots the size of a man's thumb, chittering insects that were larger still, a clutch of knee-high dinosaurs, ruddy and yellow, that screeched at them in fury, feathered ruffs billowing out to either side of their narrow-beaked maws.

Wilson ignored them.

"Photos, anyone?" he asked, and several of the men shuffled forward.

Great white hunters, Gwyneth thought, as if they'd personally felled the thing. She and Angela and Frank Stafford stood to the side, sipping cool spring water from canteens, and watched.

"Peter not well?" Stafford asked.

"No," Gwyneth said, and she felt Angela give her a knowing look.

Then they were on the move again, following the path trampled by the fleeing triceratops. Waist-high grass swayed to either side. On the far side of the clearing, the forest enveloped them once again: colonnades of towering conifers and angiosperms, damp soil underfoot. Late morning now, cool shadows under the trees, motes adrift in green air.

Gwyneth watched Wilson, lanky and tall, his neck dusky from wind and sun, slip among the trees like he'd been born of the landscape himself. Deep into the forest, the trail split.

Wilson paused, studying the sign.

"The cows went left, working their way down toward the plain," he said, pointing. "The bull climbed the ridge-line, looking for a place to hole up."

"Why?" someone asked.

"Who knows? Instinct, maybe. To protect the cows. He knows the carnivores will be coming for him."

Something coughed in the distance.

Gwyneth shivered.

"We're close now," Wilson said.

He set a faster pace after that. Winded, they trudged after him, still climbing. Wilson moved with unswerving grace, almost invisible as he cut through shadows and the golden blades of sunlight that knifed through the forest canopy.

Perspiration slid down the channel of Gwyneth's spine.

They followed some spoor that Wilson alone could see, continuing to climb—hard climbing, too, upon occasion, clutching-at-tree-branch climbing, scree sliding loose underfoot. A thin, bearded man slipped and fell, bloodying his forearm. They paused while Wilson disinfected the cut—it must have been three inches long—and applied a pressure bandage with deft, sure hands. "That'll hold it for now," he said, gripping the man's shoulder, and Gwyneth couldn't help noticing the grace of those long fingers, the blunt crescents of his nails. "You'll want to get it looked at back at the hotel," he was saying. "A couple of stitches might be in order."

They found the wounded triceratops forty minutes' hike beyond that. The ridge towered above them here, a rocky cliff face that stood sharp against the sky. A thick stand of conifers screened a wide ravine. Maybe a hundred-and-fifty yards from side to side, the chasm narrowed as it deepened. The triceratops lay inside, far back in an angle of stone.

"Can we get closer?" someone asked.

"I wouldn't advise it," Wilson said.

The binoculars made the rounds. Gwyneth studied the triceratops. The great bellows of its lungs heaved irregularly. Dirt caked the exposed wound. Insects buzzed around the glistening bulge of viscera. She could smell the thing from here, a stench of rot and shit and death. It moaned when it saw them, that long rusty sound, like a nail being wrenched from ancient wood. Wilson drew them into a blind of towering angiosperms, admonishing them to silence.

"Soon now," he said, and they hunkered down to wait.

The fronds of the angiosperms waved above them in the midday heat. Then, like God himself flipping a switch, the air went abruptly still. Gwyneth lifted her head, listening. It was more than the lack of birds. The tiny mammals in the treetops had fallen silent; the insects that moments ago had whickered in the air around them disappeared. The forest held its breath. Something big—something dangerous—was on the move. She could sense it: a charged stillness in the air, a tension in the blood.

Something snorted beyond the trees that screened the mouth of the ravine.

Gwyneth could see it in her mind, lifting its vast head to taste of the unmoving air.

Her heart quickened.

Twenty-five years, and Wilson had seen fourteen of them. Fourteen of them. And fucking Peter back at the hotel.

A callused hand touched her elbow.

"This is a time for courage, Mrs. Braunmiller. Not stupidity."

Indeed not, she thought. She could feel his breath tickle erect the fine hairs at the nape of her neck, and for a moment she was aware of nothing else, not the desperate gasping of the felled triceratops, not the expedition group arrayed in the greenery around her, not even the vast creature that shifted its weight beyond the curtain of trees—

Wilson touched her elbow again.

"There you go," he breathed, and then she saw the thing: monstrous, the beast of the apocalypse itself, like some foregone doom from the age of Revelation. It did not emerge from the trees, it simply appeared among them, ghostlike and huge and utterly silent, bigger even than the creature that had run in her dreams, invisible one moment, visible the next, like a long lens pulling focus.

And silent. So silent.

Someone moaned in terror—this wasn't what they'd bargained for, not at all—and the monster swung its vast head toward the grove of angiosperms. Another moan—Wilson hissed, *"Shut up, you fool!"*—and the tyrannosaur moved, shedding the camouflage of the trees like water, one step, then two, its great taloned feet tearing at the dark soil, its tiny, ridiculous arms—evolution's prank—folded at its breast. One slow step, then another, and a third. And did the earth shake beneath its feet? Surely not, yet Gwyneth felt it all the same, felt the earth rumble as the monster lunged toward them, gathering speed, fast, oh fast, and sweet Jesus who could have imagined the thing, death rampant and alive and more beautiful than she could have dreamed; she marveled at its sunshot hide, golden streaked and green, its bullet head weaving hollow-cheeked upon its cobra neck, its nostrils flaring, its eyes ravening and aflame.

It closed fast, forty yards, thirty, twenty-five. Someone broke and ran, she didn't see who, and then the monster—this impossible beast from an era out of time—at last gave vent to the fury that burned in its furnace heart. It roared, its jaws unhinging to reveal a shark's hoard of yellow teeth the size of railroad spikes. A gust of carrion stench blasted over Gwyneth. Her yoke seized her and she found herself careening once again toward the gravity well of the future, trying to hang on for a moment longer just to stare in wonder at the thing—

Her stomach twisted—

And then a rusty-hinge screech of agony reminded the tyrannosaur that other prey—bigger prey, and easy—was to be had. It wheeled to face the triceratops, its tail lashing, and loped the length of the ravine, its feet hammering tracks six inches into the soil. The triceratops somehow staggered to its feet; the bloody rent in its side disgorged fresh loops of tangled viscera.

And then the beast was upon it.

The triceratops lowered its head to meet the titan. Tearing at the soil with legs sheathed in swelling ropes of muscle, the tyrannosaur wheeled around the swinging horns. The wounded triceratops was too slow. One of the T-Rex's taloned feet ripped open its hindquarters. The next moment—Gwyneth looking on, choked with terror and some other strong emotion, she couldn't quite say what—the tyrannosaur closed its massive jaws just behind the triceratops's frill.

The killing blow.

The triceratops went down, feet spasming as the tyrannosaur tore lose a giant chunk of flesh and swallowed. It lifted its monstrous head to the sky and bellowed in triumph.

After that it was awful.

∞

The party that night—there were parties every night—hummed with excitement.

Three of the excursion groups had caught sight of the T-Rex, but only one of them, Wilson's, had seen the kill. Y*ou lucky bastard,* his colleagues said, shaking their heads, but Gwyneth knew that it was more than luck, that it was skill and knowledge; she recalled the swift precision of his lean hands applying the pressure bandage, she recalled his words in her ear: *This is the time for courage, not stupidity.*

She was done with stupidity, Gwyneth thought. She felt that she had opened a new angle of vision upon the world; she understood now that pain was sometimes necessary, that it ruined some things to speak of them too much, that truth could equal beauty. Her fellow guests seemed faintly diminished, their conversation—

—snapped its neck like a pretzel stick—

—magnificent creature—

—empty of any genuine comprehension of what they had seen.

Maybe the change—if there was a change—showed in her face, for as they sat down to dinner Angela said, "You look flushed, darling. Maybe this afternoon was too much for you."

"Looks like you got a fever is what it looks like," Frank opined, ordering the duckbill steak ("appropriate, eh?" he joked).

Appropriate enough, Gwyneth supposed.

The truth was, she *didn't* feel quite herself. Frank had been right: fever was the word for it. Fever—ever since she had seen that monster for herself, and felt the blast of its carrion breath. She had read about it, she had seen it on video, but not until this afternoon had she really known such things existed in the world. Fever. The fever called living, she thought, another fragment of old poetry rattling around inside her head like a piece of angry candy.

She only wished Peter had been with her.

"Where is Peter, anyway?" Frank said, as if he'd sensed the run of her thoughts.

"I think he *is* coming down with something," she said. "Maybe we both are."

"Up to the room with you, the minute you're finished eating," Angela said.

Frank grunted.

But it wasn't up to the room that Angela dragged her when Frank had finished his steak and wandered off to hold court at the party. It was to the little bar overlooking the plain, where a fire-pit burned and a pair of lovers whispered in the shadows.

"Something warm," she told the bartender, and afterwards, cupping Irish coffee as they stood by the fire pit, "Peter's not sick and you know it."

"How do you know?"

"I've been married twice, love. He's sulking. Sulking this morning and sulking at dinner, making it worse for himself every moment because he can't stay in that room forever, and he knows it. Stupid male pride. Whatever in the world has gone wrong with you two?"

"I don't know," Gwyneth said.

Down below, in the darkness beyond the tree-studded escarpment, something roared on the savannah. She wondered what it was—something big, no doubt—but nothing she could shape inside her head. And that was how it was with Peter, too, wasn't it? Something big had happened to them somewhere along the way, but she couldn't put her finger on when, or what.

She couldn't find the shape of it inside her head.

"I don't know."

She swiped at tears with one hand.

"You must think I'm an idiot."

"I think you're confused. It's okay to be confused."

"But there's nothing wrong. There shouldn't *be* anything wrong. He's a good man, he's kind and he's gentle and he's handsome—anyone could see that he's a good man."

Angela wrapped an arm around Gwyneth's shoulder and pulled her close.

"I know. I—"

"He said—" Gwyneth sobbed discreetly.

The lovers had departed.

The barman found something pressing to do at the far end of the bar.

"He said that what was wrong with us wasn't in the Caymans or in Paris or in the Cretaceous. He said it was inside us."

"He's probably right about that."

"I thought that I could save us by coming here. I really did. I risked everything on it, everything we had." She sniffed and met the other woman's gaze. "Somehow I thought that I could save us. I don't know how."

"Do you love him, Gwyneth?"

"I don't know. We just drifted away from each other," she said, and that image came to her once again: continental drift: landmasses on the move, so slow you didn't even notice it until an ocean lay between you.

It would have been easier if one of them had cheated.

"Shhhh," Angela said.

Gradually, the sobs subsided.

The barman brought them another coffee. The night had turned cool, and the moon had just started to slide over the massif to their back, laying down a patchwork of shadows on the ridge below them. Once again, Gwyneth felt that new knowledge take shape inside her: that some things could not be spoken, that truth could equal beauty, that pain was sometimes necessary, and real.

"Why on earth did you ever come here?" Angela said.

◈

They caught up with Frank at the party, but soon after, he and Angela departed—another shot at Kronosaurs had been promised for the morning, and Angela had shamed him into going along this time. "We didn't come here to play tennis," she said. "Besides you'll be wearing a lifesuit. It's not like you can drown."

Afterwards, Gwyneth floated ghostlike through the party, waiting for Peter. She had resolved to kiss him on the stairs when he came, but he did not come, and at last it was late. The moon had risen high into the alien sky. The fires had dwindled to coals. Even the hard-core drinkers were pouring themselves one by one into their rooms.

Somehow—afterward Gwyneth could never quite figure out precisely how it happened, how the decision came to her or if it had been a decision at all and not some foreordained conclusion—she found herself at the concierge's desk. Inquiries were made. The concierge responded without lifting an eyebrow. Apparently such inquiries were not uncommon.

The corridor was in the basement of the hotel.

She knocked on the door.

Robert Wilson opened it.

"Are you sure?" he said.

"I'm sure."

His hands were callused. They felt real against her flesh.

Later—it must have been three or after—Gwyneth slipped through the door of her room. Peter stirred in the depths of the eggshell bower.

"What time is it, Gwen?" he said in the darkness, as though he didn't know, as though his voice wasn't wide awake, and waiting.

"It's late, Peter."

He was silent for a long time. Gwyneth stood by the door until her eyes adjusted. She made her way across the shadowy room. She stood by the window, staring out into the Cretaceous night. It had grown darker, but the moon in its long descent still frosted the leaves outside the window. If she squinted, she could see—or imagined that she could see—something moving out there near the forest floor. A low-slung night grazer, maybe, or maybe just the wind-drift fronds of some ground-hugging fern.

"The party must have gone late."

"I guess it did."

"The T-Rex and everything. People must have been excited."

"It's all anyone could talk about."

"I'm sorry I was ill. I wish I could have been there."

She said nothing.

"What was it like?"

"The party or the T-Rex?"

He laughed in the gloom.

She had no words for it, no way to begin.

"There was something spiritual to it," she said. "I don't know how to explain."

Now his laughter had a bitter edge.

"Spiritual? Seeing one giant animal tear another one to pieces?"

"It's not that"—

But it was. The blood sport of the thing had excited her.

—"or not that alone, anyway. It was the thing's purity of purpose, I think. So devoid of confusion or . . . or ambiguity. Just pure appetite. Every sinew of its body had evolved to serve it."

She said, "It doesn't make any sense. I know it doesn't make any sense."

In the silence that followed, she felt once again the distance between them: continental drift, something so big she couldn't quite shape it in her mind.

"You weren't ill," she said.

"No."

"You could have come." Then: "What are we going to do?"

He was silent for a long time.

"Was it worth it, Gwyneth?"

She stared into the moon-silvered dark.

Peter turned on the bedside lamp.

Her face hovered in the glass, hollowed out and half transparent, ghostlike.

"Turn it off. Turn it off, Peter."

He did, and the Cretaceous dark rose up to envelop her.

"Another shot at Kronosaurs, tomorrow," he said, and she felt a doorway open between them.

Some things you could not speak of. Some wounds healed in silence.

"We should get some sleep," he said.

Gwyneth stood unspeaking. Her body was wide awake. She felt like she might never sleep again. Peter swept back the veils of the eggshell bower and stood, tall in the darkness, and came to her. He put a hand to the small of her back and leaned over, brushing her ear with his lips.

"Come to bed, Gwen," he said.

But she only stood there, his hand at her back, his breath at her ear. The night deepened. Even the moon was gone. Something huge and bright streaked across the sky. It erupted on the horizon, red and orange, a god-light towering into vacuum far above. Shockwaves followed, flattening the trees on the distant ridges in a broad expanding circle, as though a great fist had slammed down upon the planet, rocking them so that they had to clutch at one another to stay on their feet. The thick glass spider-webbed in its frame. Somewhere in the depths of the hotel, something crashed. Someone screamed. Then the fire, burning from horizon to horizon as it ate the dark. Some things could not be saved, Gwyneth thought. Some wounds did not heal. Then the yoke took her. It was just as Wilson had said: it was like being turned inside out.

A Rumor of Angels

He lay restless in the dark, a boy on the precipice of manhood or a man freshly plunged over the other side, he couldn't say which and maybe it didn't matter. Change troubled him: a snake shedding its skin, a locust shucking its husk. He was fifteen years old. The crops withered in the fields that summer and savage winds scoured the land, rocking the old house to its rafters. His father's father had laid its foundations and cultivated the rich prairie in the first great wave of homesteaders to sweep westward, and it had come to the boy's father in his turn. Someday, he supposed, it would fall to him, motherless and alone, the only son of an only son.

That was a season of mysteries. Day after day, a slow tide of humanity streamed down the rutted track that ran not two hundred yards from the boy's door, driven alike by hope and despair. Before them California and the dream of a better life, behind them drought and devastation. Sometimes strangers tarried to talk with his father. *You might as well come along,* they told him. *The land's all played out. There's nothing here but waste.* His father just hooked his thumbs in his suspenders, hawked, and spat into the dust. *Come west,* they whispered then, a queer light coming into their faces, *we hear rumors of—*

Nonsense, the old man said, turning back to his fields. But the boy lingered, transfixed. They were strange tales he heard. He couldn't countenance them. He was too much his father's son. Yet they fixed and fascinated him all the same, and now, as the wind hurled dust at his window and he plummeted toward sleep, his dreaming mind took them up anew.

His name was Tom Carver.

Rumors of angels trembled the air.

His feet decided for him, the day Tom left home.

It was nothing he had planned, nothing he would have said he wanted, though in that strange season—the third year of the drought—who could say for sure what anyone wanted? In the first year, the corn had produced a meager harvest. In the second year, the sheaves grew crisp and brown, and if you stripped back the ears, the kernels were scant and stunted. In the third year—

In the third year, disaster. The sun scorched the land into submission. Vast clouds of rolling dust swept out of the north, so thick that a man caught outside without a mask might well choke. In April, the storms came. In May, in June, in July. When the gale died, grit filmed every surface; you could draw your finger across a counter top and puzzle out your name. The boy and his father emerged to fields of bare stalks, tangled in parched ruin upon the plain. The boy's father hunkered down to crumble sere earth between his fingers. He kicked at the broken stalks. He cursed, and Tom, who had never heard his father curse, flinched as he had sometimes flinched at the silence that ruled that house.

Pap, Tom called him, just Pap.

Mulish and gaunt, with pale, appraising eyes, a fight-broken nose that had never been properly set (before Tom's time, though not so hard to imagine), and big hands, callused with labor, his knuckles scarred from fighting too with the recalcitrant, second-hand tractor against which he'd nursed a perpetual grievance since he'd purchased it somewhere (Tom never knew where), riding it home at dusk, belching blue smoke into a green evening sky a decade gone. He was a man of grievances, Tom's father, grievances against the tractor, against the sky when it withheld rain and when it poured forth a deluge, grievances against the earth itself.

Tote the water, he told Tom between the dust storms. Slop the pigs. Hoe the garden. And Tom toted water, slopped pigs, hoed the withered garden, imagining a mother almost beyond the reach of memory. With a kind of fatal obstinance, his father unclogged the tractor and plowed under the dead stalks. Soil that had once turned up black and moist under the blades lay itself in barren furrows upon the earth. In mid-July, a rare and narrow rain spat from the sky. The next day, they re-seeded. Sputtering, the tractor dragged the rusty planter across the dead land, spilling handfuls of corn from the buckets and covering them over in a single hypnotic motion. Ten yards alongside, Tom drove a plodding mule-drawn wagon loaded with bulging sacks of grain. When the buckets ran empty, he reined up and climbed down to refill them. It was hot work. It might never have rained it was so dry, and they had tied scratchy bandanas around their faces against the dust. They'd eaten two hours ago by the arc of the sun in the flat colorless sky, leaning in silence against the wagon and washing down gritty bologna sandwiches with the last of the cloudy water Tom had pumped up from the well in the baking dawn. Thirst clawed at his throat.

"Ain't it hot?" he said, heaving down a burlap sack the next time they stopped. He slit open the sack and tilted it clattering over the first of the buckets. "Ain't it hot, Pap?"

His father grunted.

"Let's go get a drink of water," Tom said.

"Reckon we'll finish this field first."

Squinting, Tom studied the prairie. He wiped a forearm across his brow, then dragged the bandana down around his neck. Five or six more passes by his calculations, another hour's work. It was like an oven out there. The mules stood sweating in the heat. They might as well have been burying stones for all the good it would do.

"We need to water the mules," he said, though he knew the mules had another hour of work in them.

His father said nothing, merely sat on the idling tractor and stared out across the field, to the fence line. Change worried Tom: snake and locust, shedding the husk of a former life. He was fifteen now.

Fifteen. And what he did next he did without thinking. He started walking. That's how simply it began—he started walking—with a few steps down the lane between the newly planted rows of corn. He just walked. The tractor backfired behind him as his father eased it into gear. The house, faraway against the enormous vault of sky, drew closer: a silhouette, stamped dimensionless and black against the horizon; a model, a toy; a house at last, the only house he'd ever known. There the broken fence and the derelict barn where pigs rooted in the fruitless earth, here the corroding pump where he bent to the lever until at last the pipe coughed and cleared its throat and spat a gout of water. A rusty stream guttered forth. Tom splashed his face. He drank deep from cupped palms, then deep again. Slaked at last, he started to walk. His feet carried him down the arid drive to the road, and without thought, but with a kind of distant awareness of his boots scuffing the dust and the whisper of the desiccated weeds that grew by the road and the faraway grumble of the tractor fading at last into silence behind him, Tom turned west.

The silence of the prairie rolled down over him. Some time later—how long Tom could not say—the choked rumble of an engine loomed up behind him. A battered truck jolted past, its cargo lashed under a ribbed tarpaulin. Tom swung himself up, worming his way deep into the labyrinth of scarred furniture, crates, and mothball-smelling cardboard boxes. Sunlight suffused the canopy with a crepuscular glow, and with the canvas fluttering overhead, he wondered for the first time what it was that he had done.

If you weren't careful, you could walk yourself right out of your life.

⁂

Tom's stomach woke before he did. Rich aromas crowded the air—corn bread, and salt pork simmering in pinto beans—and his dreaming mind conjured up a fleeting image of his mother, little more than a shadow on the threshold of memory. In the next instant, he was alert, or nearly so, back sprung and sore from the splintered planks of the truck bed. He thought of his father firing up the old tractor and wondered to what end his feet had brought him.

Hunger snaked him through the maze. He clambered over the tailgate and dropped to the ground. A fire snapped somewhere invisibly, bronzing the side of a neighboring truck, packed likewise with a teetering mass of household goods. Down the flickering alleyway between them—Tom could have stretched out his arms and lay his hands flat against either vehicle—he glimpsed a temporary encampment: two or three wagons and half again as many beat-up trucks and cars, parked nose in among a scattered grove of towering cottonwood and oak. In the rough circle between, a handful of children chased each other in some game impervious to adult logic, their clamor flitting in the dark. Their fathers here and there hunkered in circles, lean and grim, peering out from under their hats as they drew sticks through the dust or smoked hand-rolled cigarettes.

Tom made no move. He just stood in the shadows, staring the length of the narrowing lane and scheming how he might get some of the beans and corn bread to quiet his belly. He didn't see the boy—he couldn't have been more than five or six—until he heard the pent-up splash of urine—he could smell its pungent tang—just inside the shadows at the other end of the alley. Tom shrank into the dark. He might have passed unseen had his heel not caught a root, sending him staggering into the truck with a thump. The boy's stream halted abruptly as he gazed wide-eyed at Tom down the narrow alley between the trucks. Then he reeled away, his fly still unbuttoned, screaming, "Mommy, there's a man back there, there's *a man—"*

The clatter of spoon and cook-pot, the rustle of skirts, a harried voice: "Now what are you going on about, Charles—"

"*There's a man—*"

Calmly: "There's no one there. You've just scared yourself, that's all—"

"There's A MAN—"

Tom might have made his escape then, but he couldn't bring himself to move, pinioned alike by panic—the boy wouldn't stop screaming—and hunger. A second later, the opportunity had passed. A woman's shadow loomed up in the narrow space between the trucks, her flyaway hair and thin face half-lit by the unseen fire. "See, there's nothing there at all," she was saying, and then her gaze fell upon Tom. "I see," she said, and then, calmly, to Charles, "Go fetch your father."

The boy stood there, unmoving.

"I said get your father," the woman snapped, and this time the boy darted away into the circle of light. Alone, they just stood there, Tom and the woman, she at her end of the alley, he at his. Finally, he worked up the spit to speak. "My name's Tom, ma'am. Tom Carver. I don't mean no harm. I'm just hungry that's all."

"We're all hungry, aren't we, Tom Carver," she said, and he could see the truth of it in her face, in her thin lips and in the bony orbit of her single visible eye, in the sharp jut of her cheekbone, edged by flame.

"You figure you'd find something to eat poking around back here?"

He said nothing.

"Answer me, now."

Tom saw the man at her back then, striding out of the light to drop a hand across her shoulder. "That's enough now, Lily," he said, a biggish man, six foot, maybe six-one, heavy set. "You head back over to the fire," he said, "Charlie's waiting," and just like that all the ferocity dropped out of the woman, the way wind will drop suddenly out of a billowing sheet, leaving it limp on the line. And Tom saw something else, too—it was maybe the first true insight of his adult life. He saw her ferocity for what it really was: terror at being out here on the road, under the sky, with no roof to call her own. Terror for her family, for the man she loved and the son she'd maybe longed for, only to see it all crumble into dust.

The woman—Lily—did as the man said. As she turned away the light fell across her face. She was younger than Tom thought, and prettier, and tired. He didn't think he'd ever seen anyone who looked so tired.

The man leaned against the neighboring pick-up, the heel of one boot resting on the running board. He glanced away like Tom wasn't anything that concerned him at all. Taking a cigarette from behind his ear, he snapped a match alight on his thumbnail and smoked in silence. Tom could smell the smoke in the flickering yellow light.

"I seen you on the road back there," the man said at last. "You hook a ride in the bed of the truck?"

"Yes."

"Yes, sir."

"Yes, sir," Tom said.

"What's your name?"

"Tom Carver, sir."

"You run away, Tom?"

"Yes, sir."

"Well, what'd you do that for?"

"I don't know," he said. But what he thought of was angels. Rumors of angels—westward, always westward, just beyond the nearest curving of the earth—trickling back, whisper by whisper, down the long migratory sweep of the continent.

Nonsense, the boy's father said inside his head.

The man snorted laughter. He drew on the cigarette. The brightening cherry cast into relief cragged features: deep-set eyes, a jaw blue with stubble. "Well, hell, son, who ever does?" He shook his head with another snort of laughter, fatalistic but not unkind.

"Not much charity on the road these days. You must be like to starving by now."

Tom's voice cracked. He hated himself for it. "Yes, sir."

"You aiming to steal something?"

"Pap taught me better than that."

The man sighed and straightened. He exhaled a stream of smoke from his nostrils and ground his cigarette under his boot. "Well, I reckon we can spare a bowl of beans, anyway," he said. "C'mon, now."

The woman was angry. She ladled Tom's beans into a cracked porcelain bowl in clattering and resentful silence, but the man—his name was Frank Overton—didn't seem to notice. He leaned against the truck's fender and spooned beans into his mouth, staring into the darkening circle where the children had lately begun to drift back to their parents, and their own sparse meals, and sleep. But Charlie didn't sleep. He huddled under a blanket and stared at Tom, wide-eyed, clutching a tarnished silver chain in his fist.

The woman—Tom supposed he ought to think of her as Mrs. Overton—sat by the boy, caressing his hair and lulling him into sleep. The woman wouldn't look at Tom. She curled herself against the boy's back, and after a time she too slept. A fingernail paring of moon entangled itself in the cottonwood trees.

Overton wiped out the dishes with a rag and stacked them in the cab of the truck. Afterward, he resumed his place against the fender and smoked.

He didn't look at Tom, but he didn't seem to mind him either.

Finally Tom worked up the courage to speak. "Where are you heading?"

Overton took his time answering. "West," he said finally.

"Everybody's going west."

"Nowhere else to go."

"You got a job waiting?"

Overton laughed without looking at him. "No. Picking peas maybe."

Tom was silent after that. He moved closer to the dying fire. He wanted to lay down, but he was afraid to. The moon hove up out of the trees and climbed the ladder of the sky. Finally, Tom stretched out. Overton didn't say anything.

Tom lay awake for a long time, staring into the flames and thinking of Pap, wondering if he too was sleepless on this first night with his son walked away into the blazing afternoon, wondering too when he would give up on the farm—or if he ever would—and drift west, another ripple in that relentless tide sweeping across the prairies. Somewhere in the night he drifted off, and Frank Overton threw a rough woolen blanket over him. Curled up against the fire like that, Tom looked like a child, not the man he was striving to become.

Overton prodded Tom awake with a boot in the gray dawn. He surfaced out of a dream of his mother: her voice a soft contrast to her work-roughened hands, nothing more. Not much of a dream at all really, he thought as he sipped a cup of strong coffee Mrs. Overton had boiled and strained—still clattering with unspoken fury—over the fire. That was it for breakfast, coffee—even Charlie had some. As for Tom, Overton had passed him a cup without expression, as though he had done so a thousand times in the past.

Camps broke gradually around them. People packed up, huddling to horse trade a bag of dried beans here, a sack of flour there, whatever could best be spared for whatever was most needed. Children once again chased through the chaos, but Charlie clung to his mother, staring at Tom, always watchful. One by one the families departed, bouncing through the trees into the field beyond and finally into the narrow path that passed for a road.

Overton seemed to be in no hurry, though. He drank a second cup of the thick coffee and smoked in silence while his wife packed up the camp, slamming pots, rattling spoons. Then, he set about stowing their gear in the bed of the truck. Tom lugged boxes to him. Overton secured each one among the furniture and cartons that he'd roped there long ago—the boy couldn't guess how long—when wind and dust and drought had stolen away his livelihood, compelling him on this quixotic odyssey across the continent, where talk of work and angels drifted listlessly, forever unfulfilled.

"Thank you," Tom told them, the work done. "I'm sorry if I scared you. I never aimed to steal nothing."

"I reckon we could spare a bowl of beans," Overton said.

That was all.

Tom turned away and hiked back to the road. He could feel Charlie staring after him until he turned west. The sun bludgeoned him, and it not yet ten o'clock. Overton's truck rumbled to life, its springs complaining as it lurched over the field into the road. Tom moved aside to let it pass. It jounced to a stop beside him.

"You know how to drive?" Overton said, his elbow cocked on the window ledge. Tom met Lily Overton's eyes. They were a pale blue in the sunlight. She turned away and stared straight ahead, pressing her lips into a thin white line. Charlie leaned forward from his place between his parents to stare at the boy.

"Yes, sir," Tom said.

Frank Overton nodded at the truck bed. "Climb aboard," he said.

The rhythms of the road never changed. The creak of the worn suspension as the truck rocked over each new hummock. The stink of sweat in the cab as the sun mounted the sky and set fire to the stained cloth interior. Charlie's everyday litany of complaint: *It's hot* and *I'm thirsty* and most of all *Are we there yet?,* as though there were anywhere to get to except another stretch of featureless prairie or the next stand of cottonwood trees.

What for Tom had the allure of novelty had for Overton passed beyond tedium into something close to despair. Every mile of road the same road, every town the same town: a handful of buildings blasted clean of paint by three years of wind-blown grit, where he stopped to refuel the truck from his hoard of ever-diminishing cash and cast about for work where a hundred men had in the last week or so cast about before him. Occasionally, Overton was lucky: a storekeeper needed an extra hand organizing the back room or a widow needed fire wood chopped and stacked by the door. More often, he was not. The little work he did find mostly paid barter. Money—when it could be had—was a rare and precious thing.

The talk around the campfires never changed either—if you could call it talk at all. It was mostly silence, the strangled, inarticulate silence of men who had no words to convey their anguish, who had neither the gift for tears nor the grace of hope. Deft hands rolled cigarettes when tobacco was to be had. Grimy handbills passed from man to man, advertisements for peach pickers in the orchards of California, or pea pickers, or apple pickers, menial farm work for men who had once owned farms themselves, foreclosed, barren, snowed under by dust—seasonal work and even that a chance. But nothing permanent, nothing where a man could sink roots, build a house, raise a family. Only the eternal road before them.

And sometimes, late at night, when the women had bedded down the children and were themselves drifting off, sometimes a bottle would make the rounds and the talk turn strange. *They say angels have been seen to the west,* a man would say, and another scoffing, *There are no angels.*

North and west of here, another man would say, *I had it from my brother who had it from a man in Littleton who had it from a man he'd worked with as a ranch hand*, as though this chain of whispers across the middle west constituted some kind of evidence or truth.

There never were no angels anyway.

Aggrieved: *I had it from a man from Texas who'd had it from a preacher hisself, and why would he lie?*

They say, they say, they say. The news came third hand, fourth, or fifth, or more; no one could testify to the evidence of his own eyes. *Great winged monsters, they say,* and *they never stay for long* and the more devout among them *messengers from the Lord* and this required no abjuration, for God had perished in the dust, in the wind-torn wheat and in those smudged handbills that fluttered across the prairie. God? God had perished in their hearts. As for Overton, he held his counsel and when the bottle came round he took his sip and lit another cigarette, his face expressionless as a slab of stone. Tom, who had no voice in these deliberations, hovered on the periphery of the circle, and listened with a kind of wonder to the men and their cramped debate.

Talked out, the bottle empty, the men drifted back to their own camps. Tom followed Overton to their fire. Overton seemed to need no sleep. He was leaning against the truck smoking when the boy nodded off; he was awake when the boy awakened.

"You find what you were looking for yet?" he asked one night from his place against the fender, and when Tom didn't—couldn't—answer, he said, "Maybe it's the walking that matters." Tom had realized that much anyway, that he wasn't walking away from anything and maybe never had been: he loved Pap in the only way the old man had allowed, a constricted, stunted kind of love, but love all the same. Not a night went by that the boy didn't think of the old man grieving, sitting at the kitchen table maybe, tracing out by oil light the names in the family Bible that neither he nor the boy had the words to read. Not a night went by that he did not wonder where his feet had deposited him, and where they might yet lead him still. Not a night that he didn't wonder what future it was he was walking into, what hungers he had still to assuage, what thirsts to slake. Not a night that he didn't blink back tears.

If he noticed, Frank Overton never let on.

"My brother seen an angel once," Overton one night volunteered. "The beauty of it killed him."

But it was late by then, and maybe Tom only dreamed it.

The rutted path spilled into a narrow road. Overton took the wheel most afternoons, relegating Tom to the canopied bed, where he reclined in the yellow heat, rocked to sleep by the swaying of the ancient truck. More and more often Charlie joined him there, that tarnished silver chain clutched in his fist.

"What is it?" Tom asked one afternoon.

"Mama's necklace," the boy said, unfolding his grubby fist to reveal the locket secreted there. "She gave it to me so she'd always be with me." He pried it open and handed it to Tom. In the dim light under the tarp, the photo inside was hard to see: the shadow of a woman's face, featureless and gray. Tom returned the locket and closed the boy's fist around it.

"It's beautiful," he said, laying back, and the boy lay back with him, burrowing his head into the crook of Tom's shoulder, the both of them dozing the afternoon away.

Lily didn't like it—Overton could read it in the set of her mouth (Tom could, too)—but Charlie wouldn't have it any other way. "Why'd you leave home, Tom?" he would ask sleepily, and Tom, not knowing why, too drowsy to answer, could only murmur, "I don't know," but Pap hove up in his dreams, and he felt grief like a fist squeeze his heart. He woke to hunker down at the tailgate, steady himself with one hand around the nearest spar, and stare back at all the long miles he'd come. And for what? He knew only an aching sorrow. The body had its own imperatives, the soul its discontents.

Gas grew harder to find, work harder still. Sometimes they were stranded for days before they could move on. The camps doubled in size, and Tom, used to life on the farm, felt cramped and uneasy. He wasn't the only one: he could see the tension in Lily Overton's face. The lines bracketing her mouth deepened. Her rare smile (and there had been none for him) grew rarer still. Tom, sensing that the Overtons were hard up against it now, began to think of moving on. He didn't want to be a burden.

Yet something held him back: Charlie too had developed wandering feet. It scared his mother, Tom could tell. It scared her to be alone while Overton foraged the camp for beans and ham and gasoline and maybe a caged chicken or two—whatever could be had in trade to make it for another day. It scared her when Charlie slipped away, swept up by the packs of half-feral children that roamed the camps.

"I'll find him," Tom said, "I'll keep an eye on him."

A hot, dry afternoon, that was, and Tom had been out gathering wood when the boy disappeared. When he returned, dumping a load of kindling by the truck, Lily was in a panic, teary eyed, her mending dangling forgotten from one hand. She looked up in surprise when he said it and a fleeting expression—what it was, he couldn't say—passed across her face. Tom fetched the boy, and so, without a word between them, it was decided: he would stay. After that, Tom spent his days in camp with the boy, improvising games or contriving rollicking yarns about their fellow refugees (who knew he had so many words bottled up inside him?) while Lily went about her chores. They ate at dusk. Soon afterward, Charlie would doze off, locket in his fist. Lily, exhausted, most nights fell asleep beside him.

After dark, the camp grew tense with frustration. Pressure hung in the air, palpable as smoke. Men drank with purpose now—somebody always seemed to have a bottle—and conversations had a way of turning ugly. There were always rumors of work. And there were always fleeting glimpses of angels on the road, men dead of beauty and despair. More than once, when the talk grew heated, Frank Overton laid a hand across Tom's shoulder and steered him back to camp. Tom laid himself by the dying embers, and Overton took up his accustomed place against the fender of the truck and smoked.

"Tell me about your brother's angel," Tom said one night.

"It was an angel of death that took him," Overton responded, and after that Tom didn't ask any more.

On the day that followed they made it another sixty miles. In the dark, over a spare meal of pinto beans and jugged water, Charlie said, "Don't you have no mother, Tom?"

"Hush. You shouldn't ask such questions, Charles," Lily Overton said.

"Tom doesn't have to answer if he doesn't want to, Lil," Overton said. He set aside his bowl and began methodically to roll a cigarette, creasing the paper, spilling in a wisp of tobacco, and twisting it, thumb and forefinger, into a cylinder. He moistened the gum and sealed the cigarette and put it behind his ear. His eyes glinted in the firelight.

"No, I don't mind," Tom said. He was silent for a long moment. "I had a mother, Charlie. It was a long time ago. I don't remember her very well."

"What was she like?"

"Well," Tom said. He could feel the blood pulsing at his temple. He summoned to mind what he could of her: that arc of cheekbone, the touch of her hand, the sound of her voice as she read him Bible stories before bed—

And here was something new. Bible stories. Her ringing schoolteacher's voice (that much he knew; she'd been a schoolteacher once) reciting the words to him as he huddled under a pile of quilts, his breath steaming in the prairie winter night. The oil lamp threw looming shadows around the room. Her voice was steady in the black cold. And recalling (or imagining) it, Tom thought of the elaborate tales he unwound for Charlie—was this her gift to him, this spendthrift flow of words?—and wondered where recollections ended and imagination began, and how to draw the line between.

"Well," he said, "she was very beautiful, my mother. She was tall and she had blonde hair, and blue eyes—just the color of your mother's eyes," he said, and across the campfire, for reasons he didn't fully understand, he sought those eyes.

Lily Overton regarded him without expression.

Now, warming to his subject: "She used to read me stories at night."

"What kind of stories, Tom?"

"Bible stories." He cast about in his memory. "Remember the story about the angel coming to announce the birth of our Lord?"

"Mama says there are no angels."

"Maybe there were a long time ago."

Again he flicked his gaze at Lily Overton.

"Well, I never saw one," Charlie announced. And then: "What was your mother's name?"

"Olivia," Tom said. "But everybody called her Livy."

"Where is she?"

Lily tousled Charlie's hair. "I think that's enough for tonight, little man."

Overton scratched alight a match and put fire to his cigarette. "Let the boy talk, Lil."

Tom hesitated. The fire crackled, shooting sparks into the dark sky. He looked at Lily, then at Charlie.

"She died."

Charlie considered this soberly. "What did she die of?"

"Fever," Tom said, but what he thought was, *It was an angel of death that took her.*

"Maybe my mama could be your mother," Charlie said.

Lily Overton cleared her throat briskly. "And that really is enough." She glared at her husband. "Take him to pee, Frank. Make sure we haven't taken in any other stowaways."

Overton pitched his cigarette into the fire. "C'mon, Charlie," he said, climbing to his feet. Together, they disappeared into the shadows beside the truck, the boy already fumbling with his fly. Lily busied herself with the dishes. Porcelain rang against porcelain. The shards of a bowl rolled into the fire. Lily put down its surviving sister. Tom could see the divot carved in its lip. He looked up at her, her lips a gash in her narrow face.

"What did you have to go and tell him that for? Death and angels. What kind of notions are you trying to fill my boy's head with?"

"I'm sorry—"

"Don't you think he has enough to carry, and him just six years old, without having to worry about his parents dying?"

"I said—"

"I know what you said."

Tom gazed at the broken bowl in the coals, already streaked with soot.

"He trusts you," Lily said.

"I know. I didn't mean—"

"I'm glad I'm not your mother," Lily snapped, and then Charlie and his father came striding back into the little clearing where they had pitched their camp, and it was like she and the boy had never spoken—like he wasn't there at all. She enfolded the child in her arms, and when he pointed at the broken bowl in the fire, she merely smiled. "Mama had an accident, didn't she? Now come on, let's get to bed."

That night, Tom didn't walk the camp with Overton. He bedded down instead, and when tears came, he turned his back to the fire, his muscles taut with the effort of holding them in. As for Lily Overton, she watched him sleepless through the flames where the shards of the bowl slowly blackened. The rigid line of his shoulders bespoke his tears, but she did nothing to comfort him—could think of nothing to do and did not anyway wish to comfort him. Yet when her sleep came at last, it was fretful and uneasy.

None of them slept well that moonless night. Not Lily and not her boy, who dreamed his own mother's death. Not Tom, who had never known the color of his mother's eyes. And not Frank Overton either, who returned to camp late, propped himself against the truck for a final smoke before sleep, and studied the boy with his own deep thoughts, slow as silted rivers, and dreamed, when he dreamed at all, of the reckoning of angels.

&

It was dreams that drove the Overtons, as dreams had driven their forbears across the vast expanse of the continent—dreams of a better life, nightmares of the life they'd left behind. It had all crumbled in their hands, and if salvation glimmered before them like a mirage, always just beyond their grasp, the past forever ran them down. So much loss already behind them. So much terror of loss still to come that they closed their hearts against him. Overton tried not to love this boy he'd taken in, for better or worse, impulsively and against his wife's objections. Lily would not let herself say his name. Even Charlie's love had a fierce intensity, as if Tom might any moment disappear, evanescent as the air.

It was angels—their own better angels—that drew them on as far as they could go: to surrender up to Tom the warmth of their fire, a meager portion of their already paltry rations, a pittance of the affection that hammered upon the sealed valves of their attention. The future was a mystery they were always plunging into, back sore and weary in their sweat-darkened clothes, masked against the ever-present dust.

"Tell me more about your mother," Charlie said, and so, as they sprawled together in the bed of the truck, perspiring in the heat, Tom told him—of the flowers his mother had cultivated in front of the house and the vegetable garden she had cultivated in back, of the way the earth bloomed underneath her fingers, bringing some rare beauty into the world. "Tell me the stories she told you," Charlie said, clutching his chain, and so Tom summoned them to life in the dead air, mysterious tales gleaned not from those his mother had read at his bedside (there had been no tales, or if there had been he could not recall them) but, with more imagination than accuracy, from the color plates bound into the family Bible—the wave-pitched ark and David with his sling and the terrible angel come to announce the miraculous birth that would redeem the fallen world.

"Do you believe in angels?" Charlie asked.

"I don't know," Tom said, and then Charlie slept.

The truck jolted and the load creaked around them. Charlie began gently to snore, and Tom lay still, brooding over memories of Pap and the mother his half-imagined tales had summoned into the dusky air. Tom was dozing himself when Charlie stirred and flung an arm across his chest, spilling the chain from his open palm. Tom reached out to retrieve it. He held it at arm's length, watching the chain unwind itself, the locket sparking in the dim. He eased out from under the boy. Charlie whimpered in his sleep and Tom smoothed the hair from the boy's damp forehead. Then he slipped out to the tailgate of the truck and propped himself against the wooden slats that anchored the fluttering tarp. With the full sun of midday upon his face, Tom pried the locket open. Here in the light, the photo was clearer. Lily Overton—a rare and smiling Lily Overton he had not known before and could hardly have imagined ever existed—gazed up at him from within. He could not say how long he sat there like that, only that the truck braking and pulling off the road startled him back into himself. In the gloom under the wind-snapped tarp, Charlie stirred to wakefulness.

"Tom?"

"I'm right here, Charlie," Tom said, thumbing closed the boy's locket and slipping it into the pocket of his trousers.

The truck shuddered to a stop. Tom swung himself over the tailgate into a howling chaos of wind. As he reached up for Charlie, Overton appeared beside him. "In the cab!" he cried over the wind. "Get in the cab!" Without thinking, without pausing to ask why, Tom hurried the boy before him, and lifted Charlie into the truck. Lily Overton huddled against the passenger-side door. Tom snatched a glance over his shoulder. Wind whipped out of the east, driving before it a billowing cloud of black earth that towered a mile into the sky. Grit lashed at Tom's eyes. He could taste it in his throat and clogging his nostrils, yet still he stared back at the oncoming cloud with a kind of paralyzed horror. He might have stood there until it rolled over him had Overton not shoved him hard—Tom cracked his head a glancing blow on the doorframe—into the cab. Overton followed, struggling to slam the door against the wind. The truck rocked with the impact.

The storm hurtled down upon them. The world beyond the windows disappeared into darkness. Fingers of wind scrabbled at the crevices around windows and doors. Dust swirled in the air. Half-blinded, Tom dragged his bandana over his mouth and nose. Powder settled on his face and hands, working its way stinging into his eyes and between his lips, where it tasted gritty on his tongue. The contained stink of unwashed bodies filled the air. The battering ram of the wind shrieked as it hurled itself against the truck. Charlie wept and huddled against Tom, burying his face in the boy's ribs and gripping his fingers until the pressure made them ache. And through all the long storm—fifteen minutes? an hour? it felt like longer, it felt like forever—the locket burned in Tom's pocket like a flaming heart.

And then, as suddenly as it had begun, the storm blew itself out. One by one, they stumbled forth. A stark wasteland met their eyes, gray and flat as far as the eye could see. A diamond of sunlight flashed from the metal carcass of another truck, maybe a mile in the distance. Otherwise, nothing. Looking out across the waste, Tom imagined Pap, doggedly seeding a desert earth that had once thronged with stalks of succulent green corn, as if somehow, through sheer blind determination, he could summon it all back: the land that had withered beneath his feet, the wife buried beneath the weathered wooden cross in the back yard, the son he had lost. Recalling it, Tom fingered the silver oval in his front pocket, and a knot welled up in his throat. He rubbed burning grit from his eyes and surveyed the truck's wreckage: metal dimpled with a thousand tiny pits, tires half buried in sand, tarp torn and dangling from a broken spar.

"What now, Frank?" Lily Overton said, her voice rising. "What now?"

And Tom saw Charlie digging in his pocket for comfort.

Frank Overton spat brown dust. "Same as always, Lil. We push on."

Laughing humorlessly, she turned away.

Charlie though, Charlie was not so strong. "Mama," he said, "my locket, it's gone—"

"Oh, Charlie, honey," Lily said, kneeling to look him in the eye. She gripped his shoulders, drew him into her embrace, and scanned the sea of dust that stretched lone and level as far as she could see; she imagined her son staggering through the wind that had swept down upon them to carry it all away—everything they had ever loved or dreamed of—and she knew that Frank was right: the only thing to do was move forward into the bleak mystery of the future. You moved on. There was nothing else to do.

And Tom? Listening, he flushed, knowing that this was his opportunity to return the necklace. Yet there was something in him that could not surrender it, not now and maybe never, not even to this boy he had come to love as he would have loved the brother he'd never had. There was something in Lily Overton's smile, something in her eyes, gazing up at him from the tiny portrait, that gave him hope, a reason to go on, to keep following the path his feet had laid out for him.

Lily mended the tarp while Overton and Tom repaired the spar that had held it taut and Charlie grieved the loss of that lone, precious thing that his mother had given him to clasp and comfort him through the long prairie nights. Light faded from the sky. Trucks crept past, grim men unsmiling at their wheels, and they did not stop to help, for what help could anyone provide when even the land itself had been stripped clean of sanctuary? Then the hard business of dislodging the truck from the sand. Lily took the wheel, goosing the accelerator. Charlie watched as the boy and the man took places at the rear, shoulder to metal, and rocked the battered vehicle in its ruts until at last they worked it free.

Tom stumbled to his knees when it gave and fishtailed onto the road, where runners of dust snaked across the packed earth. Frank Overton laughed and clapped him on the back. Tom wiped sweat from his forehead. He wound the necklace in his pocket about his probing fingers.

It was full dark by then.

They camped alone, huddled around a niggardly fire Overton built from wood he had stored away against such a day. Charlie wept himself to sleep, and the boy lay long awake as the fire burned itself into embers. When even Overton slept, he dug from his pocket once again the silver chain and wound it tight around his hand. With a dirt-encrusted thumbnail, he pried open the tarnished locket and squinted down at the tiny photograph there, which he could not see in the darkness except with his mind's eye. At last, tucking the locket away, he slept, unaware that he was not the only one awake.

Lily Overton, curled close against the fire with her arm tucked around her boy, had watched him through slitted eyes slip the chain from his pocket. She'd seen its dull glimmer by the glow of the dying fire, and had known it for what it was, or had anyway suspected, and felt course through her something stronger—something stranger—than the resentment alone that should by all rights have been hers: a sorrow deep as rivers that she had lived to see such a world that had such children in it.

~

Lily never spoke of it, not even to Overton. Why the boy should want the locket, she could not say; but her own child looked upon him with such boundless adoration that she would not deny him that light in an otherwise dark and hopeless season. So she held her peace, and when he slipped free the locket in the late morning hours to stare down into the portrait which by the dying embers he could not see but only imagine, she watched with half-lidded eyes and wondered. By day, for Charlie's sake, she managed to keep things as they had been between them—distant, known but unnamed.

Time slipped on in the eternal rhythm of the road—seventy-five miles at a stretch, a hundred on a good day, as much as the wheezing old truck could bear—three days, four, five, she could not say how many. Only the talk of the men around their midnight fires changed. Angels were on every lip now, luring them onward, and Tom felt once again that familiar itching in his feet. Yet something held him back, something he dared not speak aloud even in the privacy of his own mind: a sense of something impending, like the crackle of air in the moments before a storm. So he was not surprised when it happened. None of them were surprised, not truly: it had the sense of something long ordained, an inescapable doom that had all along been hurtling toward them.

For Overton, at the wheel that afternoon, it began as thickening traffic. He gained upon the truck in front of him until they were creeping along, hood to bumper, and the car a mile or more behind them closed the distance. Overton glanced at his wife, squinted through smoke at the windshield, took a long last drag, and pitched his cigarette out the window. Soon they were barely moving at all. And then they weren't. That was how it began for Tom and Charlie—with the long, slow swing of gravity as the truck braked to a stop, stirring them to wakefulness. They hunkered down at the wooden tailgate, splinters digging into their fingers, and stared out at the sunlit afternoon: cars and trucks piled high with the salvage of a hundred broken lives, idling by the dozen in the hard-packed dirt road or parked helter-skelter along the weedy shoulders or abandoned altogether in the fields beyond. Sunlight flashed off metal, the smell of exhaust hung in the air, and where there should have been noise—the blat of horns, the cries of frustrated drivers—an eerie silence prevailed. Men stood in the crook of open doors, looking west into the baking sky. Women stood beside them, hands slanted across their eyes. Somewhere a child was saying, over and over, in a whisper that carried in all that endless silence, "What is it, mother? What is it?" And even here the great migration never ceased. Staring soon gave way to walking: entire families, small children clutching at their mothers' hands, every one of them silent and entranced, blank faces turned to the sky as they wound among the cars, the noon sun bleaching the world of color. There was no hurry—no one ran or cried aloud. There was only a blind imperative, as if in this, like so many other things, they had no choice.

Overton turned off the engine, and met them as Tom and Charlie came around the truck. "What is it, Tom?" the boy said. "What is it?"

But Tom, if he heard the boy at all, did not respond. He only gazed at the horizon, where dark specks hurtled upward into a porcelain sky. It could not be, Tom thought, so much his father's son. But his feet had a mind of their own. Overton, standing by the open door of the truck, took his shoulder—

"Tom," he said.

—and for a heartbeat they stood like that, man and boy. Overton's words echoed inside Tom's head—*It was an angel of death that took him*—and an instant of blank horror seized him. Charlie hugged his waist, weeping. Even Lily gazed at him across the hood of the truck. And then the horror passed.

"Don't," Overton said. "Please, Tom, wait—"

"I have to, don't you see?"

"We'll go together, then," Overton said, as if he'd known it would come to this in the end, and so they did, the four of them, wending their way through the maze of cars, struck dumb with an irresistible compulsion to see it, to know it for themselves, angels of death or angels of light or no angels at all. Others walked beside them, men and women, their faces haggard with care, and children, too, boys on the very precipice of manhood (or already plunged over the other side), and girls ripening into the fullness of their bodies at last, silent, their expressionless faces turned to the sky, where, ever more clearly, the dark specks resolved themselves into human figures flung up into the vault of heaven. Their boots scuffed the earth. Their breath labored in their lungs. Their tongues moistened chapped lips, and somewhere a woman—no two women, or three, or more—wept. Charlie clung to Tom's hand as they ranged ahead. Overton and Lily followed, and what thoughts came into their minds—if any thoughts at all—none of them could say: only the relentless magnetism of the west and a blind, white roar inside their heads.

Gradually, the snarled traffic fell behind them. The throb of abandoned engines faded. The stench of gas dissipated. They emerged into a belt of treeless prairie, wind-swept and hot. Beyond it, a crowd had gathered, a ragged crescent a hundred strong or more, Tom couldn't say for sure. More people than he'd ever seen in one place anyway, as though three or four or ten of the gypsy encampments had piled in on top of one another, all of them silent, all of them staring blankly ahead. Tom shrugged his way among them, the boy clutching his leg now, and they parted to let him pass, until at last he drew up against the far edge. If the Overtons followed he did not know and did not think to care.

Upward they looked, upward every one, heads craned slack-jawed to the sky, their faces blank as eggs, scrubbed free of kindness or humanity, except that some of them were weeping. Beyond them—twenty feet or thirty, maybe more—a great crevasse had cloven the prairie. Tom could hardly imagine the agony of stone, the mighty crack of earth as the continent tore itself asunder. Two or three vehicles, doors flung open to the air, stood askew upon the plain where they must have slammed on the brakes when the earth split and the road crumbled and plunged into the abyss.

Tom might have paused there—it was like a great hand had scrawled an invisible line in the dust beyond which few dared venture—yet something drew him on. He could feel it beating in his breast, this blind imperative, he could feel it itching in his restless feet. Kneeling, he peeled Charlie from his leg. Looking up, he saw that the Overtons had drawn close behind him.

"Go to your mother now, Charlie," he said, and the boy snatched at him, and drew Tom close against him.

"I won't," he sobbed. "Not you, too," and once again Overton's words echoed in Tom's mind: *It was an angel of death that took him.*

"Go," Tom said, standing to thrust the boy away.

"I won't, I won't let you go."

And Tom: "Go, I hate you. I hate you, don't you see?"

The boy reeled, sobbing, and Tom stood. He met Lily Overton's pale blue eyes and turned away and the chasm drew him in, thirty feet, and twenty, and there he paused, gathering his courage. A great wind, smelling of dry and ancient stone, shrieked out of the frigid heart of the planet. It flattened his pants against his legs and pressed his shirt rippling against his torso. And now, looking the length of the crevasse, he saw other lone sojourners approach the pit. Some fled back to the safety of the crowd. Still others hesitated as he had and crept closer, step by cautious step. And still others—three, no four, five, six, and more, how they fixed and fascinated him—stepped to the edge, hesitated, and hurled themselves into the abyss. The wind flung them skyward in silence, their bodies tumbling in silent apotheosis, smaller and smaller until they ceased to be human at all, ceased even to be dark specks against the bone-colored canopy of heaven. His hand crept into his pocket and seized the necklace. He felt the terrible gravity of the pit, and found that somehow—his feet would have their way—he stood at the crumbling lip of the void. Wind scoured his face and tore at his clothes, and a fierce longing sprang up within him: to leap out into the screaming air, to step out of this hard, dry world and let it take him up into the mysteries beyond—

Then a voice came to him, a woman's voice, a thin and paltry thing in that screaming wind—

"*Charlie*!"

Tom snatched a glance over his shoulder and saw the boy wrench free of his mother's grip and hurtle toward him. He crashed into Tom, seizing his leg, and for a moment Tom thought that they were both going to stagger over the edge, no longer bound to earth, and plunge forever into the sky. An awful image possessed him—of Charlie's terror-stricken face as that cold, howling wind tore him away from Tom's grasping fingers and sent them spinning skyward, each to their separate heaven. What he thought of then was dozing away those lazy afternoons in the truck, with the small boy's sweaty head on his shoulder. What he thought of was that spendthrift flow of words, his mother's sole gift to him, and his gift alone to Charlie, wrested by imagination from the colored plates in the family Bible. What he thought of was angels.

Tom dragged the boy away from the abyss—three feet, six, ten and more—and kneeling before him, dug out the locket. He pressed it into Charlie's open palm, the silver chain whipping upright in the wind, and closed the small fingers about it. Then, step by step, Tom Carver's feet carried him away from the abyss, beyond the reach of that shrieking wind, to Charlie's waiting parents. Lily Overton went down on her knees to accept the boy into her embrace. She hooked her chin over his frail shoulder, and met Tom's eyes.

"Tom," she said.

Eating at the End-of-the-World Café

She'd seen them once, the dead and damned, hooded blind, their hands bound at their backs. She'd seen blue lightning leap sizzling from electric prods as gray men in blue uniforms harried them stumbling down from enormous canvas-covered army trucks. She'd heard their cries, their moans, the shouts and the mocking laughter of the men in blue. She'd smelled the stench of their roasting flesh.

That had been her first night at the café. Afterward, in the ashen rain, Eleanor had gotten turned around somehow, missed the train station. When the fence loomed up before her—fourteen feet high, topped with coils of razor wire, and bound at the distant corner by the skeletal shadow of a sniper tower, the smoking red haze of the pit beyond—a fist closed around her heart. Recoiling in horror, she'd turned away and fled for miles through night-plunged streets, tears streaking her face. When a taxi hove up out of the dark, she'd flagged it down, blind to the expense; she just wanted to get away from that place, it didn't matter how much it cost. But the heat inside the car couldn't warm her and the aimless chatter of the cabbie provided no comfort. She resolved to give up the job, even if it meant that she and Anna both starved, but even then she knew that she would not. She could not. There were no other jobs, not for the likes of her, anyway, and so she resolved instead to forget what she had seen, to put it out of her mind forever.

Yet she dreamed of it still.

She dreamed of it now—the stench and the mocking laughter, the blue flicker of the prods in the dark. Then she was awake. A train thundered by down below, rattling the apartment. Eleanor stood and shrugged on a robe. She glanced at the alarm clock—4:27 in the morning—as she stepped into the tiny bathroom, the light glary and over-bright as she lowered herself to the icy rim of the toilet seat. She showered and dressed, shivering in the cold, and then she let herself into the living room.

Anna dozed amid damp, twisted sheets, bone thin, fever sweat beading her forehead. Eleven, she looked infinitely older—sixty, seventy even, a wizened old woman curled fetal around a hoard of pain. As Eleanor caressed the child's head, she thought of the curls that had grown there not a year ago, thick and lustrous and dark. Anna: sick unto death, unable to die. Degrees of punishment, Eleanor thought, degrees of pain. And she wondered whose punishment this was, hers or Anna's, and whose pain?

The kitchen—spotless—stank of rancid grease and an older, deeper corruption that no amount of scrubbing could eliminate, the ghosts of a thousand meals cooked into the cracked plaster, the peeling yellow-gray linoleum, and the rot-sodden wooden floor underneath. A round schoolroom clock hung above the stove: 5:01 now, Mrs. Koh due any minute. Eleanor cleared a spot among the avalanche of bills on the rickety table, set down her cup and poured boiling water over a basket of two-day-old coffee grounds. Setting it aside to steep, she brushed back the curtains to peer out.

Acheron dozed, dreaming its unquiet dreams. On and on it went, street and tenement, tenement and street, shot through with commercial avenues, decaying storefronts and dusty offices where men in suits labored at inconceivable tasks. Craving the warmth of sunlight against her skin, Eleanor had tried once to beat the city—everyone did, sooner of later—jumping from line to line, yellow line, blue line, red line and more, until the primary colors failed and still the network of trains went on, each fresh stop spilling her up into the same squalid warren.

Eleanor lifted the coffee basket, dumped the grounds, and screwed the cap down atop her cup. She stole another glance at the clock, 5:17 now—*where was Mrs. Koh?*—tilted the weak, bitter coffee to her lips and twitched back the curtains. Beyond the age-rippled glass, Acheron stirred. To the east the sun glowed, a polluted cinder, wreathed in fog; to the west, the dawn burned. Night and day, it burned: the pit, sleepless and terrible, casting its sickly red pall over the successive rings of the city that surrounded it. And night and day now, Eleanor felt its pull. As it did with each successive generation, the city had drawn her slowly in, ever closer to its bleak and desperate heart. Even now she could feel it, its dark allure, as irresistible as the drag of a dying star.

In the living room, Anna cried out. Eleanor tensed, knuckles white around her coffee cup. And then Anna was sobbing. Eleanor let the curtain fall, turned from the window, and slipped through the beaded curtain between the rooms. Anna half-sat against the headboard, rocking, her interlaced hands clenched over her belly in agony.

Eleanor put her coffee down. She sat on the edge of the bed and rested her hand against the child's forehead: hot, so hot, a fire burning deep inside her; just feeling it, Eleanor had to choke back the tears. "It's okay. It's okay, baby. Let me get your pills"—she stretched for the orange bottle on the nightstand—"Here. They'll help."

"They *don't* help," Anna gasped between sobs, but Eleanor had already loosened the cap. She was spilling the silvery caplets into her palm—one, two, and two more for luck; the prescribed dosage had ceased to help a long time ago—and reaching for the cup of tepid water Mrs. Koh had left the night before, when Anna screamed—

—*"They don't help"*—

—and lashed out with one hand. Pills and water went flying like glistening rain. The prescription bottle and the water cup fetched up spinning against the rump-sprung sofa.

"Dammit, Anna!"

"I don't want *the pills!"* Anna hissed. *"I* want *Mrs. Koh!"*

Confused emotion erupted at the base of Eleanor's ribcage: fury and dull resentment and something else—

—*face it, why don't you?*—

—something darker and more loathsome, something she didn't want to name. It was all she could do not to slap the child.

Then the buzzer. Mrs. Koh. Eleanor rang her up. The diminutive Asian woman, her face as shrunken and wrinkled as a dry apple, bustled into the apartment, spilling umbrella and purse, a canvas sack stuffed with her knitting and her romance novel, and a spate of apologies even as Eleanor snapped, "You're late."

"I said I'm sorry," Mrs. Koh told her, shrugging off her coat. "Sorry, sorry sorry." She flapped her hand. "The trains, you know. What can I do about the trains? Hire somebody else, you don't like it."

"The trains!" Eleanor said, snatching up her cup of bitter coffee. "I'm late, and it's you she wants anyway."

Outside, Eleanor ran for the subway, clutching her coffee at arm's length so it wouldn't slosh on her uniform. The doors snatched at her skirt, and the train lurched into motion as she was edging through the crush of grudging rush-hour flesh inside. She snagged a spot on the overhead rail and steadied herself, already framing the morning's excuse—

—*Anna it was always Anna*—

—in her mind.

An in-bound train hurtled past the windows, light and shadow, scattering her thoughts. The car leaned into a curve. Eleanor shut her eyes, breathing air thick with the funk of coffee, cologne, stale sweat. It was okay.

Everything was going to be okay.

"Avernus Street Station," the PA system said, and the train braked, gravity swinging through her like a pendulum.

The doors hissed back. In the rush on the platform someone jostled her, splashing coffee across her breast. "Hey—" she said, swiping at her blouse. "Why don't you watch where y—"

A low menacing growl drove her back a step.

A man lean and sharp as a straight razor gashed the air before her, uniformed in a short double-breasted black tunic buttoned to the neck, with a pair of tiny red eyes affixed to the tips of his stiffened collars. His own eyes were glittering chips of mica, set deep over cheekbones like upturned blades. His mouth was a slit, unsmiling. She could see the coffee stain, darker on the dark breast of his uniform. And a dog, vicious and lean as its master, straining against its leash, teeth bared and slavering.

"I'm sorry," she said. "I'm sorry."

Clutching the coffee against her breast, Eleanor fished in her purse with one hand for a wad of napkins to blot the stain. "Here, let me—"

"Don't touch me," the man said. And then: "Sit, Cuth."

The dog dropped to its haunches, gazing up at her out of mean, narrow eyes.

"I'm sorry," Eleanor said. "I'm—"

"Move along," he said.

And she did, swallowing the word like a stone. She let the crowd carry her away, feeling those eyes take her measure as momentum swept her past. She glanced back from the turnstiles, but he was gone, lost amid the welter of blank morning faces. Vendors clashed back their storefront cages, and someone screamed into a cell phone—

—"it was at *six*, doesn't anyone listen"—

—and the train shrieked as it pulled away, dragging up a rooster tail of candy wrappers and newsprint.

Just gone, like he'd never been there at all.

And she was late.

Yet he wasn't gone, not really. His twin gazed down at her from enormous banners over the escalators, right arm crossed over his breast, hand curled into a fist over his heart, the words *Ever Watchful* inscribed in red above his close-cut hair. And then she veered away, into one of the labyrinthine corridors to the street. Her shoes unleashed a chorus of crêpe-soled accusations on the tile, *late again, Eleanor, you'll be late for your own funeral*—

Charlie's voice. Screw Charlie, she thought, and stepped out into the rain.

The sky clamped down like the lid of a pressure cooker. Even now, even in the rain, the air reeked of the pit, a sulfurous miasma of cinder and ash, charred flesh rendered down to bone, air so tainted not all the rain in the world could ever wash it clean. Clear days you could see it, an oily black haze that masked the sun, filming everything—sidewalks and windows, skin too—in clinging grime; worse, you could feel it, a sub-aural throb in your bones.

A tangle of secondary enterprises had sprung up to feed it, tributary veins wound tight into the fibrous heart of the tumor, newsstands and snack shops mostly, cigarettes and lunch, for people who worked in the pit would just as soon wash their hands of the place afterward, she supposed. Shed their uniforms and the knowledge of the things they did in them and do their real shopping elsewhere.

And there was the diner, too, of course.

The End-of-the-World Café, Tank's idea of a joke.

It glimmered across from the station in the murk, crimson neon bloodying the rain-slick pavement. Eleanor poured out her coffee—rancid with the memory of her collision on the train—in an overflowing trash bin, and dashed across the street. Pausing, she glanced back at the dark mouth of the subway.

For a moment—a heartbeat—she thought she saw a figure standing there. Thin and black, that hateful cur at his side, straining at its leash. Both of them watching her. She brushed the water from her eyes, blinking: gone now, if they had ever been there at all.

Eleanor ducked inside, the dining room jumping with the first-shift crowd, damp heat and the rattle of crockery, the tang of frying bacon in the air. Philippe, bussing table six, winked as she rolled through. Noreen smiled from behind the counter.

"Today's the day," she said.

"What are you talking about, Noreen?"

"Loverboy, that's what. Ten bucks says he makes his move during the lunch rush."

"Right."

Shedding her coat, Eleanor swung into the kitchen, already awhirl with the sizzle of grease and the tinny thump of the radio propped over the prep table, a wire clothes hanger jammed into the hole where the antenna used to be. Tank grinned at her from the grill, his clean-shaven skull shining, the roll of dark flesh at his collar stippled with sweat. "Darla laid down on me this morning," he told her as she punched in, half an hour late, half an hour without tips, the clock grinding down her hours. "Said she was puke sick, if you believe that. You wanna pull a double?"

"I'll have to make a call, see if Mrs. Koh can stay with Anna."

"You know you gonna do it. You late, and both us know you need the hours." He shook his head as she buzzed by in the other direction, tying on her apron. "You be late for your own funeral someday," he said, and then the kitchen door swung closed at her back and the roar of the dining room engulfed her.

Loverboy rolled in just after one—

"Ten bucks," Noreen hissed, sweeping past with a tray of iced tea. "Betcha."

—and took the last booth in Eleanor's section, same as he always did; the dining room teemed by then, blue uniforms most of them—pitmen, the ones who did the really dirty work—their oily, sulfurous smell strong in the place, them and a handful of their supervisors, gray men clad in gray, their uniform collars emblazoned with a stylized flame, and a handful of locals, shop girls and countermen, hunched in nervous silence over their meals. Nobody talked much when the pitmen were around. They sucked the air out of a room, leaving other folks gasping for breath, stricken with the certainty that it wouldn't do to cross them.

Loverboy, though—Loverboy was an exception.

Eleanor had noticed that much even before Noreen had saddled him with that ridiculous name. Yet she couldn't quite figure out what it was: the way he carried himself maybe, confident but empty of swagger or maybe just that he always ate alone or maybe—though Eleanor didn't like to admit it that he reminded her of Charlie, rangy and raw boned, with a beak of a nose that looked like it had wound up once or twice on the business end of someone's fist. He had the same dark hair, unkempt and shot through with strands of gray; the same hands, thick knuckled, knowing. Occasionally—and she didn't much care to acknowledge this either—Eleanor found herself alone in bed after Anna had drifted off to sleep, her mind fixing on those hands and how it might feel to have them touch her. Aside from the simple exchanges he needed to order, though, he'd never spoken to her—so when Noreen's bet came in it took Eleanor by surprise.

She was making a coffee run through her section—just warm it up a little for me and how bout another one of those rolls and you got a straw, miss, the usual—when she swung by his table—

"Coffee?" she said. He pushed away his sandwich—tuna on rye—half eaten. He looked up and met her gaze, his dark eyes spoked with gray.

"Sure," he said. And then, just as she was about to pour: "I've been watching you."

She stood there frozen for a moment, carafe in hand, wondering if Noreen was right, and this was some kind of creepy come-on. And then she thought of Charlie, the way he used to step in when some guy forgot that he was paying just to look and got too friendly with his hands, the way he'd get right down in the guy's face.

"Well you enjoy the show, hon," she said. "I've been watched before."

"That's not what I mean."

"Thing is, mister, I don't care what you mean. I got seven tables here, I don't have time to play whatever game it is you're—"

"Listen. The last guy you rang up," he said, and something shifted inside her. She was still suddenly, utterly still. She could feel a vein pulsing at the corner of her eye.

"I saw what you did."

"I didn't do nothing."

"Sure you did, I've been watching you."

"I don't know what you're talking about."

"I'm talking about the habit you got of collecting full price, but ringing up something less. You did it to me the other day, didn't you?"

She had, too; it had seemed too easy to pass up. He was so insular, so private and apart from the rest of them, like he wasn't but halfway in the world. She stood there another moment, and then—just to fill the silence—she leaned over and refilled his cup. Her hand shook, coffee lipping the rim to puddle on the table. She straightened, ignoring it.

"You need something else?"

"I'm not trying to scare you. I'm—look. My name's Carl. Don't get me wrong, I'm not judging you"—He glanced at her badge—"Eleanor. Really. I'm just . . . warning you. You wanna be careful, that's all I'm saying." He leaned toward her, lowering his voice. "All I'm saying is you're ripe now. They're going to come for you. I'd like to talk to you. I'd like to hel—"

"Thanks," she said. "You let me know if you need anything else."

Heart hammering, Eleanor turned back toward the counter, intending to slip the carafe back atop its burner and duck into the restroom. She needed a minute to pull herself together. Her mind had slipped into some kind of vicious feedback loop: she was ripe now, they were going to come for her? What did *that* mean? And if *he'd* seen her, then who else—

A hand shot out from a booth as she passed, closing around her elbow.

"Coffee, miss?"

She poured without looking—four cups, one two three four—emptying the carafe. Still the hand clutched her elbow. "Why don't you look at me?" its owner said.

So she did, stumbling back a step as his features—those deep-set eyes, that lean hard face, the black tunic—impressed themselves upon her. She glanced wildly at the soot-grimed windows and there was the dog, too, Cuth, chained to a post on the sidewalk, unmoving, impervious to weather. And still the black tunic did not release her. He just reeled her in, utterly without effort, not so much as lifting his other hand from its place flat atop the table. She looked at his companions, four of them, black tunics all, watchful red eyes pinned to their collars, searching their faces each in its turn, not knowing what it was she hoped to find there but not finding it all the same, not finding anything at all, their faces flat and without affect, like stone, their eyes as empty as orbs of painted glass, until her gaze rounded the circuit and settled once again upon her captor.

He smiled.

"I saw you on the subway this morning, didn't I? You caught my eye."

"I'm sorry, it was an acc—"

Still clasping her elbow, he tilted his head and lifted his other hand to silence her. An inch or two, that's all. And smiling. Still smiling.

"No need for that. Accidents happen. You caught my eye, that's all. And just now—just now I couldn't help overhearing your conversation with my"—He pursed his lips, considering—"my . . . colleague—though the phrase is a little grandiose for the likes of a man in a blue uniform, don't you think? Such a lowly . . . servant . . . of our regime, don't you think? I could have him in the pit in a minute, if you know what I mean. On the other side of the equation: experiencing the pain rather than dispensing it."

"That's—" Eleanor swallowed. "I don't know what he was talking—"

Again he silenced her with a wave. "Be that as it may. One thing you want to know—a very good thing to know—is that our organization is always looking for someone anxious to put their shoulder to the wheel. Someone willing to get their hands dirty. There are opportunities for advancement. We all end up in the pit sooner or later. It's just a question of which side of that equation you want to be on." And now, at last, he did release her, but still she stood there, unmoving, waiting to be dismissed, like a kid called in to see the principal.

He lifted his coffee, still steaming, and drained it in a single long swallow. He set the empty cup on the table—gently, oh so gently—and then, surveying his companions, he said: "Gentlemen."

They stood as one.

Eleanor drew back to let them pass, but the man from the subway—she could see the coffee stain on his tunic now—wheeled back to face her, lifting his hand. She recoiled, thinking that he was going to strike her—something broken inside her almost welcomed it—and then she saw that he had magicked a sheaf of papers out of some hidden pocket. He folded them with one hand, his fingers dexterous and swift, once, twice, and then again, a neat packet the size of a business card. Leaning toward her, he tucked it down inside her breast pocket. His fingers lingered there, skating the rim of her nipple. Her cheeks flamed with impotent rage.

"We can take you away from this . . . *place*," he said, the disgust audible in his voice; without another word he turned away. Outside a gray rain poured down—Eleanor could smell it, the gusty wet and the damp smolder of the pit beyond it, when the door swung jingling closed behind them.

The airless bubble that had formed around her burst; the clatter of the diner—the clink of silver and the muted babble of conversation and Tank bellowing *Order up!* from the kitchen—rushed in to fill it. Eleanor looked around, mystified that no one—

—not even Carl not even your precious loverboy—

—had noticed anything amiss: the world was as it had been always, spilling over with things to do and never time enough to do them, the clock by the serving window propelling her willy-nilly onward, onward, into a blind, imperious future where someone somewhere faraway was always wheedling her, "Excuse me, ma'am, excuse me, but is there any chance we could get some refills?"

She looked around at the grimy windows, the cracked vinyl benches, the stained and scarred formica tabletops, and there was nothing at all for her there, nothing but a phrase rolling through her thoughts like a stone: *We can take you away from this place.*

Then it was late.

Philippe headed home, the street wound up its business for the night and still the rain came down, the dining room empty but for a couple of blue uniforms at a table, male and female, lovers maybe, whispering over pie and coffee. Eleanor was restocking the soda coolers when Tank stuck his head in the service window.

"Can I see you when you get a minute, Eleanor?" he said.

"You go ahead," Noreen told her, "I got this," so Eleanor slipped back through the kitchen to the office, a cramped cell jammed with furniture: a pair of battered filing cabinets, an oversized desk, and two chairs, Tank's capacious leather throne and a rickety monster of molded yellow plastic that looked like he might have fished it out of a dumpster. Eleanor stood, shivering—Tank kept the window unit running full blast year round, as if to compensate for the constant blistering assault of the kitchen—and when she saw what he had on his desk, the temperature seemed to plummet another ten degrees.

He'd pulled the till and arranged the cash in neat stacks on the blotter in front of him. "How you doin, Eleanor," he said, flipping methodically through a sheaf of yellow receipts, a pair of wire rim reading glasses perched at the tip of his nose. The fingers of his other hand danced over the keys of the adding machine. Eleanor stared at it as she tried to work up the spit to speak, watching in doomed fascination as the extruding tongue of white paper stroked out line after damning line of faded purple figures.

"Fine—" she said. She said, "I'm fine."

"That's good. I'm glad to hear that. And what about that little girl a yours, what's her name, Hannah—"

"Anna." Eleanor swallowed. "Her name's Anna. She's okay."

"Is she? I know she's been sick, Noreen says—"

"She's as well as can be expected."

"Well, I'm sorry to hear you're having trouble. Seems like all we get is trouble sometimes." Tank thumbed the last receipt face down on the desk, picked up a pencil, made a note. He rocked back in his chair. "You want to sit down, Eleanor."

"I'm fine."

Tank shrugged—have it the way you want it—laid his glasses on the desk, and rubbed his eyes, thumb and forefinger, sighing like he didn't want to do what it was he had to do. Then he looked up at her. Looked her square in the face.

"You stealing from me, Eleanor?"

"Someone say I was? Darla maybe? You know she can't stand me, Tank."

"Wasn't Darla and you know it. I mean, don't I got eyes?"

She said nothing.

"Thing is, I do most of the cookin' myself, specially on days when Frank doesn't come in. I know what goes through that serving window, I know what it costs, and I got a head for figures. I'm not stupid. How you think I got to where I am today." Eleanor, looking around the ugly cell of an office, had to suppress a bark of hysterical laughter. To think of such a place as a destination, rather than—rather than what? The last station on a long doomed journey to . . . where exactly?

Once again, those words pinballed around inside her head:

We can take you away from this place.

Tank said, "You tipped out yet?"

She swallowed. "Yeah."

He leaned forward and drew the money toward him with his forearm, clearing a place on the desk. "Why don't you empty your apron for me, Eleanor."

"Tank—"

"Tank nothing. You ain't stealing, you got nothing to worry about."

Eleanor stared at him, hating him suddenly with a white hot resentment—

—I want Mrs. Koh—

—that burned inside her like the sun. She stepped to the edge of the desk, and upended her apron. Coins scattered everywhere—Eleanor watched a dime roll spinning to rest on the battered oak veneer—a handful of pens and paper-wrapped straws, her order booklet, a much-creased photo of Anna, and a damning clump of folded bills. The stack of bills collapsed in an untidy heap. In the silence that followed, Tank whistled.

"You done alright for yourself today, didn't you?"

He reached out, pushed most of the mess back at Eleanor—he didn't even glance at the photo—and picked up the cash, tapping it sidewise against the deck, like a poker dealer edging up a deck of cards. He leaned back, licked the ball of his thumb, and began to count. Once, twice, a third time. Then set the stack of money down on the desk, where it lay between them like a bomb.

"Get your stuff off my desk, Eleanor," he said, not ungently. But when she reached out for the money, he laid his big hand over it.

"How long's this been going on? How much you stuck me for? Three or four grand? More?"

"I didn't— I don't—"

"You telling me you tipped out at two-hundred fourteen dollars, when Noreen—yeah, I asked Noreen—tells me she's lucky she clears a hundred dollars a night. You telling me that for real? Don't you bullshit a bullshitter, girl. What I asked you was, how much you stuck me for?"

Eleanor opened her mouth to speak, but—nothing. No words came.

"Let's call it five grand, what do you say?"

"You going to call the cops, Tank?" she asked, thinking of the pit, those smoldering depths spiraling down into the bowels of the earth.

"I don't *want* to call anybody, Eleanor. I know about that girl of yours, I don't want nothing bad to happen to her. But I can't just let you steal from me, can I?"

Eleanor didn't respond. She just stood there, feeling like the floor had slipped out from underneath her feet, like any moment now she might slide right off the daylit surface of the planet and into some black abyss where everything was weightless and still.

It was Charlie all over again, kicking back at his favorite table with the new spotlight dancer, Lena, his brand-new best-girlfriend-ever, the love of his life, lithe and high breasted and barely twenty if she was even that, guzzling his lies and his liquor both and cutting out his share of her stage money every night, blind to Eleanor, blind to the future incarnate standing right there in front of her, the clock already glutting itself on the beauty that wasn't hers to keep: Charlie saying, *you're a sweet girl, Elle* (and had anyone else ever called her that?), *but this ain't no job for a woman of your age, you know what I'm saying. Since the baby you know. Don't get me wrong now, you still look damn good, but—*

"Eleanor."

She looked up. "What do you want, Tank?"

He ran his tongue across his lips.

"A man has his needs," he said.

"What are you trying to say?"

"I'm not *trying* to say anything. What I'm saying is you're a fine looking woman. We could work this thing out between us, the two of us. I don't have to begrudge you the money, that's what I'm saying."

It was like he'd been sitting there this whole time, listening in somehow on the run of her thoughts. It was like something had been caged up inside her, some small fierce animal, furious and impotent, gnashing at the bars of her heart. Her voice broke when she started to speak. She hated the sound of it, the words hanging helpless and weak in that icy air.

"You've been good to me, Tank. Don't do this to me now."

"*Me?* I haven't done anything, Eleanor. You done this yourself."

Then: "Look, we're all of us damned in this place, Eleanor. We every one of us going to wind up in the pit, one way or the other. Why not have a little fun along the way?"

"It wouldn't be fun for me, Tank. Not this way. Can't you see that?"

Tank said nothing.

Eleanor bit her lip, swiped in fury at her eyes, hating the tears that trembled there unspilled.

"Please."

Tank heaved his bulk up behind the desk. He leaned over splayed hands, thick fingers mashing aside the neat stacks of bills.

"Don't do *me* like this. What I'm saying, it ain't nothing new to you, Eleanor. I know what you used to be. A leopard don't change its spots."

He straightened, picking up the stack of cash. Then he leaned over to tuck it down inside the pocket of her apron.

"You worked hard to steal this today, so you take it home with you, you hear. You take it home and you think things through. Think about that little girl of yours. You think about her real hard. We'll talk this over again in a day or two."

He lowered himself into his seat, put his glasses on, turned back to his paperwork. Eleanor just stood there, silent before him, fists dangling at her sides, that animal inside her heart hammering so hard at its cage that for a moment she thought she might just keel over. Without looking up at her—it was like she wasn't there at all—Tank reached back to adjust the air conditioner, kicking the window unit into higher gear. Chill bumps erupted on her forearms, tiny hairs shivering themselves erect.

Then Tank *did* look up, peering over the tops of his spectacles at her like he was surprised to see her still standing there, he thought she must have left hours ago.

"You can go now," he said.

The tears came the instant the bathroom door swung closed behind her, an onslaught that drove her into the last stall. Eleanor thumbed the lock and put her back to the wall, drinking in the soothing chill of the cinderblock, like water drawn up from some untapped well in cool depths of earth, to slake a thirst she hadn't even known she had. She couldn't say how long she stood like that—five minutes, she supposed, maybe ten, but it felt like forever, it felt like some central line had burst inside her and the tears wouldn't ever stop. Except they did finally, wearing down in stages: sobs, then sniffles, then nothing but the hollow aftermath, her breathing labored and her makeup shot, her nose plugged with snot.

She leaned over to tear off a length of toilet tissue. The sheaf of paper—forgotten—crinkled in her breast pocket. Eleanor blew her nose, folded the tissue, blew it again. Dumping the soggy mass in the toilet, she took a breath. Settled herself. Dug out that neat rectangle in her pocket, memory stinging her, the humiliation of it, the way he'd touched her. As she unfolded it, a little flume of paper, it must have been folded up inside, sprayed out like it had been spring-loaded and fluttered to the floor at her feet: the familiar yellow rectangle of the ticket and something else. Three bills.

Eleanor knelt to retrieve them. Counted them out, one two three, and then again. Three one hundred dollar bills. Enough to cover the tab ten times over. She dropped to the filthy tile, her legs abruptly boneless, folded the cash, slipped it into the pocket of her apron. She leaned her head against the tile and closed her eyes, trying to think things through.

When she opened them, she turned her attention to the other paper, the one he'd wrapped everything up in: a heavy stock, textured and creamy, folded over three times like a letter and gummed closed, *Application for Employment* printed neatly on the outside.

Eleanor laughed.

She shook her head in disbelief. She didn't bother unsealing it, just shoved it down into the apron's pocket with everything else. Her finger brushed the scalloped edge of the photograph, her personal talisman, a snapshot of Anna two years gone, the last one she'd ever taken before their life had turned itself inside out, not so much a life at all anymore but an endless campaign, a battle waged against photographs and mirrors and panes of night-drowned glass, a war to protect her little girl from understanding what it was that was happening to her, and maybe to protect herself as well.

She pulled the snapshot out, the lacquered surface creased with a thousand touches. Held it there before her with trembling fingers, Tank's words—

—*think about that little girl of yours*—

—unleashing a torrent of memory. Anna hunched over the toilet, her narrow shoulders heaving. Anna in agony, her face limned red by the digital clock on her night stand, whittling down the hours until she could have another dose of morphine, twisting with skeletal fingers her threadbare sheets, her drug-dulled eyes unseeing. She thought about the hair, clumped anew in the teeth of the comb with every fresh pass, the wastebasket in the bathroom already brimming over with the stuff, all that beautiful, beautiful hair. She thought about Anna's labored breathing in the deepest slough of night, about the ammonia stench of the treatment center and the avalanche of unpaid bills claiming inch by inch the kitchen table and how long it had been since she'd had even a little bit of anything for herself, a drink or an hour alone or the touch of a man's hands and when would it end, God, when would it ever end?

And something else: Anna's face twisted ugly with fury, smashing the pills out of her hand, the glittering shower of tepid water.

I don't want the pills! I want Mrs. Koh!

Eleanor's fingers, unbidden, crumpled the snapshot. Then she was crying again—or trying to, anyway—as she struggled to smooth out the fresh creases in the photo, but it was too late. Too late. Somewhere along the way the tears had dried up, some microscopic internal plumber had gotten around to patching up that burst line at last. She felt nothing. She felt nothing at all. And so, still holding the snapshot in her hand, Eleanor climbed wearily to her feet and unlocked the stall and headed back out to work.

As Eleanor turned the corner into the corridor, still staring at the photo, a voice broke her reverie—

"Careful, miss—"

Startled, she looked up too late. She had a confused impression of a shadow looming before her, backlit in the fluorescent glare of the dining room. A heartbeat later, they collided. She stumbled back, overbalanced, and for a single panicky moment she thought she was going down. Then hands reached out to steady her. Strong hands, work roughened, with corkscrews of dark hair at the knuckles.

"You okay?"

She looked up.

Gray eyes, knotted nose: her friend the voyeur. Loverboy.

Carl.

He released her, smoothing down her sleeves where his grip had rumpled them and she pushed herself back, away from him, shoulders to the wall. He knelt before her, and when he stood, she saw that he was holding the photo of Anna. He studied it for a moment, trying to smooth out the creases himself, and then he extended it to her.

"Sorry about that," he said.

Fingers trembling, she took the picture and tucked it away in her apron.

"I'm off. Noreen'll take care of you."

"Actually, I came back here hoping I'd run into you. In a manner of speaking."

She let the joke pass unremarked. "What do you mean?"

"You've got to be worn out. Let me buy you a cup of coffee."

He coaxed her into the dining room, empty now, and as she slid into a booth, split red vinyl rasping against the backs of her thighs, Eleanor realized that she *was* tired, and not just tired either: weary, a bone-deep weariness bigger than the exhaustion of fourteen hours on her feet, so big it stretched all the way back past Anna and beyond, to Charlie and the club, almost seven years now. Sighing, Loverboy—Carl, she tried to think of him as Carl—slid into the seat across from her. She turned away. Beyond the transparent mask of her face in the window, steady gray rain slanted down.

Noreen flounced up to the table, winking at Eleanor. "Tell you what," she said to Eleanor after he ordered—coffee, nothing more, "I'll go ahead and clock you out. We're about done anyway."

Then she was gone, leaving them to the rain and the hum of the soda coolers back of the counter, the steady beat of the clock by the serving window, chewing down the hours. Funny how you never noticed that when the place was hopping; now each bite the second hand took sounded like the detonation of a tiny bomb. Then Noreen reappeared with the coffee and time vanished once again, swallowed up in the ritual bustle of sugar and cream, the clatter of spoons. He picked up his coffee and blew across the top of it.

"You afraid of me?" he said. And when she didn't answer: "People are, you know. This . . . uniform"—he pinched the blue fabric at one wrist—"all you have to do is walk in the door when you're wearing it and you see it. You see it in every face."

She stared at her coffee.

"This afternoon at lunch. I saw what happened. You were afraid then."

"I'm not afraid anymore."

"Sometimes it's better to be afraid."

"I have other things to be afraid of."

He nodded. Sipped his coffee.

"That picture. That your little girl?"

"Yeah."

"She's cute."

"She's sick."

"That one of the things you're afraid of?"

She didn't answer.

He held her gaze for a moment; then he looked down, his thick hands restless, turning his cup, turning it and turning it.

Eleanor pushed her coffee away.

"Look—Carl—I don't have time to play games. I'm tired. I've got a little girl I need to get home to. Whatever it is you think you saw me do, it doesn't matter. That's over now. So thanks for the coffee. And have a great life, okay. You probably won't see me around here anymore."

Putting her hands flat on the table, Eleanor shoved herself to her feet. She'd almost reached the pass-through in the counter when he spoke again, so soft she wasn't sure what he'd said. But something in his tone—something grievous, something lost—stopped her cold. She drew a breath. Turned. Stared back at him gazing down into the muddy depths of his coffee, like he could see something down in there that no one else could see.

"What did you say?"

"This is how they do it to you." He laughed. "It's so easy. That's the thing about it: it's so goddamn easy. They wait until you don't have anywhere else to turn, and then they take the best thing you have inside you and turn it into a razor and they cut your throat with it."

She took a step back toward the table. "What do you mean?"

He looked up. "Don't fill out that application."

She laughed. She couldn't help herself.

She folded herself into the seat across from him.

She said, "You think I can steal enough? You think enough money comes through this place in a week to pay for the help she's going to need? I could steal every dime of it and it wouldn't be enough."

She leaned forward, lowering her voice, laughter—strangled, humorless laughter—bubbling like madness in her guts. "Fuck you," she said. "You've got a lot of nerve, sitting there in that suit, holier than thou, like you know something about me I don't know myself. Well fuck you."

She pushed herself back from the table once again, but before she could stand, his hand shot out, shackling her wrist. His coffee—what was left it—went over, the cup rolling on the stained formica like a spun coin. He tightened his grip, bones grinding in her arm. His hands were cold, she thought as he dragged her close to him. In Acheron, everyone's hands were cold.

"You don't know what I have to do in this suit. You have no idea."

But she did. She *did* know, she could feel it in the way he held her wrist, she could see it in the crusted black crescents under his fingernails, in the tension of his jaw and the cold light shining in his gray-spoked eyes. She knew something else, too, something she'd been pining to know in the secret recesses of her heart: what it would be like for him to touch her; she'd been touched like that before, not a man on earth who didn't have that down inside him.

"Let me go," she whispered.

But he drew her closer, so close she could smell the taint of coffee on his breath. And worse: the reek of the pit. It had started to seep into his pores, a stench of blood and iron and soot that no soap on earth could ever lave away.

"It's not enough," he said. "No amount of money could ever be enough. And that's not the worst of it. The worst thing is, you do it long enough—and you can't ever stop, you can't just walk away—you do it long enough and little by little you start to enjoy it, little by little it starts to eat you up, it just . . . devours whatever it was you thought you were, whatever it was you thought you wanted to be."

And then he did release her.

She sat back, panting.

Cradling her wrist against her breast.

"Look, I've got money," he said. He shook his head, fixed her with his gaze. "You'll have plenty of money, they said, and they were right about that. I've got all the money I could ever want. So let me help you."

Eleanor stood.

She stared down at him. "Why? What do you want from me?"

"Nothing," he said.

He reached out to her, and though she flinched, she didn't pull away. She just stood there, her breath suspended in her lungs as he traced the livid ghosts of his fingers on her wrist, his touch so light she could barely feel it, yet it seemed to fill up the silence that ached between each contraction of her heart, it seemed to chime inside her like a bell.

He had that in him, too.

"I just want to do one right thing before I disappear," he said. "I just want to help."

"I don't need any help. I'm doing all right by myself."

Eleanor turned away.

She didn't look back as she slammed past the counter and into the kitchen, Tank behind closed doors in the office, the radio tuned to something jazzy and light.

"You and Loverboy make out okay?" Noreen said from the prep table.

"Shut up, Noreen."

"Had his eyes on you for weeks now, that one. I told you so."

Eleanor draped her apron over the rim of the laundry bin and started emptying the pockets, angling her back to Noreen as she shoved the cash into her coat. "It's not like that."

"What's it like then, honey? He's just a man, isn't he? I don't care what color suit he wears. *Or* what he does in it. Long as he brings home enough money I can put my feet up and catch up on daytime television."

"Well I do." Eleanor glanced over her shoulder at the other woman. "I care, okay."

Noreen shrugged. "All I'm sayin is what a man does ain't necessarily what that man *is*."

"That's all any of us ever are," Eleanor said, "the things we do. We don't have to agree about that."

"No, I guess we don't."

Noreen turned her back—*so there*—and started wiping down the grill.

Eleanor finished cleaning out the apron—a handful of straws, the application, the photo. She dumped the straws in a bin and crushed the application into a ball. The hell with it. She started to chuck it in the trash, all of it, the application and the ruined photo, too; instead, she found herself staring down at the snapshot—at Anna's gap-toothed smile, her tongue probing the hole, a perfect paradox, frozen that way forever, as if the world wasn't full of clocks, every last one of them mocking the endless era of her misery. She'd tried to stay awake that night—she'd wanted to see the tooth fairy, she'd been so excited—but when Eleanor looked in at eight, she'd already drifted off. And then the words came back to Eleanor, the twisted look upon her small face—

I don't want the pills! I want Mrs. Koh!

Eleanor shrugged on her coat, shoving the wad of paper deep into one pocket. "Thanks, Noreen. Night."

"You think about what I'm saying, Eleanor."

"I will," she said, and maybe she already was, for when she stepped back through the kitchen door and saw what was waiting for her on the other side—just emptiness, the sterile glare of fluorescent lights hung low over battered countertops, just nothing at all—she felt something give way inside her, some final parapet she hadn't even known was there.

He'd cleaned up after himself, or tried to anyway, sopping up the spilled coffee with napkins from the tabletop dispenser and shoving them inside his righted cup. And something else: a fifty-dollar bill.

Eleanor picked it up, crumpled it, flung it to the table.

Noreen could have it.

Headlights dazzled her, igniting in their thousands the rain droplets that jeweled the window, counterfeit every one of them, and a million million more falling by the minute. Looking up, Eleanor caught a flash of blonde hair behind the wheel, a woman's smile; then she saw him circle around the car to climb in beside her, a blue uniform like all the other ones, another loverboy.

The car pulled away from the curb, and Eleanor stepped out into the rain.

It slammed down around her by the bucket, soaking her through in the space of a breath, pummeling her scalp and shoulders and drumming down on the pavement and the parked cars like stones, unleashing all the thunders of heaven in wave after pealing wave until the sky split open in a smoky crimson gash and the earth itself trembled underfoot.

Eleanor paused, uncertain how she had come to be here: the chain link fence that loomed stark and black above her, slashing the turbid sky to bloody rags; the coiled thickets of razor wire and the towers and the dogs and the cold-eyed men with guns; the broken streets she walked upon; the husks of buildings; the pustulant wound inside the fence, a blight upon the land, or a tumor metastasizing to consume at last the strength of the city that had so long sustained it.

Not thunder.

Oh no, not thunder.

It was worse: the boom and din of vast, infernal engines in the midnight hollows of the planet, and in the intervals between, other sounds more terrible still: the creak of the whip and the rattle of the chain and everywhere around her bleeding up into the sodden air the pleas of the damned, the fruitless and eternal cries for succor of human souls hoisted on the cradle, rack stretched and flayed and broken on the wheel, time and time again, forever.

The word rang inside her mind—

—*forever*—

—forever without cease.

Eleanor reeled away—away from the blasted soil and the terrible coppery stench that hung like a pall in the humid air. Away from the futile moans that coiled up to shackle her and drag her down. Away from the searing conflagration that smoldered in the spiraled hollows of the pit, in the ruined chambers and recesses where sweat-slick men in blue coveralls, human beings not so much unlike herself, bent to the tasks assigned them and plied the tools of their terrible trade.

What kind of God could permit such an obscenity? What kind of God?

Eleanor reeled away.

Back to the street and the mouth of the subway somewhere awaiting, back to her dank apartment, to a wicker basket that had once overflowed with the hair of a child, to a bottle of pills that had long since ceased to have any effect at all, to the flat unfeeling face of Mrs. Koh.

What kind of God?

They spun her on her heels, those images; they marched her down to the spiked gates and the adjacent guardhouse, a squat bunker of yellow block that might have been mined out of the pit itself in some dim, forgotten era, and the whole time she could feel it, the tense circuit of that fierce little creature that had been caged up inside her, turning and turning as it paced off the measure of its prison.

She touched the door.

It swung open to admit her.

Eleanor stepped inside.

The door clapped into its frame at her back, and that quickly the noise faded. That quickly it was silent, utter and pristine.

And cool. Eleanor hadn't realized how hot it had been out there, but she felt it now, a trickle of sweat down the channel of her spine.

She looked around.

An empty room, a fluorescent light flickering overhead. A reception window. A round schoolroom clock paring down the hours.

Eleanor rapped on the glass.

An old man, bloated and enormous, his thinning hair greased back over the dome of his liver-spotted skull, hove into view. He slid back the glass and peered myopically out at her.

"Help you?"

"I'm here about the job."

"I see." He sucked at his teeth, considering. "You got your application."

"Yeah, it's—"She dug in her pockets, looked up—"Here it is."

Eleanor placed it on the counter, ironing it flat with the palm of her hand before she unsealed it, and by that time the old man had conjured a pen from somewhere. He slid it over to her. She picked it up and looked down at the form, smoothing it out again with her other hand. And then she looked up, puzzled.

"Is this some kind of joke?"

"It ain't the most complicated form in the world," the old man said.

"No it isn't, is it?"

"That's it, though. That's all you need."

She looked down at the page again: *Application for Employment* at the top, and below that, maybe a third of the way down the sheet, a single black line, and under that a word:

____

Name

"Okay, then," she said.

She took a breath and then—*no regrets, just do it*—Eleanor wrote her name.

She handed the sheet across to the man. He eyed it in silence for a moment—like he'd expected more from her—and then he looked up at her.

He crumpled the application into a ball—

Eleanor gasped.

—and tossed it under the counter. Straightening up, he pushed a fresh copy of the form across to her.

"Maybe you misunderstood, ma'am. We don't need *your* name. We've had your name for a long time now. What we need from you is somebody *else's* name."

"I don't—" she started to say, but the final word—

—*understand*—

—died on her lips, for she did, she did understand, she understood all too well, and the day swept back over her in a tide of gray misery, Tank and Carl and the awful man on the subway—the way he'd seemed to look right down inside of her, knowing things about her she didn't know herself—and Anna most of all.

Anna in her sickbed, waiting with Mrs. Koh, her sponge bath yet to come and then the sheets because you had to be careful of the bedsores and the avalanche of bills upon the table, which one to pay first, and why even bother?

Because there would never be enough.

No matter what she did, there would never be enough.

She licked her lips.

The old man held her gaze, phlegm rattling in his chest.

Eleanor picked up the pen and the clock overhead notched another second. She could hear it now, the steady electric whirr it made as it shaved down the hours.

Eleanor wrote down a name.

Lightning Jack's Last Ride

They say Lightning Jack died in a fiery crash just outside of Atlanta, racing west toward freedom, into the teeth of a setting sun. I remember the scene in digital video, the way I saw it then, on the ancient flatpanel affixed to the wall of a dingy apartment in Biloxi. He'd rolled coming out of a curve on I-20, and even then that struck me as laughable: three lanes of abandoned highway, all that room for error and him the finest driver that had ever lived.

Yet there it was on the screen. The networks looped the tape over and over in the days that followed, snippets of Lightning Jack's blistering death interspersed with archival footage of the moments that had made him a legend: hoisting his trophy in triumphant youth at his first Talladega, squiring Julie Marina down the red carpet to collect her Oscar, slamming into the wall as he roared out of the third curve at the last legal Daytona.

But they always came back to that final cataclysmic sequence. Captured by antiquated cameras installed in an era when I-20 still saw civilian traffic, it had, even then, the look of video you'll be seeing for the rest of your life, the flat inarguable reality, the banal composition of history in the making: Hitler at the Reichstag, Kennedy in the motorcade. The opening images have the archetypal familiarity of a scene apprehended in a dream. The leaden vault of sky looms over a sweeping plane of empty asphalt. But for the heat rippling above the pavement it might be a still photo. It's that static, that timeless. And then, suddenly, like an apparition, the car appears, a low-slung black blur, tires smoking as it clears the curve. The rear end slews to the right, threatening to send the vehicle into a spin, and then—impossibly, inconceivably—the driver overcorrects. It's over almost as soon as it begins, an anti-climax; only our knowledge of the man inside the car—only our knowledge of Lightning Jack's myth—redeems the paucity of drama. One moment the car is skidding. The next moment, it's airborne, skipping across the pavement like a stone. Then it smashes into the concrete crash barrier and jolts to a rest atop its shredded tires.

A moment of stillness follows, a moment in which I always expect the door to fly open and Lightning Jack to step out, cradling the Heckler & Koch G40 he cosseted like a baby, his lean face creased in a roguish grin as he prepares to go down in a hail of New Federal lead. He always vowed they'd never take him alive. But the door does not open. The car merely sits there, frozen beneath an armor-plated sky for a heartbeat longer. Then, suddenly, it bursts into flame.

New Fed officials turned the tape over to the newsnets not thirty minutes later. The story of Lightning Jack's final caper unfolded in the hours that followed. Soon enough the network faces had that footage, as well, cobbled together from vehicle-mounted military cameras. It showed Jack's standard operating procedure for cutting a gasoline tanker out of a military convoy, a task as audacious as it was dangerous, requiring six people in the kind of rolling iron that would stiffen a gearhead's pecker: a Midori Spyder, a Mitsubishi Gilead and, God help us all, Lightning Jack's sweet sugar itself, a modified black Chevy Dragon straight out of the heart of old Detroit. Three vehicles, two to take out the gunners in their crow's nests atop the tank, and one more—Jack's Dragon—to match the trucker wheel to wheel. Then, hurtling along at seventy, eighty, ninety miles an hour, the swingman would lever himself out the passenger side window of the Dragon, fling himself across the void of racing gray pavement to the running board of the tanker and take out the driver with a single pistol shot to the temple, bang through the window glass. The most perilous moments of all followed. The truck veered out of control as the swingman wrenched open the door, shoved the dead man aside, and took the wheel. If things went as planned, they'd coax the tanker with its three car escort down the nearest exit and disappear into the tangle of surface streets below.

Fifty years previously the maneuver wouldn't have been possible. A law enforcement satellite would have lit them up the minute they cut that tanker loose. But in these days of peak oil and global warming, a satellite is lucky if it can punch a signal through the atmospheric murk once in a million pings. Still, it was a daring crime. In a U.S. of A coming apart at the seams, with D.C. irradiated, Manhattan blown clear off the map, and insurgencies booming from sea to shining sea, a single thermos of petroleum was a hell of a thing to lose. There must have been half a dozen gangs working the black market in gasoline in those days, from Gallant Jim's up around the lakes to Victor Albertini's out on the left coast. But famous as some of them were, none of them could match Lightning Jack's crew or his legend. None of them could match his style. He'd sign in on Channel 19 to mock the truckers on their CB radios as the shit rained down, and he'd send thank you notes—he had the prettiest script—when he was done.

But this time things had gone wrong. They'd taken out the driver and cut the tanker free of the convoy all right, but as the eighteen-wheeler swerved across the lanes, it clipped Lola Bridger's Spyder. She went spinning back into traffic where a tanker crushed her like a bug and jackknifed in the middle of the highway. The next fish in line slammed it side on, igniting an explosion so big that it must have singed God's beard. A heartbeat later, the swingman rolled his own rig, reducing Joe Hauser's Gilead to a greasy stain on the pavement. Lightning Jack dropped the hammer, and that Dragon leapt forward like a rabid Doberman fixing to break its chain. Four and a half minutes later, it struck the crash barrier on I-20. That fire burned hot and clean. By the time it was done there was barely enough left to put in a pine box. The networks reported it all the same, and DNA confirmed it: the Feds had gotten their man.

But there are those who'll tell you that the charred carcass they pulled out of that car was a ringer and that Lightning Jack lives to this day. Some say he'd finally made his nut and retired to some clement place like the Upper Peninsula of Michigan or maybe Edmonton, others that he took his thieving ways out west, where he gave Victor

Albertini a run for his money. That's the way with famous outlaws. Some men will attest to this day that Jesse James died of old age, and that John Dillinger wasn't the man the FBI pumped full of holes in front of the Biograph Theater.

I'm here to tell you that they're wrong. Lightning Jack died almost forty years ago. Don't bother telling me otherwise, because I'm the only man who knows the truth. After all, I was there. I knew Jack, you see. I knew him from the time he was a bean.

He'd already acquired the nickname—some say he gave it to himself—by the time I met him, and he was barely out of diapers then. The man—if you can call a seventeen-year-old boy a man—was flat great behind the wheel from the start, and I'll swear to that until my dying day. I knew it the first time I ever spoke to him. I'd been knocking around the Truck Series for a year by then, trying to catch on somewhere, when I saw him blow a sticker at the Charlotte Motor Speedway. I'd had my eye on him for weeks. He'd been in the lead until the tire betrayed him. This was maybe a flaw in his driving—he hadn't pitted as often as he should've—or maybe a flaw in the tire, I couldn't say for sure, but as he coasted into pit row, flapping leather, the field sped past him. I figured the wheel was too bent to mount a new scuff, but we'll never know for sure: the front tire carrier fumbled the exchange. Lightning Jack came out of that truck like a piston firing. His helmet went one way and Jack went the other, straight up into the tire carrier's face. He probably would have hit him—he *did* fire him—if Joe Hauser, the rear tire man in those days, hadn't simmered him down.

I'd known Joe since we'd been boys racing go-karts together. It was by his invitation that I was in the pit in the first place. I had an inkling that Joe might be able to broker me a job, and I had planned to show Jack that I knew my way around an engine, nobody better. But sometimes it's better to be lucky than good. Even so, I might have slipped the opportunity like I've slipped so many others if it wasn't for my own big mouth. I always was a talker, and an opinionated bastard to boot, and those traits have gotten me into more trouble than they have gotten me out of, but just then they worked in my favor, for as Jack vaulted the wall and strode into his pit stall, I couldn't help myself. I said, "You left money out there on the track."

Jack turned to face me, and I saw then what a handsome devil he already was and would become. He aged well, Jack, and even when a New Fed bullet creased his forehead during the Tallahassee job a decade later, the scar it left behind only gave him a rakish look that seemed to make him more popular with the ladies. Some men you just can't beat.

"What did you say?" he asked, and the whole time Joe is standing behind him, slashing the edge of his hand across his throat. *Shut up, shut up*.

But I never could. So there we stood in the maintenance stall, me and Lightning Jack, everything stinking of spent oil and smoking rubber and sweat, and what I do is, I turn up the volume. "I said, you left money out there on the track."

"How do you figure?"

"Two ways. One, you were too aggressive. It ain't all about driving, son"—this though I didn't have but five years or so on him—"it's also about timing. You got to judge your tires and your fuel, and pit at the right time."

"I reckon driving has got me this far."

"Well, it's not likely to get you much farther. NASCAR is big-time racing, son."

"Don't call me that again," he said, and I never did. Some men you have to learn not to push, and others you just know. Jack was one of the latter. I never met a man who had a more charming disposition, but you didn't cross him but once, not Jack. The front tire carrier could attest to that.

"What's the second way?" he asked.

"Hell, you know that. Prize money. Who knows whether you could have loaded a tire on that front wheel, but if you'd let the guy try, you might have placed. You don't have to win every time."

"The hell with placing. I want to win."

"Of course, you do. But you have to take the long view. Rack up enough points, you win the series and step up to the next division. From there it's only a short hop to the show, Jack."

"You go on and get out of my garage," he said. "I don't know how you got in here anyway."

And he put his back to me.

I should have let him go. But no one ever missed a turn in hindsight, did they? Instead, I said, "You need me, Jack. There's not a thing about cars that I don't know," and I think that's what did it. I wasn't asking, I was telling. And if Lightning Jack liked anything in a man, he liked confidence. He had it himself in spades. He wasn't a bragging man, but he knew there wasn't much he couldn't do with a car and he didn't get in his own way when it came to doing it. I think that's why he spun on his heel to look me over, a long, appraising look, like a man who's getting ready to drop a fair chunk of change on a brand new piece of iron and wants to make sure he doesn't get taken.

"What's your name?" he said.

"Gus March."

"Well, Gus March, I reckon you can lug a tire as well as any man. I seem to have an opening in that department."

"It's a start I guess. But I'll be running your crew inside a year," I said.

"That so?" He smiled as if he'd let go of some internal tension, the strain maybe of the race and losing it, and he looked simultaneously like the boy he was and the man he would become. There was something golden in that smile, a kind of glamour that would charm the knickers off just about every woman that swung into his orbit and that would make the men give up everything and follow him to the ends of the earth. I know because I felt it then, and before it was over I *did* follow him. He made a kind of chuffing noise, something between a snort and a laugh. Then he turned away again. "Don't let me down, Gus," he said, and his glamour hadn't rubbed off on me so much that I promised I wouldn't—not aloud, anyway. But I felt the promise in my heart. In the end, I did let him down, though. We always do, I guess. It's what makes us human. Still, that was a long time coming. In the meantime, I had other promises to keep, among them my pledge to be his crew chief before the year was out. I did it, too. It's true: there's not a thing about cars I don't know, and there's less that I can't fix. I'm not a bragging man myself. It's not bragging if you can do it.

Those were the twilight years of motor sports, of course, and if I grieved to see them go, I was glad that I'd gotten in soon enough to see them at all. Sponsorship was way down and so were ratings. Things had gotten a lot like it was in the beginning, when a man with a car didn't have to have a twenty million dollar team to buy his place on pit row. He could earn it, the way Jack did, with his smile and his talent. He breathed new life into a dying sport, same as Ali had done for boxing. You couldn't tap a newsfeed back then without Lightning Jack smiling out at you. I can see him now, the way he was before a race, that unearthly calm he had about him. "Let's ride, Gus," he always said as he strapped himself into the cockpit, and for a while the ride was a wild one, like an out-of-control elevator hurtling to the top. You'd have thought the other drivers would have hated him, but Jack was funny like that, incandescent as the lightning bolt he'd painted down the hood of his midnight-black Dragon. He lit a room up, and people loved him for it. But even that wasn't enough to save us.

By then the soup we all took in with each breath was so thick that in some of the bigger cities—Tokyo and L.A., for instance—people wore surgical masks every time they stepped out the door. Electric vehicles had never caught on—they'd never solved the battery thing—and though public transportation had skyrocketed, plenty of people still gassed up to go. There's just something about a gasoline motor, the sense of contained deviltry in it, pistons hammering as gas explodes—actually *explodes*—in the cylinder and drives the crankshaft like a dervish in his finest hour. Meanwhile, the Feds down in Washington steadily whittled away at drivers' rights. It wasn't much more than window dressing really. Peak oil had taken hold and the flow dried to a trickle. By the time Jack crashed coming out of the third turn in the last Daytona, there just about wasn't any place left where a man could wind a motor out anymore.

When NASCAR disbanded, Jack's team broke up. Me and Joe Hauser and Lola—the finest jack man I ever saw—stuck around for a while. Jack was glad to have us. We wanted to drive, even if it meant running thousand dollar drags in the middle of the Birmingham night. Amateurs all around us, and Jack ate them up like candy hearts, so charismatic that they didn't mind watching him fold away their money. Jack was all about winning even then. But a time came when even Joe and Lola and I began to drift. The last of the street gas began to run out for one thing. First it was a night or two between races; then it was a week or a month or more. Plus, there was the competition. A man can only go so long stealing lunch money before his conscience begins to nag him.

Jack fell into a funk. He took to drink, thickened up around the middle. I got to where I had to get away from it all. Before you knew it, I had a straight job, working on hydraulic lifters in Montgomery. Joe Hauser drifted out west and started pushing paper for an insurance company. Lola—the only one of us with a college degree—landed a position as an executive at a fiber optic plant, and before you know it, she was running the place.

Then the NRA's dirty bomb put the quietus to D.C. The New Feds relocated to Buffalo, but by the time they got themselves organized, it was too late. Insurgencies had begun to break out like a bad case of the clap. State's Rights and all that. I'm talking secession, the seizure of all military assets by right of eminent domain, and vigorous defense of self-declared borders. A dozen other special interest groups followed the NRA into terrorism.

Jack, with his usual prescience, had seen the way things were headed. He showed up at the hydraulic plant one afternoon and took me to lunch. It was the kind of Alabama day where just breathing you sweat through your shirt. When we got into the air-conditioned diner, I heaved a sigh of relief. "Goddamn, but you're a sight for sore eyes, Jack," I said and for a moment I couldn't do much more than stare at him. He was his old self, sinewy and lean behind a pair of Aviator glasses, his unruly mop of hair close cropped.

"It's good to see you, too, Gus," he said. "Hell, not a minute goes by I don't think about you and the old days."

"Good times," I said, and for a moment we were silent in contemplation.

An icy cold Coca-Cola appeared—you could see the glass sweating it was so cold—and then a couple of menus. I ordered a burger and fries without hardly noticing the lady serving us. Jack and I chatted in a desultory way about past times as we ate.

"You and Lola ever have anything together?" I asked at one point. I'd often thought about trying my hand with her myself—she'd have probably shot me down like a clay pigeon—only I feared horning in on Jack's territory, and I would never do a thing like that.

"Lola?" he said. "She was too important to the organization."

After that, the conversation turned in other directions. We were both melancholy by then, anyway. We missed the track, the stink of exhaust and the sizzle of anticipation as we took the pavement, the burst of activity whenever Jack slipped in to pit. I ran the fastest crew on the circuit—I can't tell you how many times other drivers tried to poach my guys—but every time we rolled out onto the asphalt we strove to shave a tenth of a second off our time. In a close race, a tenth of a second can make the difference between winning and losing.

So we chewed over what we'd been doing in the year or two since we'd last seen each other. I didn't have much to share. I worked at the hydraulics plant eight hours a day and saw a lady named Mary occasionally, but neither one of us really had our hearts in it. Jack didn't have much to say either. He'd spent a long time in that funk and then he'd pulled himself together, stopped drinking, hit the gym. I thought the conversation had hit that lull that old friends who've grown apart so often do, when they find themselves staring at each other across the gulf time has opened up between them. It saddened me. I didn't have many close friends in those days, and I hadn't realized how much I missed the easy camaraderie that grows up between men bound together in a common enterprise.

"How come you to get yourself together like that?" I asked just to break the silence, and Jack got quiet all over again. He looked me over, and I recalled the first time we met, the way he'd studied me, like he was getting ready to surrender some serious change for a hunk of rolling iron, and he wanted to make sure he liked what he was seeing. I realize now that he was wondering whether he could trust me, and I'm glad that he decided he could. Things would have gone differently if he'd chosen otherwise, and I might have been a happier man now, but it would have hurt something awful to know that Lightning Jack hadn't trusted in our friendship.

He didn't answer me. Not directly, anyway. What he said was, "Real tragedy what happened in Washington, wasn't it?"

I allowed it was, though I hadn't been especially fond of the party that was in power at the time. Nor the one that wasn't, either, if it came to that.

"This is only beginning," he said. He leaned forward, lowering his voice. "The whole thing's going to come apart, Gus. Wait and see. Nothing but spit and baling wire ever held this country together anyway. If it were a car, it would be a jalopy sure."

I allowed that this was true, as well—with the caveat that, all due respect, it didn't take any genius to see it. "Hell, Jack, Georgia's already gone and you hear the same rumbling right here in Montgomery."

"Sure," he said, and now he leaned back, flung one arm across the back of the booth, and grinned. I thought our waitress, who was just then delivering the check, might go into heat. When she was gone, he ticked the rest of the secession risks off on his fingers. He finished up with California and the Midwestern Alliance and said, "You know what that means."

"War."

"That's right. And a hell of a big one, too."

"Best thing you can do is keep your head down when the shooting starts."

"I got a different perspective," Jack said. "The way I figure it, the New Feds are going to win this thing. I reckon that at least half the military are going to stay loyal. You're going to see pockets of resistance to just about every insurgency that springs up, and soon enough Buffalo will be coordinating them. And the New Feds have the codes to the nukes. It's going to be a hair-raising ten years, but I think we have a window of opportunity here."

"Opportunity for what? To get our heads blown off?"

"We run that risk no matter what. There's no keeping out of the fray."

"Well, what do you have in mind?"

"Tell me, come war, what's the most valuable commodity on earth?"

"I don't know. Those nukes, I guess."

"Weapon of last resort, unless a terrorist gets hold of one. The New Feds are going to try to keep it conventional—and you can't fight a conventional war without—"

"Oil," I said.

"You got it." He aimed a finger at me and dropped the hammer. Bang. "Just try firing up an Abrams tank on a Sears Diehard," he said, grinning that cocky grin of his, "and you'll see what I mean. The New Feds are already moving convoys of tankers down the old interstates. It's only a matter of time before someone picks one off."

"You're a crazy man. Let's say—just for the sake of argument—you can manage it. Who are you going to sell it to?"

"Anyone who wants it. Insurgents. Gearheads hungry to fire up their old iron. Hell, I'll ransom it back to the Feds. I don't care. I'm an amoral son of a bitch, Gus. I just want to drive."

"How do you plan to do it?"

He leaned forward and sketched it out for me, and I saw then that he *was* a madman. But something in his voice made me keep listening—the lure of the open road maybe or the hunger to feel a car come to life under my hands one more time. Maybe it was money and maybe it was love for Jack himself. A crew chief lives in the shadow of his wheelman, after all. Comforts him and cossets him and makes sure his car is purring like a kitten every time he takes the pavement. So, yeah, I listened. Most of us never can say why we do the things we do. Oh, we can count out reasons like we count out change, but those are just rationalizations. We're mysteries to ourselves. That's the one true thing I know, so in the end I can't say why I did it. I can say only that I started off by telling him no. I thanked him for lunch and sent him packing, to pitch his crazy scheme to someone else—Joe maybe, or Lola. Anybody but me, brother. Hydraulics were the thing for me, and when the war came I'd follow my own advice, keep my head down, and hope that the draft board needed a gearhead more than another grunt.

Three months later, Alabama seceded from the union. I got my draft notice from the Citizens' Militia two months after that. I didn't make the appointment, though. I called Jack up and skipped town instead. He met me at the gate to tell me he'd pulled the crew back together. "Welcome home, brother," he said, clapping me on the back. "Let's ride."

Our first job was a disaster. The gunners in the crow's nests took one of our chase cars straight out of the game, spinning it off to the shoulder where it slammed into a guardrail. A minute later it was moving again, but by then it was too late. The action had moved on. It limped to the rendezvous point, where we learned that the man in the turret—Vance Tyler, my gasman for a good half-dozen years—had caught a face-full of lead. Worse yet was the swingman, Paul Harrison. He'd worked behind the pit wall, wrangling air hose, and I think it was that more than anything else that caused him to volunteer to make the leap. He'd always longed to work the dangerous side of the wall. He miscalculated his jump and rolled up under the truck. The tires thundered over him, unwinding him like a ball of twine as Jack peeled away toward the exit.

Jack and I both took it hard. When we sheltered up at an abandoned garage, Jack told me he'd never matched speeds with the tanker. Paul hadn't had a clean shot at the running board. "Bullshit," Lola said later.

"Sure," I said. "Doesn't help *me* any, though."

"What do you mean?"

"Vance," I said.

"Well, don't cry about it," she told me. "Armor up."

We disassembled the gun turrets and rolled home under cover of darkness, just another band of gearheads testing the night air. We weren't hot, not yet.

While Jack calmed our client, my crew and I went to work on the cars. The biggest challenge was balancing speed and weight. Jack was used to hitting 200 on the straightaways of a fast track like Daytona, and that was with restrictor plates. The question was how to maintain that kind of velocity on a vehicle that weighed considerably more than 3300 pounds.

"That's the wrong question," Lola insisted.

"Then what's the right one?" I demanded one day in the garage. I'd been complaining about the weight and drag of the aluminum armor we'd begun bolting to the Dragon's exterior.

"How to achieve your objective," she said. "Speed is not your objective."

"Then what is it?"

"You want to snatch a forty-ton vehicle off the highway. What do you think it is?"

Me, I thought about Vance Tyler, and did just as she'd told me to. I armored up. I reckoned that top speed for a loaded tanker couldn't be more than a 100, 110 miles per hour on a long straightaway, and that without a convoy to slow it down. We had plenty of weight to give. We upgraded to rolled steel armor and we were still hitting 150.

Like I said, there's not anything I can't do with an engine if you give me enough time.

◇

Which is enough car talk. I could talk about cars all day long if you let me, but this story is about Lightning Jack, and how he finally went under the running boards himself. The next job—and don't worry I'm not going to belabor every one of *them*, either—went down outside of Baltimore. We scooped the tanker off 70 West and dropped it into Ellicott City. You have to understand, we never held on to the rigs for long. It was all very bang bang. Our job was to acquire and deliver. After that it was the customer's problem, and what they usually did was put it under cover somewhere quick and drain the tank into an idling fleet of smaller vehicles. But as I said, they could blow the thing sky high on the spot if they wanted. We didn't care what they did with it. We were in it for the cash and—this was true especially of Lightning Jack, I think—the thrill of the thing.

And there were plenty of thrills. I took the gunner's position in Lola's Spyder after Vance died, so when Jack said, "Let's ride, Gus," it had a personal immediacy I'd never felt before. A night job, this was, and in the dark you couldn't see much more of that car than its tail lights. There's tape of the raid, but the video has the cheap washed-out quality of CCTV, and in the dark it has no resolution at all. You can see muzzle flash as the team breaks cover, swings in behind the convoy, and takes out the crow's nests on the last truck in line. There's some return fire from the truck's escort vehicles, but most of them are farther up in the convoy, already out of play. There are maybe two bringing up the rear, it's hard to tell. But none of that can communicate the sheer adrenaline rush of being there. I took out one of the escorts from the gun turret on Lola's Spyder. The other one rolled and skated down the highway on its roof, throwing up a rooster tail of sparks.

Up ahead, Jack's car veered in beside the tanker and locked speed. The dark swallowed the swingman—Dean Ford, the front tire changer who'd volunteered after Paul kissed the deck—but I knew he'd made the exchange because the truck began to drift out of true. For ten seconds, twelve at the most, everything hung in the balance.

The trailer swung to the left and the right front wheels of the tractor started to come off the ground. I thought the thing was going to ditch and go skidding across the pavement on its side. Then it righted itself and hit the exit to Ellicott City, the chase cars on its tail. It nailed the street going maybe sixty miles per hour, and that quick it was over. Ten minutes later Jack makes the exchange with the client, and ten minutes after that, we're undercover in a bankrupt Toyota dealership on Baltimore Pike.

This is pit work, as exciting in its way as any tanker raid. The objective is to break the cars down as swiftly as possible—you can't cruise the streets in armored vehicles with gun turrets—and get the hell out of Dodge. My crew is fast. We've simulated this a thousand times, just like we did in the old days. The turrets come down, and roof panels slide into place. Street tires replace sticky ones. Off comes the armor. Everything goes into a chaser van. Fifteen minutes later we hit the street, and branch off onto different routes, running by night to a second rendezvous point, two hundred, maybe three hundred miles away, wherever Jack has us sheltered up until we do it all over again. And there you have it. The anatomy of a job.

If we'd only run the one, everything would have been okay. But there was no chance of that, not now. Jack loved to drive too much. As for me and Lola and the others, we loved the feel of an engine beneath our hands. There were just six of us by then. We doubled up on the road team and in the pits, doing half a dozen jobs each. We were all junkies and road dogs, hardwired for gears and adrenaline. I think that was what sustained us over the next nine months. I want to emphasize that. Months. You're reading this, you probably carry around a truckload of myths and misconceptions: that we had a ten- or twelve-year run maybe, that we pulled off dozens of jobs before Lightning Jack's last ride. The truth is, we pulled seven tankers off the street in all, four in quick succession before we garaged the cars and laid up in Memphis, safe from the Feds in the heart of the New Confederacy.

After Baltimore, Jack sent out thank you notes, leaking them to the news hounds. And sometime along the way—I think it was before number three, down in Charleston—he painted that incandescent lightning bolt from his NASCAR career down the rolled-steel armor on his hood. It was just like the old days: an express elevator to the top. His footage was playing every time you tapped a newsfeed. Like many race drivers, he was a little guy, Jack—5'10" and 160 pounds or so. That weight to speed ratio again. But he seemed like a much bigger man. He was as handsome as Old Scratch himself, and he inspired loyalty like no man I've ever seen. For a while, he kept a suite in the Adler Hotel, wearing his brand-new scar from the Tallahassee job, entertaining women and dining out on his notoriety.

But the New Feds had taken notice. We were plenty hot by then. Word on the street was that Buffalo was aiming to scalp us. After a month or so of jumping at shadows, Jack picked up the Heckler and Koch, a lethal-looking bastard if I ever saw one. Soon we were all sporting ordnance, pretending to be gangsters, or maybe not pretending, though in my heart I was never anything more than an old pit boss. But Jack still had a case of the nerves, so we moved shop to a farm outside of Little Rock. It belonged to Eileen Sheldon, one of Jack's girls from the NASCAR circuit, and if she'd put a few miles on the odometer since then, well, who hadn't? She was still a fine-looking woman—big boned and kind of rangy—and she took Jack into her bedroom that very night. More important, she had a big barn where we got to work upgrading the vehicles.

By then, Lola and I had started sleeping together. As I've said, I'd had a hankering for her all along—she was a petite kid, with dark hair and eyes so black you could catch reflections of yourself if the light hit them right—but like Jack, I'd known she had too much value as a jack man to even think about it. A crew is a finely oiled operation. The last thing you need is personal tension to gum up the works. But thinking wasn't part of the equation. A driver and his shotgun man have to trust one another completely, and a close brush with the grave—and every job counted on that score—left you with a yen for a little human warmth. When we reached the safe house after the job in Baltimore, we just kind of fell into the sack together. Nobody said a word about it, but after that it was understood: Lola Bridger was my girl. I count this as the biggest mistake of my life, but I couldn't know that then. And God I loved that girl. In my heart I love her still.

A gentleman doesn't speak of such things—and I don't intend to in any detail—but late one night we found ourselves futzing around alone in Eileen Sheldon's barn. The radio was playing some old dance tune, slow and easy, and we'd both had a beer or three too many. Me,

I was poking under Jack's hood, when Lola says something I don't hear. I straightened up to listen and, bonk, knocked myself dizzy on that rolled-steel armor. Next thing I know, Lola's saying, "You okay?" and we both got to giggling and one thing led to another and we ended up having it off right there in the hay. What I'm trying to say is, there was some heat in that relationship, if you take my meaning, and if neither one of us ever professed our love aloud, we didn't need to. It was understood.

We lingered three months on Eileen's farm, and it was a kind of idyll. Joe Hauser was a mean hand with a spatula. We ate like kings, and afterward Joe would sit back like a sultan and watch us wash up. Everybody but Jack took a hand in the suds. Nobody caviled either. Jack was a different order of being. It would be unseemly for the wheelman to dirty his hands scraping leftovers into the disposal. But Jack and Eileen had it sweet and steady, and so did Lola and I. In retrospect, I think that was the best time of my life. If I could have stretched it out forever, I would have. But all good things, right?

Jack wanted to drive, and he'd gotten some intel on a convoy coming out of Buffalo and heading toward Nashville. Everything Jack had predicted had pretty much panned out the way he said it would. The United States had splintered along lines geographic and sectarian—and these weren't always in agreement. The New Feds were trying to put down insurgencies on a half a dozen fronts. The insurgents themselves were engaged with pockets of New Fed loyalists in their midst who needed reinforcement and resupply: guns, grub, and gasoline. The convoys would have been impossible in another era, but the satellites were useless and the fighter jets had been grounded by particulates in the atmosphere. The air war was a joke, leaving the convoys to defend themselves against occasional skirmishes—and us. I was against the whole thing. I worried about Lola behind the wheel of the Spyder, and I was none too enthusiastic about taking more fire myself. But you didn't cross Lightning Jack, and besides, part of me wanted to see what the rebuilt vehicles could really do. I was a gearhead at heart.

The answer was, they did fine. We cut a truck free of the convoy on 65 South, just north of Bowling Green, broke down the cars, and hit the road again by nightfall, three hundred thousand New Confederate dollars richer. I think Jack sold the gas back to the New Fed loyalists who'd been scheduled to receive it in the first place, which was good for a laugh, especially when the update hit the newsfeeds. We pulled off two more jobs in the next two weeks: Raleigh and Frankfort. We were really hot by then, and we scooted for home under cover of darkness. A Fed patrol—maybe twelve guys armed with popguns and rocks—stumbled across us at the second rally point, but between Jack's G40 and five other buzzsaws we cut through them like a good wheel man cutting through the pack. By this time we were back in New Confederate territory, and we didn't face any more resistance on our way to Eileen Sheldon's farm. When we rolled up, Eileen was waiting at the door to meet us. We'd escaped pretty much unscathed—Lightning Jack was nothing if not lucky—though the iron plating on our vehicles had been dinged dozens of times and Dean Ford had taken a round clean through the shoulder. Eileen disinfected and packed the wound—Lord, I've never heard such a racket—but Dean pulled through. His arm was never quite the same, though, and his days as swingman were over.

Me, I hoped our days as outlaws were over too. And they were, though we didn't know it at the time.

For a while, the idyll resumed. We spent the stifling Arkansas days working on the vehicles. We ate Joe's cooking. Evenings it cooled down into the 90s. We sat on the porch drinking beer, while Lightning Jack lounged on the hammock strung between two big oaks out front. Everything seemed free and easy, but the truth was the Feds had turned up the heat on Lightning Jack. He'd heisted three tankers in three weeks, and they needed to stop the bleeding. Plus, he was more famous now than he'd ever been in his NASCAR days. Taking him out would be a coup for Buffalo, and it might curtail the ravages of Gallant Jim and Albertini and the half dozen other gangs that had sprung up in our wake. Worse yet, the rumors of undercover Federal agents that had forced us out of Memphis had started floating around in Little Rock. It was enough to make a man nervous.

Despite all that, Jack was anxious to get on the road again.

"I want to drive, Gus," he told me one afternoon out in the barn. He leaned against the hood of the Dragon and crossed his legs at the ankle. A shaft of sunlight pierced the roof—the barn had seen better days—limning him in a golden nimbus. The scar from the Tallahassee job was a vivid white streak across his forehead. A millimeter to the right—less even—and it would have splattered his brains across the rear window of his black Dragon. Sometimes I think it would have been better that way.

"Remember when we met? You blew that race on the truck circuit because you were too aggressive."

"I remember."

"Sometimes you got to know when to pit, Jack."

"I want to win," he said.

"Well, the stakes are a lot higher than they were in Daytona."

I didn't say it—I didn't have to—but the stakes were life and death. I didn't know how many crow's nest gunners I'd killed, but I figured in all that shooting I must have taken my fair share. And that didn't include the seven tanker drivers that had gone down, or the boy I'd shot in that New Federal patrol that had stumbled across us after the Frankfort job. I still remembered him. I favored an older daisy cutter, the G39-X, a predecessor to Jack's Heckler and Koch, but it was still lethal. It had cut that boy nearly in half, and I couldn't stop seeing that image in my mind—the shocked look on his face as the bullets tore into his midsection and his mortality dawned on him for the second or two it took him to bleed out. He probably hadn't thought about it before, not in any real serious way, and he didn't have long to think about it then. But you could tell it made an impression. He was the one who stuck with me most, but none of them were very far from my mind in those days. I couldn't lie to myself that I was merely a crew chief anymore. The knowledge of what I had become and what I had done sometimes woke me up in the night to gaze out the window into the dark rolling hills of the farm. When I'd showed up at Jack's gate after the Citizens' Militia had drafted me, I hadn't realized I was signing on for this.

Lola too seemed to be having some trouble coping—or that's what I thought anyway. She grew distant and quiet, and while she still shared my bed, there were no more good-natured tussles in the hay. Sex became perfunctory, a grim duty. It's not that I didn't love her anymore. But a river of blood flowed between us now, and we couldn't find a way to bridge it. We didn't spend much time in the barn together, and when we did we kept our conversation to the point: "Reach me that spanner, will you?" or "Can you give me a hand with the lift?"

I guess the rest of the crew must have known before I did—love can blind you that way—but no one said a word. You didn't cross Jack for one thing, but I think the true reason is that none of them wanted to break the glue that bound us all together. We'd divorced ourselves too much from the world for us to risk it. With those rumors of Federal agents in the air, even Little Rock was off limits. So we lived for one another, and we lived for the cars, and we lived for Lightning Jack. He was the most solitary of us all, I suppose. As the wheelman, he stood a step above his crew, isolated by his skill and by his fame and by the scar that forever marked his identity. The easy days of living in the Adler Hotel and making the social rounds were over. He was a marked man, and I think he knew that he was living on borrowed time. I believe that's why he was so anxious to hit the road and boost another tanker—it was the only time he really felt alive anymore. And I think that's why he started sleeping with Lola, as well. For the thrill of it, nothing more. To this day I don't believe he meant anything personal.

It was Eileen who finally broke the whole thing open for me, like lancing an angry boil. We were in the kitchen alone, chopping up vegetables, when she said, matter-of-fact like, "He's sleeping with her, you know."

In my heart I think I'd known it all along. When Lola came to me that night, I turned on my side and lay awake a long time, staring into the dark. I'd trusted Lola, sure. But I'd trusted Jack even more. I'd trusted our friendship, though he'd as much announced the truth himself, hadn't he? "I'm an amoral son of a bitch, Gus. I just want to drive."

But Lightning Jack's driving days were over.

❧

Which brings us full circle, I guess.

Jack didn't wind up puttering around his garden in the Upper Peninsula, and he never gave Victor Albertini any competition out in the Golden State either. But the conspiracy nuts are right about one thing.

The I-20 tape is a put-up job. You can argue that the video was manipulated, or even created from whole cloth, and don't think I haven't heard plenty of speculation along those lines. I've known people who could talk themselves blue in the face when it came to crash trajectories and video grain—and would, too, if you'd let them. But when it comes down to brass tacks, I agree with them. I've been around cars my whole life, and back in my NASCAR days I must have seen half a hundred crashes or more. Simply put, the overcorrection on the video isn't sufficient to cause the Dragon to roll. I know. I built the damn thing. The air dam was low and wide, never mind the weight of the rolled steel armor. The downforce on that car was tremendous. Even in the skid, those tires would have stuck to that pavement like glue.

But let's assume for a moment that I'm wrong. Let's assume that the video *is* real.

The question then is the matter of provenance. It can't be confirmed that the tape came in only half an hour after the crash. We have only New Fed assurances on that score, and the files remain closed. And what about the cleanup? Where are the investigators and where the glib network newsfaces doing stand-ups in front of the wreckage, their flawless features sculpted by the strobing blue and red beacons of the emergency lights? The most notorious outlaw of his era had just been killed. Where are the boots on the ground?

As for Lightning Jack, I did for him myself.

I suppose you've figured that out on your own by now, but I don't think any of us—even me—knew that I was capable of such a thing. Tension weighed heavily upon the farm by then. The sense that New Fed agents might any moment sweep down out of the hills was palpable, and we kept our weapons close to hand. After Eileen's revelation, Lola and I continued to share a bed. As long as she didn't leave, we could both—we could all—pretend it hadn't happened. But Eileen put Jack out of her room. Without explanation—he was the wheelman, after all, and he owed no explanations—he took to sleeping in the hammock, in the warm summer air. It was there that I did the thing.

It was nothing I had planned. I was drinking whiskey in the darkened kitchen one sleepless night, that's all, and I caught a glimpse of him through the window, dozing there. The knife lay in the drainer, close to hand. Without thinking about it, I took it and stepped outside. My foot fell upon the squeaky riser of the porch steps, but he didn't wake up. If he had, everything would have been different. We might have talked the thing through. I might have let his charm seduce me yet again. But he merely stirred, murmured something unintelligible, and lapsed back into slumber. He never knew a thing until I slipped the knife between his ribs—I can still remember just how easy it went in—and even then I don't think he believed it. He gazed up at me with a question in his eyes—a kind of wonder, I think, that I could betray him. He opened his mouth to speak, and I laid my hand across his lips. I leaned in close to his ear and began to slowly twist the blade, like a man tightening a lug nut.

"Shhh," I said. "Be still now, Jack. It's time to sleep."

A heartbeat passed, and then another, and then he did.

It's the rest of the thing I've never been able to figure to my satisfaction. We're entering the realms of pure speculation here, but I believe New Fed agents really *had* infiltrated Little Rock, and they must have been watching the farm for days, maybe longer. I slipped the noose, that's all. I hoofed it past dawn. Somewhere around eight AM I flagged down a bus out of Conway. I changed at the East Washington station in Little Rock, surrendering up a handful of cash for the first stagecoach out of town. It dropped me in Jackson, Mississippi, where I holed up in a cheap motel for weeks, living on vodka and takeout. As best I can figure, some time during that period New Fed agents must have taken the farm. I can imagine it all too clearly: the stark white flare of muzzle flash in the darkness, the hiccup of automatic weapons, the crew falling one by one, their bodies riddled by New Federal slugs—Joe Hauser, Dean Ford, and all the others, Lola most of all. I can see her lying in the doorway to the farmhouse, her arm flung out toward the still-smoking SAR bullpup she cherished, her body cooling as the sun rises over the Arkansas hills. I can see the blood. Imagination, I know, but sometimes imagination is enough. Sometimes it's too much, and I wonder that a man as practical as I am—an engine man to the core—should be cursed with so much of it.

The New Feds must have been furious at being deprived of their prize. Three months after I landed in Biloxi and nailed down a straight job—hydraulics, again—Buffalo released the tape and Lightning Jack's saga came to an end. But the oil raids weren't over, not yet. Lightning Jack had shown how the thing was done, and the Midwestern Alliance and the New Confederacy both had borrowed the technique, upped the firepower, and started knocking off entire convoys. The Feds—as Lola had put it to me in Birmingham all those months ago—armored up. Military escorts tripled in size, heavy ordnance came into play, and the tankers themselves became rolling dreadnoughts. Cutting one out of the pack was a suicide mission—as Gallant Jim found out in the Oak Park Massacre. Not two months later Federal agents killed Victor Albertini in the lobby of a San Francisco hotel. Mason, Cholewinski, and Smilin' Susie Samowitz all went down in the months that followed. The Age of the Gasoline Outlaw was officially over.

Me? I kept my head down and waited for the New Feds to come for me. They never did. It's been a lonesome kind of life these last forty years. There've been women now and again, but no one steady. I had too much road behind me to really settle down, and I don't think I ever did get over Lola. Now that I'm an old man, with eighty looming just beyond the horizon, I find myself thinking of her more often—and the truth is not an hour has passed in all those years past that I didn't think of her already. You probably reckon that I dwell on her betrayal at the end, but the truth is I think mostly of the good days that came before. There were a lot of those good days, more than our fair share, considering the circumstances. We loved each other with a ferocity and desperation that only the hunted can know. And more important still, we had the things we loved in common to bind us together—love of the pavement and the rolling iron that ran across it and the mighty engines that made them go. As for the betrayal, I don't blame her much. As I've said, there wasn't a woman on the planet that Lightning Jack couldn't charm out of her knickers in ten minutes flat. She never had a chance, and neither did I.

If I'm going to be honest about it—and I don't see why I shouldn't be—I don't think Jack did either. I guess I miss him most of all. I forgave him. I believe he was a prisoner: to his charisma and to his ego, to his skills and to his hunger for victory, and to the fame all those things together bought him. And despite all the harm we did—and we did great harm, I'll be the first to admit it; every night I am borne to sleep on a tide of blood—for all that harm, I believe to this day that Jack didn't have a bone of true malice in him. He just wanted to drive, and like a thousand other gearheads who cruised the night streets on black market gasoline in those days, he was going to find a way to do it. The only difference is that he was Lightning Jack, had been all his life, and couldn't find a way to stop being Lightning Jack. He was a competitor, he had to have a stage. He never could pit before it was too late, and in the end he got everyone he loved—and he did love us in his way, I'm sure of that—killed. I have many regrets about those days, but I guess what I regret most of all is that I wasn't there to take my final stand with Lola and the rest of them. I betrayed them all. I should have stood by my wheelman to the end. There is something sacred about the work that binds a crew together, and I profaned that bond, and I have lived too long with my regret. I'm glad the finish line is in sight at last. I don't think I could stand another lap.

Troop 9

Every Girl Scout knows that good homes make a country great and good; so every woman wants to understand home-making.

Scouting for Girls (1920)

Girl Scout Troop 9 went feral sometime in mid-July, during a camping trip in the lower Adirondacks. This happened just after the war, when the lean, hungry years of ration cards and scrap-metal drives were still fresh in everyone's minds, women had only lately returned home from the munitions factories, and a week-long idyll in the mountains, sleeping in tents and reciting the Girl Scout Laws, seemed like just the thing. Later it would become terrible, of course, but then you could hardly imagine such a thing, so no one objected when Scout Leader Betty Grishnam proposed the trip.

By this time the girls of Troop 9 had been together eight years or so. They were all fourteen or fifteen years old—they'd started together as Brownies—and they had grown up in a world without men, aside from those too old or enfeebled to carry a gun. The girls' mothers worked night and day riveting together massive flying fortresses and shipping them to the front, so the girls of Troop 9 spent virtually every hour together. They practiced the art of building campfires. They learned that the buds of the slippery elm were safe to eat, while the Amanita toadstool was not. They hiked the foothills for days at a time, until their muscular, brown thighs grew smooth and hard as stones beneath their skirts, and they could slip off the path and into the woodland murk as silently as shades.

When they met, they performed the Girl Scout handshake with their left hand and the Girl Scout salute—three fingers upraised—with their right. They were respectful to their elders and devoted to the principles of *Scouting for Girls*. They had been together so long by then that their cycles moved in synchronicity and they could almost understand one another without speaking. They no longer had much need to talk. On that first night in the woods, when they unrolled their mats around the fire to toast hot dogs, they sat in a companionable silence so complete that it faintly unnerved Betty Grishnam, who remembered her own girlhood days as a time of endless giggling about boys—which boys were cutest and which ones were funniest and which ones they liked best and why. The girls of Troop 9 didn't seem to care much about boys one way or the other, or if they did they didn't talk about it.

A full moon looked down through the trees, swathing everything in webs of shadow. Ann Miller's hot dog slipped off its stake into the coals. Susan Hardesty, who had been Troop Leader for as long anyone could recall, smiled, and a brief titter, not unkind, ran around the fire. Ann didn't seem to mind. She just skewered another hot dog and crossed her strong legs Indian-style before her. And Susan Hardesty? She bit into a hot dog without bothering with a bun, and when the grease squirted out onto her hands, she licked her long delicate fingers clean with the fastidious precision of a cat, her eyes half lidded with pleasure.

Something in Betty Grishnam shuddered to see it. "Susan," she said, "that's no way for a lady to eat." Susan smiled sweetly and apologized, but Betty had had enough. "I'm going to bed," she announced. "I expect you to be in your sleeping bags by ten." She was snoring raucously herself well before that, and the girls of Troop 9, sitting silently around their campfire and eating hot dogs, tittered once again.

A Girl Scout's Honor Is To Be Trusted

They had gathered to begin their expedition that day in the eye-splitting glare of the July morning, five cars wheeling one by one into the sunbaked parking lot of the A&P, where Betty Grishnam awaited them in her husband's old pickup. There would have been eight cars—eight girls to every Troop! *Scouting for Girls* dictated—but Ann Miller and Jo Anderson had spent the night together (they always did) and Susan Hardesty had met her Corporal, Louise Jackson, for breakfast at Simm's Diner to put the last touches on the week's activities schedule. They had walked the two blocks to the A&P together, swinging their packs with the grace of young girls poised on the brink of adulthood, still beautiful in their youth. You would have wept to see them.

No one could have imagined what would happen later, least of all John Hardesty, who'd been a corporal himself once, snaking up Omaha Beach as German 42s spanged off tank barriers, and men screamed and cursed and died all around him. His best friend—Frank White, who was twenty-nine, and had two daughters of his own—peering out from cover, more or less disintegrated in a scalding spray of blood and bone that Hardesty still felt on his cheeks some mornings. But he didn't talk about it, any more than he talked about the surrendering German soldier he'd spontaneously executed two days later in revenge. Blood for blood, he'd thought at the time, taking the German's rifle as a trophy, and if the equation didn't balance quite as well as he had planned—Hardesty didn't know what he regretted more, the blood on his face or the blood on his hands—well, some things you just didn't talk about.

But he wasn't thinking about that now. This morning he had nothing more on his mind than swinging by the rendezvous point and saying a quick goodbye to the baby girl he doted on—the baby girl who'd been all grown up when he got back from overseas and whom he still didn't really know yet. He'd already said goodbye once—he and Mary both—when Susan slung her pack over one shoulder and departed for Simm's in the gray half-light of dawn. Mary was pregnant again—better late than never—and Hardesty had his heart set on a boy this time around. He ached to teach a son to fish and shoot and throw a football. But there was something special about a girl: you wanted to hug her close forever because you knew what an awful place the world could be and how ill prepared she was to meet it. He sometimes thought it would be better if Susan would never leave home at all, but the truth was, she'd have a husband of her own someday soon, and probably a couple of little ones to boot.

His girl was growing up and the best he could do was stop by the A&P to deliver up one last piece of advice (again) and hold her tight for just a moment longer, which is exactly what he had planned when he slid his Chrysler into a spot by the little cluster of girls loading their gear into the back of Ern Grishnam's battered old Ford.

"Hey there, you gals," he called, climbing out of the car. "Suze here yet?"

Suze—she hated the nickname, but Hardesty couldn't break himself from using it—wedged her pack in with the others and turned to face him. Credit her with smiling, anyway, he thought. He could already see that it had been a mistake coming. He'd embarrassed her in front of her friends, but what could he do now? He'd set himself on the track and he'd have to follow it through.

"Hi, Dad," she said.

"Hi yourself," he said, pulling her into a rough embrace—if she'd been a boy, he'd have knuckled her scalp. "Watch out for yourself out there, okay?"

"I know what I'm doing, Dad."

"Well, see that you watch out for yourself, anyway. Okay? Promise?"

"Scout's Honor," she said, relenting at last. She flashed him the sign and turned away to help Kate Robinson wrestle a bundle of tent poles into the truck bed, and Hardesty just stood there for another heartbeat, looking on like an idiot, taken with his daughter's beauty—with all their beauty, really, standing golden in the sunlight, on the fleeting edge of childhood. "Listen," he said, "Can I give you a hand loading up?"

"We've got it, Dad."

"Sure. Right."

He smiled and waved at Betty Grishnam. "Take care of my girl, you hear?"

"You can be sure that I will, Mr. Hardesty," she said, and that was that.

Hardesty climbed behind the wheel of the Chrysler and spun it back toward the street. Betty Grishnam smiled at him as he passed. Neither of them knew just how wrong she was.

A Girl Scout Obeys Orders

When Betty Grishnam woke, late, with the sun casting wind-drift leaf shadows on the canvas of her tent, she woke to a silence so pristine that she knew in her heart—even before she skinned out of her sleeping bag and stumbled into the little clearing where they'd set up camp—that something had gone terribly wrong. According to Girl Scout procedure, the girls should by this time have been well into the process of policing the area—boiling water for oatmeal over the campfire, inspecting the tents, stowing gear and pulling on shoes for the day-hike down to the lake. None of these duties were especially loud, but taken together they should have produced at least a low electric hum of activity.

Instead, nothing. Nothing at all. Just the sound of the midmorning breeze rustling canvas and the call of a starling somewhere in the trees. And when Betty fumbled her way outside, her eyes confirmed her suspicions. The fire had been carefully banked, the equipment stowed, the tent flaps secured—but the girls were nowhere to be seen. Maybe they'd set off on the hike without her (they would never do that) or maybe they were playing some kind of mean-spirited joke on her (also not true, though she sometimes wondered about Susan Hardesty). But in her heart she knew the truth: the girls were just gone. And here was a further mystery, she realized, sweeping open the neighboring tent: they'd left their equipment behind. Knapsacks and walking sticks, snacks, shoes—*shoes?*—and clothes. Their clothes lay neatly folded atop their sleeping bags. *Their clothes!* And their sleeping bags had not been slept in.

They'd simply vanished.

And Betty Grishnam, who once upon a time many years ago had lost a child of her own, plowed back into the center of camp, her head lowered like a bull's with terror. "Susan?" she called, and then, louder: "*Susan? Louise?*"

Nothing. Leaves rustled in the breeze. Sweat beaded on Betty's forehead in the July heat and she could suddenly smell herself, the bright, glittering whiff of panic, as she staggered in a circle around the dead fire, cupping her hands around her mouth and calling their names until she was throat-sore and hoarse.

At some point—she'd lost track of time by then—the panic tipped over into dread and she found herself in Ern's old truck, bouncing down the rutted track toward town. By one, she'd alerted John Hardesty that their children were missing, by two the whole town knew, and by three the men were organizing a search party. It was four-thirty when two pickups—one of them Ern's battered Ford, which had already earned its keep today—jounced to a stop at the edge of the campsite. Twenty men spilled out of the beds, rifles in hand—though why they needed rifles no one had paused to consider.

Hardesty, with military precision, had divided the woods into a rough grid, although he knew with a heavy heart that these same woods—forest would really be the better word—extended miles and miles on every side of the town, climbing high into the Adirondacks, where they gave way to true wilderness. The men lurched into the trees, and the Girl Scouts, naked and streaked with mud, watched them blunder by. Their eyes sparkled with the fun of it. From a thicket of lilac, Susan Hardesty squatted on her hunkers and peered out at her father, hardly recognizing him as he searched for sign. She laughed, knowing they had left none. It was the best prank ever, she thought in a remote corner of her mind. They would go home tomorrow.

But when the men finally gave it up for the night, Troop 9, by silent consent, moved deeper into the woods, beyond the lake. Shafts of moonlight among the trees lit their way. They settled down at last in a grove of white pine. The thick-piled needles were soft, the flesh of close-huddled sisters comforting. Tomorrow, some of them thought as they drifted toward sleep. Or the day after that, for sure. But no one spoke and some of them thought nothing at all.

A Girl Scout Is Loyal

The next day, the search was more organized. Hardesty and the other men were forced to wait on the sidelines as cops scoured the campsite and the woods beyond. The police had laid out a tighter grid than Hardesty's, this one based on doctors' estimates of how far the girls could have gotten on foot. (Not far, was the official verdict, not on bare feet; none of them knew how often over the war years the girls had kicked off their shoes and hiked the trails around the lake without them.) And there were the dogs. "The dogs'll hunt 'em down," the sheriff told Hardesty. "You wait and see." But the dogs couldn't hold the scent, not as many times as the girls had crossed and re-crossed the network of streams that drained into the lake.

There was a single close call toward dusk, as a lone, deeply discouraged state trooper named Asa Wilson trudged back toward the desolate camp. The Girl Scouts had taken shelter in a blind of dead brush, and as Wilson passed, one of the girls—it was Kate Robinson—shifted ever so slightly, rustling the undergrowth. Wilson paused, turning. In the same breath, Kate froze. Wilson stood there, trying to puzzle out the shape in the gloom. Was that pale smudge a face? For her part, Kate endured a moment of intense longing. From the time they had melted into the woods that first night, driven by some wild consensus they understood no better than Betty Grishnam or John Hardesty would have, they had all sensed in an inarticulate way what they were becoming, and what it might cost them. Now, Kate had a sudden visceral understanding of what was truly at stake—an almost unbearable yearning to hold her baby brother one more time seized her—and she would have stepped out into the open had not Susan Hardesty's hand closed around her wrist. Kate felt then the titanic will of the troop bearing down upon her. It was a prank, that's all, she thought. The most wonderful prank in the world. They would go home tomorrow, or the next day, or the day after that, for sure. Until then, she would stay with her sisters. And so she held her breath until Wilson spat into the mulch, snorted, and pivoted back toward camp.

A moment later the oncoming night swallowed him, and the girls—they really *were* sisters, just as the Girl Scout Laws commanded—were alone again. That night they slept in a ravine on the far side of the lake. The next morning they were on the move again, and if Kate Robinson still nursed a spark of regret so deeply buried that even she no longer felt its glow, Susan Hardesty felt nothing but animal freedom, unfettered by thought or conscience, and the other girls, as they always had, followed her lead. So another day passed, and another, the men conducting their fruitless search around the lake, the girls effortlessly eluding them. They had learned their woodcraft from *Scouting for Girls*, and in their eight years together they'd learned the woods around town even better.

Two weeks passed, and then another. The case gradually faded from the headlines. A month later, just as the heat of August broke and Indian summer fell like a benediction across the land, the search was discontinued. John and Mary Hardesty grieved their loss deeply and long, and John often spent his weekends tramping the woods around town. Early in September the new baby—a boy; they named him Frank—was born. They were busier after that, but they still met with the parents of the other girls two or three times a week. And not a night passed that Hardesty didn't lay rigid and sleepless long into the morning, thinking about that other Frank, dissolved by a German buzzsaw on Omaha Beach, and the German soldier he had executed in retribution, and his lost daughter most of all.

Rumors of the girls still floated through town. They always would, Hardesty supposed. The Lost Girls of Troop 9. Ed Grier claimed he'd seen a pale blur in the underbrush as he fished for bluegill out on the lake, but everyone knew that Ed did more drinking than fishing out there most days, and most folks agreed that he'd poured his testimony out of the bottom of a fifth of Ten High. But it was harder to dismiss the testimony of Max Brock, a deacon down at the Baptist Church on Main Street, who claimed to have seen two or three girls scatter like coyotes as he topped a hill west of the lake, deer rifle in hand, or Fred Stockton, the assistant manager of the A&P, who said he'd seen a naked girl hovering in the stunted copse of woods behind the store one Saturday night. He must have spooked her when he stepped out on the loading dock for a midnight smoke. She'd disappeared into the shadows as soon as the door clanged shut behind him.

In any case, each fresh rumor gave Hardesty hope. Daily, hourly, he imagined Susan home again, holding her baby brother in her arms. And the occasional sightings haunted him. "Maybe it's just a phase," he said to Mary one night as she put his dinner on the table, cradling the baby in one arm.

"Maybe," she said as she sat down across from him. "Maybe it is."

A Girl Scout Is Thrifty

They were filthy by then, so grimy with dirt and mud that the whites of their eyes were startling to behold in the dim forest. Tangles clotted their hair, and the bottoms of their feet had hardened into pads of callus so thick that they could splash through a stony creek bed without so much as wincing. They moved without speaking among the trees, their feet silent in the bracken. An easy and unspoken understanding ruled them. They took their cues from Susan Hardesty. They were still when she was still, they moved when she moved, and their minds were as blank as midnight silence, when even the wind falls still and only the stars gaze down in their supreme indifference.

They were all sinew and muscle, ribs visible beneath their fleshless breasts. They slipped through the woods like deer, and they ate like deer as well: rosewood buds and apples plucked from midnight orchards in the deepest gutter of the night, wild onions and Indian cucumber excavated with work-toughened hands. As the season turned, they collected nuts—hickory and walnut, and the rare, yellow delicacy of the chestnut—and cached them away, clawing holes for them with ragged, dirty fingernails, and marking them with stones. They lapped cool water from the lake, covered their feces like cats, and marked their territory with hot streams of urine. They cycled as one, blood streaking their inner thighs. They exuded a deep animal musk that came to be as natural to them as the perfumed lotions and poultices of their former lives, dim echoes of this, their true and untamed condition.

At night they howled at the moon, and the townsfolk wakeful in these small hours cringed to hear them. John Hardesty would climb from his sleepless sheets and check on little Frank, pressing a hand gently to his breast to feel the thump of his tiny heart before turning away to test the locks on the nursery windows. Afterward, he'd stand shivering on the porch until the distant clamor died away. Then he would brew coffee and sit smoking in the half-lit kitchen, mashing cigarette after cigarette into a beanbag ashtray that they'd inherited from somewhere, he couldn't say or imagine where. The loss of his daughter had stripped his life of such petty details. By day he drove to his office and sold insurance to people who bought it out of pity and terror, inspired by his bereavement. In the evenings he drank Falls City Beer and ate the meals Mary set upon his table, barely tasting the food. And at night he held these lonesome vigils, until sometime in the dead hours before dawn, Mary would join him, her eyes rimmed red from midnight weeping. In little Frank alone they found some shard of solace. So they lived—a mere existence really—stranded on a narrow isthmus between grief and joy.

The season turned.

The leaves fell in their spendthrift beauty. In the woods, Troop 9 huddled close against the cold, and glided like wraiths through the naked trees. In town, Halloween came, but few parents risked their costumed children to the howling streets, and those who did squired them quickly from house to house, snatching glances over their shoulders for pale shapes that moved in the shadows beyond the bright circles cast by the streetlights.

In November, the first real cold spell clutched the town. Snow flurries drifted through the pristine air and the Girl Scouts of Troop 9 caught them on extended tongues, crying aloud with animal joy. They scraped lichen from stones and stripped the bark from pine and birch, elm and cedar, to feast upon the rich meat that lay closest to the wood. Then the snows came for real, driving icy storms that stung their upturned faces and piled in drifts against the trees. They nested in stands of tall pine, in bowls under the low snow-burdened branches where the scalpels of wind could not carve them up. When the lake froze over, they used stones to batter their way through the ice to the brutally cold water underneath. They grew thinner still. Their deflated breasts lay flat upon their chests, and their ribs ridged their flesh like the curving spars of a sunken galleon. During the days leading up to Christmas—a cheerless holiday in the Hardesty household and not even a ghost of memory to the girls—they began to push aside the stones that marked their stashes of nuts. For a time, their thrift paid off. But by the middle of January, they had exhausted even these feeble stores.

There were two months of winter left. They were starving.

A Girl Scout Is a Friend to Animals

The Girl Who Had Been Joan Brown saved them. Handy with a stone, she stunned an inattentive rabbit. The pack tore it apart alive, fighting like wolves for handfuls of bloody flesh. Afterward, in the vigilant dark, The Girl Who Had Been Susan Hardesty stayed awake to watch over the pack. There were only six of them by then. The Girl Who

Had Been Jo Anderson had sickened during the first bad cold spell, and died after three days of hacking up clots of blood, bright red splashes in the snow. And The Girl Who Had Been Louise Jackson had slipped upon a patch of ice and smashed her head against a stone. She died convulsing, leaking brain and blood from her shattered skull. Each time, the Girl Scouts of Troop 9, weeping in distress, had lingered by the bodies for days, poking them with sticks to prod them back into life, but the dead girls had lain unmoving, and at last the pack turned away, back to the forest and their own blank, animal lives.

The Girl Who Had Been Susan Hardesty alone nursed some dim memory of these losses. If they were to survive until the seasons turned again, she sensed, she would have to save them. And her impulses told her that the arm of The Girl Who Had Been Joan Brown could not alone sustain them. Not in the wild. They would have to go back.

In the dark, in silence, they returned. They stuck to the outskirts of town at first, raiding trashcans and scurrying back into the shadows if lights anywhere sprang to life. But soon, emboldened by success, their forays into the night streets grew more daring. They burrowed into restaurant dumpsters, feasting on a rich pottage of rotting meat and putrid vegetables. And then came the animals. The memory of the rabbit's bloody succulence, its entrails hot and pulsing in her cupped palms, lingered in The Girl Who Had Been Susan Hardesty's mind. The pack began to hunt. Cats fled their wild musk and dogs feared it—they erupted into wild barking when they scented it—but they were slow and fat, their instincts dull. And the pack was six. It was easy to box them in, stone them to death, drag them into the woods, and devour them even as the warm flesh cooled. The pack moved as one now, each to her place, without thought or hesitation. The pack was swift and vicious.

Even so, they were spotted. More than once an errant shotgun blast scattered them into the trees to regroup in the depths of the forest. And once again the town turned its mind to the problem of Troop 9. The mayor called a hasty meeting and summoned the parents of the missing girls. Troop 9 had gone too far. Pets first, children next, someone reasoned, and then reason was abandoned. Complex schemes to drive the girls deeper into the Adirondacks were proposed and dismissed as unrealistic, traps were discussed, and measures to lure the girls into them, but everyone knew that the pack was too wily by far for such stratagems. And at last the debate hinged, as John Hardesty had known it would, upon hunting the girls down. His mind turned to the dead German's rifle and he felt something like despair. *They're hardly human anymore*, someone shouted and someone else—it was Betty Grishnam, who'd lost her prized Chihuahua to the pack—screamed in something like despair, *They're not human at all.*

The meeting fell silent.

Ern Grishnam tried to pull her back into her seat, but it was too late for that.

"Point of order," John Hardesty cried, but even the parliamentarian could not stand before the ire of Betty Grishnam. She was already mounting the stage.

"I knew them," she wept. "I was their Scout Leader, I knew them better than anyone else in town. I tried to discipline them. I tried to tame them. I *tried*. But you don't know how strange they were. How they never spoke, how they moved to the whims of that Hardesty girl"—and here she plunged a blunt finger at John Hardesty—"your daughter, sir, and now you dare stand up and oppose me. During the war, when you were gone, and we were in the factories doing men's work, where were they? In the kitchen, cooking for their exhausted mothers? No! In the nursery, caring for their little brothers and sisters, the very children they now threaten to devour—were they in the nursery, sir? No! And when their mothers returned at the end of a long shift, were their houses—the very houses you came home to, sir—were their houses tidy?" And now her voice dropped to a whisper. "No, sir, they were not."

Hardesty stood, his hands outstretched. "Betty," he said, "If you'll just—"

"Let her talk, Hardesty," someone said into the silence.

But Hardesty, shrugging off Mary's hand, had started down the central aisle to the stage. Little Frankie began to cry.

That didn't stop Betty Grishnam. She merely cranked up the volume.

"Where were they?" she cried. "They were in the woods, roving like a pack of wolves! They were probably hunting the small creatures of the forest even then! I saw the way they looked at your girl, sir"—she swallowed as if she could barely bring herself to speak the next words—"I saw the way they looked at her body and the way she looked at them in return, so silky and smooth. They were probably doing—"

"Shut that baby up," someone said, and Mary, cuddling Frank against her breasts, slipped down the aisle and into the lobby, so she didn't hear the words that came next, words that Betty Grishnam nearly spat, they were so repugnant—

"They were probably doing dirty . . . *sex* things!"

She ran out of steam at last.

By then, Hardesty had mounted the stage himself. "And to think you were the one we passed our daughters' care into," he said.

"I tried," she said softly. "I gave those girls my all," she said, but Hardesty ignored her. He turned and looked out over the shocked crowd. "Terrible things have happened," he said, "terrible things. They have been driven by hunger and by . . . by instinct. By forces we can hardly understand. But they are our daughters," he said, and now the parents of the other lost girls began to nod their heads.

"That's right, John," someone said.

"They are our daughters, and we must not give up on them."

"You tell them, John."

"I beg of you— I beg of you. Give us some time, a little time. Spring is coming. Spring is just around the corner. Things will get better. They will not be so driven by hunger. They may— They may even come home."

On this note of counterfeit hope, he fell silent.

And because everyone knew Betty Grishnam to be riven with griefs of her own—for the dog, for the Lost Girls of Troop 9, for her own lost child most of all—and because deep down they sympathized with these friends and neighbors who had already lost their children, and most of all because they were fundamentally decent people, John Hardesty carried his point.

The mayor, an officious little man in a dark suit, cleared his throat. "I propose we wait," he said. "We can reassess in a month or so. Until then, care must be our watchword. Do not go out alone. Keep your pets inside. And keep a weather eye"—and now *he* swallowed—"keep a weather eye on your little ones."

They did as the mayor ordered. They did not go out alone. They kept their pets inside. And they kept a weather eye on their little ones.

For a time food was scarce for the pack. They were forced to keep to the dumpsters and the trashcans, but if they were seen skulking through the midnight streets, no one spoke of it.

March came. The snow melted and the first green shoots appeared on the trees. Reveling in plenty, the girls of Troop 9 once again retreated to the woods.

But in April they came back.

In April, things got worse. In April, they became very terrible indeed.

A Girl Scout Is Clean in Thought, Word and Deed

If they hadn't been teenagers—The Girl Who Had Been Susan Hardesty would turn seventeen in May and the youngest of them, The Girl Who Had Been Ann Miller, was already sixteen—things might have turned out differently. But they were in their sexual prime, and they simultaneously came into estrus, little suspecting or understanding what was happening to them. Yet at an almost cellular level they recalled the rich aroma of pheromones exuded by the boys they had once gone to school with.

Instinct once again drew them home.

This was in mid-April, just as the first daffodils began to bloom. The Girl Scouts of Troop 9 weren't forgotten—their occasional chorus of moonstruck howls ensured that—but the townsfolk, lulled into security by more than a month without incident, had let their vigilance lapse. They still kept their pets leashed and no one was quite deranged enough to let children wander around unsupervised, but high schoolers, heady with the spring weather and their own vulnerability to the pheromones everywhere in the air—prom season loomed on the horizon—were another matter. You couldn't keep *them* on a leash, though God knows enough parents had tried. Such were John Hardesty's thoughts as he stood smoking on his porch and thinking about his daughter: where she might be in the encircling arms of the vast woods and what she might look like now and what thoughts, if any, ghosted through the wilderness of her mind. She had kept him going in North Africa and Italy, she'd walked beside him during the weary march through occupied France—visions of her and Mary and the boy he'd hoped yet to have. And now she was lost to him all over again and probably for good. He would never get to see *her* in a prom dress, never walk her down the aisle, never cradle her children in his arms—so there was a special ache in his heart that season as the high school kids in their dozens waltzed by his insurance office on their way to school or stopped in for a milkshake at Moore's Pharmacy, across the street, when the bells rang at three.

That was almost the last place anyone saw Tom Anderson—a senior that year, a star in the classroom and on the gridiron, with a scholarship in hand from Brown, where it was preordained that he would quarterback the Bears to an Ivy League championship. That Tom Anderson. The previous fall, on an October night so clear and cold that you might reach into the heavens and snatch down a star, he'd directed a game-winning fourth-quarter drive against an arch-rival the town hadn't beaten in nine years. The final play? Tom Anderson on a forty-seven yard scramble to the end zone as the clock ticked down to zero: it had been a dazzling run, so breathtaking that the local sportswriter found himself stymied for words to describe it in the next morning's paper.

The pack put an end to all that, sweeping down a wooded embankment to snatch him from the sidewalk not two blocks from home. Their winter deprivations had served them well. They knew the secrets of the hunt in their bones. Be swift, be silent. Be, above all things, merciless and cruel—though by then the concepts of mercy and cruelty had passed beyond the ken even of The Girl Who Had Been Susan Hardesty. Driven by instinct alone, they lived entirely in the moment. They no more planned the abduction than salmon plan their run upstream. They'd been scouting the town for days by then, moving unseen through the early spring nights, waiting for their opportunity. Tom, flush with the overconfidence that attends great talent and beauty, provided it. One moment he'd been sauntering along the sidewalk beneath the great overarching maples just then coming into bud, his satchel slung carelessly over one shoulder as he dreamed a lazy dream of the way Allison Baker's sweater had pulled tight across her breasts at Moore's Pharmacy that afternoon—and dreaming too of the warm pressure of those breasts against his chest as he kissed her goodbye at her doorstep (the true last place anyone had seen him; Tom Anderson wasn't the kind of young man to let his girl walk home alone even if the woods *hadn't* been haunted by the howling specters of Girl Scout Troop 9)— one moment he'd been doing all that, and the next, those very specters had come screaming silently out of the dark trees to encircle him. For a single heartbeat, maybe two, Tom's vaunted scrambling abilities might have given him a chance to escape, but he was so shocked at what he was seeing—six lean, inhuman girls, their filthy arms and legs corded with muscle—that he did not react in time. When he did, feinting to his left, the satchel tucked under his arm like a football, it was too late. His mother's admonition—

—don't walk home alone Tom whatever you do—

—rang in his mind like doom as they hurtled down upon him, their long knotted hair swinging before their faces like veils. A confusion of impressions washed over him—the stench of them and their eyes aglitter with animal cunning in the twilight, their lips skinned snarling over their stained yellow teeth, and, most of all, perhaps, the graceful, curving talons of their fingernails, ridged with strength. Then he felt something crash into the back of his skull (it was a rock the size of a softball, though he never saw it and there was anyway nothing soft about it). A flare blazed up behind his eyes, and then he was plummeting down a long well. The light receded above him until it snapped abruptly out of existence, and Tom Anderson was gone. In his place rolled the deep, subterranean waters of unconsciousness.

As the other girls faded into the shadows, The Girl Who Had Been Mildred Allen and The Girl Who Had Been Kate Robinson seized him by the collar of his letter jacket and dragged him up the slope into the trees. But for his abandoned satchel and a smear of blood upon the concrete, he might never have been there at all.

Three hours later—three hours of endless, cuticle-gnawing anxiety—his mother was on the phone with Allison Baker. Yes, they'd been together and yes, Tom had been fine when he left and no, she hadn't heard from him since and was something wrong, Mrs. Anderson? Something was, something was terribly wrong, and in virtually the same moment that Tom's mother hung up to call the police, a distraught Allison phoned her best friend, Edna Kowalski, who told her mother over dinner who called *her* best friend Shirley Thomas, and so the news hop-scotched across town until the telephone rang in John Hardesty's house. It must have been 9:30 by then—late in those days for a call—and he had a sense of foreboding as he picked up the receiver.

Mary, cradling little Frankie against her breast, could tell from the clipped tone of her husband's responses—

"Yes."

"No."

"Of course."

—that something awful had happened, and she did not want to hear the words he would speak when he put down the phone. In the months since that ill-advised camping trip, she'd had enough bad news for a lifetime. Not a night passed that she didn't weep when the pack lifted their howling faces to the moon, and the mattress sighed beneath her as John stood up to leave the room and keep his lonely vigil.

He hung up the phone.

For a moment Mary had a wild thought that if she didn't ask, it wouldn't be true, whatever it was, but the words rose in her throat against her own volition. "What is it, John?"

"Tom Anderson," he said. "Missing."

"Missing?"

He said nothing. He sat across from her, holding his body stiff, like it might shatter if he moved too suddenly. He leaned forward and put his head in his hands.

"The police are looking for him now," he said.

"They're not saying—"

"Of course they are."

"But they can't," she said. "They couldn't believe—"

But the horror of it was, if she let herself, Mary could believe it, too—*did* believe it. If she let herself, she believed it all. She believed Ed Grier, despite the drinking, and she believed Max Brock when he said he'd seen the girls scatter like coyotes into the trees. She believed that Fred Stockton really had glimpsed a naked girl—maybe Susan herself—when he'd stepped out onto the loading dock of the A&P for his midnight smoke. She even believed that the Lost Girls of Troop 9 had hunted down the town's pets and eaten them alive, and might do worse yet. And she knew that John believed it as well, whatever he'd said at the town meeting. Those howls. Those awful howls in the night.

She squeezed little Frankie so hard that he began to cry.

Rocking him on her shoulder, she said, "What do they want you to do, John?"

"We're meeting down at the A&P in the morning. We'll help in the search, I expect. They'll want all the hands they can get"—and the irony of it struck him, that the fathers had been sidelined during the official search for the lost girls, while the resources of the entire community would be mustered to find Tom Anderson. He brushed a hank of hair off his forehead with one nervous hand, and looked up at her, forcing a smile. "He'll turn up," he said. "Probably snuck off with the boys for a beer and things got out of hand. It's that time of year, the seniors'll start sowing their oats. He's probably holed up somewhere sleeping it off. You wait and see. He'll turn up yet."

But he didn't believe it—she could see it in his eyes—and he was right.

Tom didn't turn up.

Even his satchel didn't turn up until the following morning, when Sam Rogers stepped out into the chill dawn air to walk his dog, a bullmastiff named Charger. As Sam saw it, neither one of them had anything to fear from a pack of feral girls. A veteran of Belleau Wood, the old man had taken to carrying his service revolver when the town's dogs had started vanishing in February, and, at a hundred and thirty pounds, Charger could take care of himself. Still, in the dim light, the satchel gave Sam pause. At a distance, he took it for a dead animal—a raccoon or a possum maybe—but dead animals held dangers of their own, among them rabies, so he approached it cautiously. Only when he drew near did he recognize it for what it had to be: Tom Anderson's schoolbag.

An avid high school football fan, Sam had last night gotten word that Tom had gone missing. Like John Hardesty he'd told himself that the boy had gone off on a youthful bender; unlike Hardesty he actually believed it. In fact, if Sam believed anything, he believed in a man's—any man's—ability to take care of himself, so finding the bag like that, spilling its freight of books and papers like the viscera of some slaughtered animal, shook him to the core. And that was before he noticed the brown stains on the concrete. He'd seen plenty of stains like that during the Great War (even now he could hardly believe that a second such conflagration had consumed the earth;

the long span of his existence sometimes seemed to him like a never-ending nightmare of carnage, this merely the latest atrocity), and he knew without a wisp of doubt what they were: dried blood. The speculation was right. Tom Anderson hadn't slipped off on some reckless binge, after all.

The pack had taken him.

Not an hour later, Sheriff Raymond Lewis stood in the bed of a pickup, brandishing the satchel before the host of armed men thronging the parking lot of the A&P. As Lewis described the bloodstains, a sulfurous murmur passed through the crowd, like a blighted wind combing tall grass, and Hardesty, clutching the rifle he'd pried from a dead Nazi's hands, sensed the colossal will of the mob bearing down upon him. The mayor clambered up beside Raymond Lewis. At the edge of the crowd, dogs strained barking against their leads.

The mayor stared dolefully at the satchel for a moment, and then he faced the crowd. "Ten months," he said, and the host fell silent, and his voice carried. "Ten months ago our daughters walked away into the trees. For reasons we cannot fathom, they abandoned us. Long we searched for them—for six long weeks we scoured the woods—and longer still have we grieved. We grieve yet. We will always grieve," he said, and it seemed to John Hardesty that their gazes locked across the crowd. They held like that for a heartbeat, and then the mayor turned away. He stared at his feet for a moment, and when he looked up, his eyes swept the multitude and seemed to hold every man there to account. "We will always grieve.

"Yet we cannot, we must not, we shall not live in fear of them. For a while we saw them now and then, haunting the edges of our town, and we did not fear them. And then we saw them no more. We ceded to them what was theirs and we kept for ourselves these orderly streets, where our wives fulfilled unmolested their most sacred duties to home and husband and child, where those same children played freely and without danger, where our men—*you men*—could daily depart to your labors without fear of what might await you when you returned. And so we might have lived for many years to come.

"And then they came among us again. They walked our streets and stole of our discards and we did not act. They took our beloved pets and we did not act. John Hardesty pled for time, and we gave him time. We surrendered even our streets to them. We imprisoned ourselves behind locked doors that they might live, in vain hope that they would return to us, the daughters we had lost. But they did not return. And now"—He reached out and took Tom Anderson's bag from Raymond Lewis. He held it high above his head and said—"And now they have stolen away our best and our brightest, our most brilliant light. We see here the bag he left behind. We have seen his bloodstains on the concrete not two blocks from the house where his mother waited dinner for him. We have seen all this, and my friends, my friends and neighbors, *this must not stand—"*

A cheer exploded from the crowd. It built upon itself until it rolled out of the parking lot to fill the streets beyond, an enraged chorus of *This must not stand!*—and this, this was the voice of combat and discord, of blood and vengeance, that Hardesty had come to despise, in others and himself. This was the voice of the rabble and the mob.

The mayor held up his hand for silence.

There was silence.

"We must scourge the land of these vile women," he said quietly. "While there's still time we must recover the young man who has been stolen away from us. While there's still time we must bring Tom Anderson home."

But by then time had long since run out. Tom Anderson was dead.

A Girl Scout's Duty Is To Be Useful and To Help Others

He'd been dead eleven hours by the time they found him, in a grove of tall, spindly beech, not two miles from the street where the Lost Girls of Troop 9 had scooped him forever out of the world of men. He lay on his back in the khaki chinos and the crimson letter jacket he'd died in, one arm extended, his fingers curled, his cheek flat against the damp foliage, staring through cloudy eyes out into nothing at all. As the little band of four men—John Hardesty among them—stood over him, a black and yellow centipede trundled across his cheek and disappeared into his gaping mouth. Someone—Dave Brown, by the sound of it—gasped and turned away. But John Hardesty did not turn away. Death had stolen all the grace of that dazzling run from Tom Anderson's young body—but a kind of beauty lingered. Sam Rogers would have recognized it—he'd seen it a hundred times at Belleau

Wood—and John Hardesty during his time at war had seen it, too, horrible to behold. Yet it fixed the eye: in death Tom Anderson had ceased to be human at all. He'd become a surreal artifact, made lovely by the strange eruption of stillness into flesh that had been so quick so soon ago, and by the striking juxtaposition of colors, too—the black earth, and the grass almost unbearably green in its thriving, and his alabaster flesh against it, and the wash of awful sunlight, moted and dim in its dapple beneath the spectral trees.

A scrap of poetry ran through Hardesty's mind—

—how do you like your blue eyed boy, Mister Death—

—and then one of the other men—it was Jack Thompson—said, "It was his head they got him," and all the grotesque beauty of the tableau was gone. How could he ever have seen such a thing, Hardesty wondered, thinking suddenly of Frankie, thinking of his boy. There was no beauty here, only obscene travesty, a mockery of everything sane and kind. The blood-streaked rock they'd done the thing with lay nearby, the size of a large man's fist. And the boy's skull—

Dear God, they'd crushed the back of Tom Anderson's skull into a stew of red pulp and curdled brain and shocking white shards of bone. My daughter did that, Hardesty thought, and though it had not been his daughter who swung the stone—The Girl Who Had Been Elizabeth Smith had done that—The Girl Who Had Been Susan Hardesty would have done it in her place. In any case, none of them had intended it, none of them had intended any of it, even at the beginning when they *could* intend and it had all been a lovely prank, a wonderful wonderful prank, the best prank of all pranks (had it ever been a prank?) and nothing more. Tom Anderson had come swimming out of unconsciousness to find one of the wild girls—it was The Girl Who Had Been Elizabeth Smith—caressing his crotch, that's all. Horrified to find himself responding, he'd scrambled away. The beautiful boy had tried to get away and The Girl Who Had Been Elizabeth Smith wanted to keep him. They all did. And in stopping him, she'd killed him. An accident, nothing more.

They were long familiar with death by then—two of their own had died, and they'd killed countless times over the long winter—so they did not linger to prod him back to life. That possibility was gone from their minds now. Even the concept of death was gone. There was merely life and not-life; Tom Anderson dead might as well have been a stone or a tree.

The Girl Who Had Been Susan Hardesty afterward hunkered at the edge of the glade and tested the air with flaring nostrils. Nothing and nothing and nothing. Not yet. But men—though she no longer thought of them as such; they were merely other than the pack (the pack was everything), and therefore dangerous—men would come. The instinct in her loins had decreed the boy's abduction. Instinct of another kind commanded her to abandon him, and so the pack slipped into the wood, leaving the not-life behind.

The men came hours later, not long after daybreak, tramping through the trees. It would have been easy to avoid them but for their sheer number—there were so many of them. The pack splintered before the human onslaught, each of them isolate and terrified and stricken with longing for her sisters. As a quartet of policemen lugged Tom Anderson out of the woods, the search intensified. Parties of armed men blundered through the underbrush, and the clamor of dogs once again rang through the woods. Not long after nine, Jim Bildridge dropped The Girl Who Had Been Mildred Allen down by the lake. The bullet took her in the throat; Bildridge stood by and smoked as she writhed in agony, clawing at her wound. It took her thirty-two minutes to bleed out. Bildridge timed it.

The Girl Who Had Been Kate Robinson was luckier. Perhaps the men in the woods fanned into flame that spark of regret that she had from the first day hidden deep in her heart; perhaps she thought once again of her baby brother, and though she was no longer fit to live among men and could not have been tamed even had she tried to do so—perhaps at some level she longed to return. Maybe that's why she exposed herself on a trail and stood unmoving before her killer. State Trooper Asa Wilson, who had spotted her in the brush so many months before and turned away uncertain, this time took no chances. A sniper in the war, he licked his thumb and tested the wind. Then he socketed the butt of his rifle in the hollow of his shoulder and put a bullet through her left eye.

One by one they went down: The Girl Who Had Been Elizabeth Smith, The Girl Who Had Been Joan Brown, The Girl Who Had Been Ann Miller, until at last only The Girl Who Had Been Susan Hardesty remained. She'd heard the shots echoing among the trees.

As twilight closed in, she fled toward the lake, lunging across a field between enclosing arms of woodland, the panicky terror of all hunted, haunted things hammering in her breast.

It was her father who spotted her.

John Hardesty had lagged maybe fifty yards behind his party—the other three men had crested the nearest knoll—when he saw her crossing the meadow below, a hundred feet away. "Wait," he said, and her sharp, wild ears caught the sound of the word, startling her. She wheeled about in terror to face him, crouching, her arms out flung, her matted shroud of hair swinging like a rope. And after all this time, John Hardesty still knew her. He knew the lineaments of her body, he knew the shape of her face, and though he could not see them from this distance and in this light, he knew even the color of her eyes—a midnight blue so dark they were almost black. He knew her, so long had he ached for her, standing on the porch and smoking as the pack howled into the dark, these children who had in another time been children of the light, and among them she who had been the child of his life in an age when the world had gone mad, and the best friend he'd ever known had peered just inches around the edge of a tank barrier only to be torn apart before his eyes by the thundering rounds of a German buzzsaw. He knew her, this the child of his heart, who had seen him through, who had once been, who was still and always would be, his daughter. He said her name, he said, "Susan."

They called out to something in her savage breast, those two syllables. She paused a moment, puzzling over them, and in that moment, John Hardesty had a chance to think it all through—the corpse of Tom Anderson beautiful in the grass, and his own son Frank, someday to be a man, and Mary at home awaiting his return, and all the women of the town in their houses in this blue twilight awaiting their men, lights coming on one by one against the night, and the smells of dinner cooking, these frail hedges against the horrors of the world men had made—and so he lifted the stolen Nazi rifle, sighted down the barrel just as his father had taught him, squeezed the trigger, and took his daughter down.

The End of the End of Everything

The last time Ben and Lois Devine saw Veronica Glass, the noted mutilation artist, was at a suicide party in Cerulean Cliffs, an artist's colony far beyond their means. That they happened to be there at all was a simple matter of chance. Stan Miles, for whom Ben had twice served as best man, had invited them to his beach house to see things through with his new wife, MacKenzie, and her nine-year-old daughter, Cecilia. Though the Devines had no great enthusiasm for the new wife—Stan had traded up, was how Lois put it—they still loved Stan and had resolved to put the best face on the thing. Besides, the prospect of watching ruin engulf the world among such glittering company was, for Ben at least, irresistible. He made his living on the college circuit as a poet, albeit a minor one, so when Stan said they would fit right in, his statement was not entirely without truth.

They drove down on a Sunday, to the muted strains of a Mozart piano concerto on the surround sound. Ruin had lately devoured most of the city and it encroached on either side of the abandoned interstate: derelict cars rusting back to the elements, skeletal trees stark against a gray horizon, an ashen, baked-looking landscape, though no fire had burned there. In some places the road was all but impassable. They made poor time. It was late when they finally pulled into the beach house's weedy gravel driveway and climbed out, stretching.

This was a still-living place. They could hear the distant sigh of breakers beyond the house, an enormous edifice of stacked stone with single-story wings sweeping back to either side of the driveway. The sharp tang of the ocean leavened the air. Gulls screamed in the distance and it was summer and it was evening, and in the cool dusk the declining sun made red splashes on the narrow windows of the house.

"I thought you'd never get here," Stan bellowed from the porch as they retrieved their luggage. "Come up here and let me give you a kiss, you two!" Stan—bearded, stout, hirsute as a bear—was as good as his promise. He delivered to each of them a scratchy wet smooch square on the lips, pounded Ben's back, and relieved Lois of her suitcase with one blunt-fingered hand. Ghostlike in the gloom, and surprisingly graceful for such a large man, he swept them inside on a tide of loose-flowing white silk, his blouse unbuttoned at the neck to reveal corkscrews of gray hair.

He dumped their baggage in an untidy pile just inside the door, and ushered them into a blazing three-story glass atrium. It leaned rakishly over the dark, heaving water, more sensed than seen, and Ben, as always, felt a brief wave of vertigo, a premonition that the whole house might any moment slide over the cliff and plummet to the rocky white beach below. Ceiling fans whispered far above them. Two Oscars for Production Design stood on the mantle, over a fireplace big enough to roast a boar.

Stan collapsed into a low white sofa, and waved them into adjoining seats. "So the last days are upon us," he announced jovially. "I'm glad you've come."

"We're glad to be here," Ben said.

"Any word from Abby?" Stan asked.

Abby was Stan's ex-wife—Ben's first stint as best man—and just hearing her name sent a spasm through Ben's heart. When the dust from the divorce settled, Stan had gotten the beach house. Abby had ended up with the house in the city. But the last of the city was succumbing to ruin even as they spoke. A gust of sorrow shook Ben. He didn't like to think of Abby.

"Ruined," Lois said. "She's ruined."

"Ah, I knew it. I'm sorry." Stan sighed. "It's just a matter of time, isn't it?" Stan shook his head. "I am glad you decided to come. Really. I've missed you both."

"And how's MacKenzie?" Lois asked.

"She'll be down any minute. She and Cecy are upstairs getting ready for the party."

"Party?"

"Every night there's a party. You'll enjoy it, you'll see."

A moment later, Mackenzie—that was the only name she had, or admitted to—descended the backless risers that curved down from an upstairs gallery. She was a lithe blonde, high breasted, her face as pale and cool and unexpressive as a marble bust. She wore the same shimmering silks as her husband, and nine-year-old Cecy, trailing behind her, lovely beyond her years, wore them as well.

Ben got to his feet.

Lois pulled her shawl tight around her shoulders as she stood. "MacKenzie," she said, "it's been too long."

"It's so good to see you both again," MacKenzie said.

She brushed glossy lips against Ben's cheek.

Lois submitted to a brief embrace. Afterward, she knelt to draw Cecy into her arms. "How are you, dear?" she asked, and Ben, though he despised cliché, uttered the first thing that came into his head.

"My how you've grown," he said.

Yet his life had in some respects been a cliché. His poetry, while not without merit, had broken no new ground—though perhaps there was no new ground to break, as he sometimes told audiences at the small colleges that sought his services. Poetry was an exhausted art, readers a dying breed in a dying age, and he'd never broken through anyway. His verse was the stifled prosody of the little magazine, his life the incestuous circuit of the MFA program, and he had occasionally succumbed to the vices such an existence proffered: the passing infidelity, the weakness for drink and drug.

His marriage had weathered storms of its own. If Ben did not entirely approve of Stan's decision—he had loved Abby, and missed her—he could understand the allure of novelty, and he was not immune to the appeal of MacKenzie's beauty. Perhaps this accounted for the tension in their suite as he and Lois dressed for the party, and when they departed, descending the cliff-side steps to the beach, sensing her discontent, Ben reached out to take her hand.

Down here, that salty tang was stronger and a cool wind poured in off the water. The sea gleamed like the rippling hide of some living behemoth in the moonlight. The sand seemed to glow beneath their feet. Everything was precious, lovely in its impermanence, for what was not now imperiled? And an image came to Ben of the gray towers in the once-bustling city, of men and women in their millions but blackened effigies, shedding ashen debris in the unforgiving wind.

Yet it was nothing to brood upon, this slow doom that the earth or fate or the God Ben did not believe in had inflicted upon them. Not now anyway, not with another set of precipitous steps to ascend or another house of glass set back a hundred yards from the brink of cliff-side annihilation, great windows printing flickering panels of light upon the still-succulent grass, and pouring forth the dissonant, tremulous notes then in fashion. Inside, in the darkness, the intersecting beams of digital projectors cast violent images upon every available surface—upon walls and windows and the faces of the people who danced and drank there. "This is Bruno Vinnizi's place—you know, the director," Stan shouted over the music, passing Ben a drink, but he needn't have said anything at all. The movies spoke for themselves, half a dozen stylized art-house sensations that Ben had seen in the last decade and a half.

Somehow, in the chaos, Ben lost Lois—he caught glimpses of her now and then through the crowd—and found himself talking drunkenly to Vinnizi himself. A blisteringly bloody gunfight unfolded across Vinnizi's fashionably stubbled cheeks. "I have been making movies about ruin for years," Vinnizi pronounced. "Even before there was a ruin, no?" and Ben saw how true it was. "So you are a poet," Vinnizi said, and Ben answered something, he didn't know what, and then, without transition, he found himself in the bathroom with Gabrielle Abbruzzese, the sonic sculptor, chewing jagged crystals of prime. After that the party took on a hectic, impressionistic quality. A kind of wild exhilaration seized him. He saw Lois across the room, sipping wine and talking to the tattoo-skulled frontman of some slam band or other—Ben had seen him on television—and stumbled once again into Stan's ursine embrace. "Having fun yet?" the big man yelled—and then, abruptly, Ben was squiring Cecy giggling across the dance floor.

Finally, exhausted, he reeled outside to piss. He unzipped, sighed, and let flow a long arc. A husky, female voice, deeply amused, said, "Something wrong with the bathrooms?"

Ben stepped back in dismay, tucking himself away.

A tall angular woman with razor-edged cheekbones and a cap of close-shorn blonde hair stood in the shadows. She was smoking a joint. He could smell its faint sweetish scent. When she passed it to him he felt the effects of the prime recede a little.

"I know you," he said.

"Do you?"

"You're the artist—"

She took a hit off the joint. Exhaling, she said. "This place is lousy with artists."

"No"—slurring his words—"the humiliation artist. Victoria—Victoria—"

In a stray reflection from the house, a car screeched across one of those exquisite cheekbones.

"Victoria Glass," he announced, but she was already gone.

The party climaxed at dawn, when the rising sun revealed how closely ruin had encroached upon the house, and Vinnizi hurled himself over the cliff onto the rocks below.

It was accounted a triumph by all.

They slept late and joined Stan and MacKenzie on the verandah for drinks at eleven. Piano and saxophone burbled over the sound system. Stan paced, sucking down mimosas like water. MacKenzie reclined in an Adirondack chair, her long legs flung out before her. She sipped her drink, watching Cecy at some solitary game she'd improvised with a half-deflated soccer ball.

"Did you have a good time at the party?" Mackenzie asked.

"Of course they had a good time," Stan said, clapping Ben on the shoulder, and Ben supposed he had, but the night itself came back to him only in flashes: blue smoke adrift in the intersecting beams of the projectors; the taste of prime sour on his tongue; the tall angular woman who'd caught him cock in hand outside the house. Her name came to him, he'd seen a piece on her in *The New Yorker*—Veronica

Glass, the mutilation artist—and he felt mortified for reasons that he could only vaguely recall. All this and more: the headachy regret that comes after any bacchanal; the image of Vinnizi leaping off the cliff onto the jagged rocks below. No sight for a little girl, he thought, and he recalled swinging Cecy drunkenly across the dance floor.

Lois must have been thinking the same thing. "Do you really want Cecy to see things like that?" she asked MacKenzie, and Ben could sense her struggling to reserve judgment, or anyway the appearance of judgment.

MacKenzie waved a languid hand.

"What does it matter anymore?" Stan said, and Ben thought of Abby, built like a fireplug, with none of MacKenzie's lissome beauty. Abby wouldn't have approved, but then she wouldn't have approved of MacKenzie either, even if the other woman hadn't stolen away her husband on the set of a failed summer blockbuster where her blank mien actually played to her advantage. Skill was a handicap in such a role; MacKenzie'd been little more than eye candy on the arm of the star, an aging action hero long since ruined himself.

A wind off the ocean lifted Ben's hair. He leaned over to peer through the telescope mounted on the railing. Near at hand, white-capped breakers rolled toward shore. Farther out—he adjusted the focus—the waves gave way to the cracked, black mirror of dead water. Moldering fish turned their ashen bellies to the sky.

"How long, you think?" he asked Stan.

"Not long now."

"It doesn't matter. No child should have to see a man throw himself over a cliff," Lois said.

"She's not your child," MacKenzie responded drily, and Ben straightened up in time to see Lois shoot him a look of disgust—with MacKenzie and with Stan for marrying her, and with Ben most of all, for standing beside the groom and collaborating in the disposal of Abby like a used tissue, and this after more than twenty years of marriage.

But what was he to do? He and Stan had been friends since their freshman year at Columbia, when they'd been thrown together by the vagaries of admissions counselors on the basis of a vapid form with questions like: *Do you sleep late or get up early?* He slept late and so did Stan. And they'd had the same taste for girls (as many as possible, as often as possible, and no need to be choosy) and for drugs (ditto). It had been a match made in heaven. Sometimes Ben wondered why Lois had ever been attracted to him in the first place. He supposed she'd wanted to save him. The same was probably true of Abby and Stan. But old habits die hard and in his peripatetic days, reading indifferent poems to indifferent audiences, Ben had fallen into his former ways: banging nubile English majors and chewing prime. At home one man, on the road another. Jekyll and Hyde. Last night Hyde had been in the ascension. And why not? Nero fiddled as Rome burned, but what else could he do, break out impotent buckets against the conflagration?

All this in the space of an instant.

"Here," he said to Lois, "why don't you have a look?"

"I've seen all I want to see," she said, but she strode over and gazed through the telescope all the same. She'd thickened in middle age, and Ben found himself studying MacKenzie, suddenly envious of Stan, who'd had the courage to throw it all aside. A sudden hunger for MacKenzie's raw sexuality—she seemed to glow with lascivious potential—possessed him. What had Stan said, when he'd called to tell Ben that he and Abby were done? *She's a fucking tiger in the sack, Ben.*

Stan shoved another drink into his hand—they'd moved to chilled vodka, it seemed—and Ben felt his headache retreat before the onslaught of the alcohol.

MacKenzie lit a cigarette. He could smell its acrid bite.

"Mom!"

"It's not like I'm going to die of lung cancer, sweetie," MacKenzie called, and Ben thought, no, none of us is going to die of lung cancer.

"You mind if I have one of those?" he said.

MacKenzie held the pack silently over her shoulder. Ben shook one out and struck it alight, inhaled deeply. Smoke drifted in twin blue streams through his nostrils. He'd smoked in college, but Lois had convinced him to give it up; it had become another vice of the road, indulged in frenetic after-reading parties. Playing the role of the dissolute poet, he used to think. That's what they wanted to see. Yet he wondered who he really was—if the persona hadn't become the person or if the persona hadn't been the person all along.

Lois looked up from the telescope. "It's terrifying," she said.

Stan shrugged. "It just is, that's all."

"It's terrifying all the same."

She set her unfinished mimosa on the railing. "I'm going in to make a sandwich. Anyone else want one?"

"Sure," Stan said.

And Ben, "Why not?"

She didn't bother asking MacKenzie, who, by the look of her, hadn't had a sandwich—or maybe any food—in years, if ever. The door clapped shut behind her.

Ben ground out his cigarette in MacKenzie's ashtray. "I've always wondered," he said. "What's your real name?

Stan laughed without humor and downed his drink.

"MacKenzie," MacKenzie said.

"No. I mean the name you were born with. I thought you'd adopted MacKenzie as a stage name. You know, like Bono, or Madonna."

"My name is MacKenzie," she said without looking at him.

Stan laughed again.

"Her name is Melissa Baranski," he said.

"My name is MacKenzie." Her voice flat, without emotion.

Wishing he'd never asked, Ben descended to the lawn. "Throw me the ball," he called to Cecy, and for a while they played together by some rules Ben could never quite decipher. *Stand here*, Cecy would say, or *Throw me the ball*, and between sips from his drink, he would stand there or toss her the ball.

"I win," she announced suddenly.

"Sure, you win," he said, ruffling her hair.

They climbed the steps to the verandah together. By then Lois had returned with a tray of sandwiches for everyone.

Later, he and Lois made love in their suite. Before he came, Ben closed his eyes. A blur of faces passed through his mind: the features of an especially memorable undergraduate, and then MacKenzie's affectless face, and the woman on the lawn last of all, Veronica Glass, the mutilation artist, kneeling before him to take him into her mouth. He felt something break and release inside him. He cried out and drew Lois to him, whispering *I love you, I love you,* uncertain whom he was speaking to, or why, and afterward, as she pillowed her head on his shoulder, that headachy sense of regret once again swept through him.

Later, they walked by the sea, waves foaming far down the beach. At high tide, the water would hurl its force against the stony cliff itself, undercutting it in a million timeless surges. It leaned over them like doom, unveiling the faint blue tinge that gave the colony its name.

He took Lois's hand and drew her into an embrace. "It's beautiful here, isn't it?" he said, as if by the force of language itself he could redeem the fallen world. But Ben had long since lost his faith in poetry. Words were but paltry things, frail hedges against the night. Ruin would consume them.

And it was to ruin that they came at last. They stopped at its edge, a ragged frontier where the beach turned as black and barren as burned-over soil, baked into a thousand jagged cracks, and the surf grew still, swallowed up by the same ashen surface. Digging their toes in the sand, they stood in the shadow of Bruno Vinnizi's ruined beach stair and gazed out across the devastation. Vinnizi's shattered corpse lay among the rocks, arms outflung, one charred hand lifted in mute supplication to the sky. As they stood there, the wind picked up and his outstretched fingers crumbled into dust and blew away, and the sea, where it still washed the shore, retreated down the naked shingles of the world.

As ruin spread, Cerulean Cliffs retreated. On the second night, Ben stood on the verandah and counted lights like a strand of Christmas bulbs strung along the coastline; in the days that followed they began to wink out. One afternoon, he and Stan hiked inland to the edge of the destruction: half a mile down the gravel driveway, and two more miles after that, along the narrow two-lane state road until it intersected with the expressway. In the distance, a soaring overpass had given way, its support pylons jutting from the earth like broken teeth. The pavement Ben and Lois had driven in upon was cracked and heaved, as if it had endured the ice of a thousand years. Businesses that had been thriving mere days ago had decayed into rubble. The arms of corroding gas pumps snaked across blistered asphalt. The roof of the Bar-B-Cue Diner had buckled, and the shards of its plate glass windows threw back their sooty reflections.

"Abby and I celebrated our fourteenth anniversary there," Stan said.

"We used to go there every time we came down," Ben said. "Best barbecue I ever had."

"It was shitty barbeque, and you know it. The company made it great."

Laughing, Stan unclipped a flask of bourbon from his belt. He took a long pull and handed it to Ben. The liquor suffused Ben with warmth, and he recalled his first liquor drunk—he'd been with a girl, he couldn't remember her name, only that she'd held his head as he puked into the toilet at some high school revel. After that, he'd vowed never to drink whiskey again. You had to learn to love your vices.

As they turned and started back, he snorted, thinking of Cecy and her soccer ball and her mysterious games upon the grass.

"What?" Stan said.

"Cecilia."

"She's a good kid."

"The best," Ben said, taking another swig of whiskey. He handed the flask back to Stan. They passed it back and forth as they walked. The blasted land fell behind them. The day brightened. The sky arced over them, fathomless and blue. Ben took out a cigarette and lit it and blew a stream of smoke into the clear air.

"You ever wish you'd had children?" he asked.

"I have Cecilia."

"You know what I mean."

"I had a career."

"What about Abby?"

"What about her?" Stan said.

"Did she want children?"

Stan was silent for a time.

"Ah, it was my fault," he said at last.

"What?"

"You know. The whole goddamn mess." He took a slug of whiskey. "We had a miscarriage once. I never told you. After that—" He shrugged. "She never forgave me you know."

"For a miscarriage? Stan, she couldn't have blamed you—"

"Not that. Cecilia, I mean. She could forgive the infidelity. God knows she had in the past. She never forgave me Cecilia." He looked up. "She always thought that was driving the whole thing: MacKenzie had the child she could never have."

"And was it?"

"No." Stan laughed. "It was lust, that's all. Simple lust." He shook his head in dismal self-regard. "I envy you, you know. Holding things together the way you have."

They turned into the driveway. Ben kicked a stone. A wind came down to comb the weeds. Somewhere in the trees a bird burst into song. The faint sound of the ocean came to him. Envy was a blade that cut two ways.

"What about you?" Stan said.

"What about me?"

"Kids?"

Ben finished his cigarette.

"It never crossed my mind," he lied. "I wish it had."

They'd reached the house by then. Ben went to his suite and lay down to sleep off the whiskey before the party. When he woke, the sun was red in his window, and Lois was reading in the chair by the side of the bed. They walked out onto the balcony and gazed at the ocean. The dead water had crept closer. He'd lost track of time. It all blurred together, the liquor and the prime and the multi-hued tabs of ecstasy spilled helter-skelter across the butcher block of a financier who'd filled her house with priceless paintings. Her taste had run toward the baroque—Bosch and Goya—and over the course of the party she'd slashed them to ribbons one by one. At dawn she'd walked out onto the lawn, doused herself with gasoline, and set herself on fire.

"Did you know Abby had a miscarriage?" Ben asked.

"Of course, I did," Lois said, and they stood there in silence until the first faint stars broke out in the dark void where ruin had not yet eaten up the sky.

∞

The parties were Ben's solace and his consolation: the photographer whose prints adorned the walls of her house, the painter whose canvases did not, the novelist who'd won a Pulitzer. Ben had met her once before, a lean scarecrow of a woman with a thatch of pink hair and a heart-shaped pinkie ring on her left hand: a brief introduction by a friend of a friend at a Book Expo party. "What are you working on?" he'd asked as she paused. "I subscribe to the teakettle theory of art," she'd responded. "Open the valve and the energy escapes."

Ben had nodded, taking a long drink of his gin and tonic. He leaned against the wall, trying to pretend he wasn't alone. He'd come for the free drinks—he always did—but he knew that nothing was ever free; you paid the price in the coin of humiliation. And that reminded him of his fleeting encounter with Veronica Glass, the "humiliation artist," as he'd called her. He'd seen her flitting through the crowds occasionally, tall and gamine with her cap of blonde hair, but mostly she lingered in corners. If it bothered her to be alone, Ben could not discern it. She observed everything with an air of bemused fascination, the expression of an anthropologist faced with a curious custom she had not seen before.

Once or twice, they'd even talked briefly.

"Hello, again," he'd said, as he squeezed past her in the scrum around the bar, and briefly he felt her taut body glide against his sagging middle-aged one.

Another time, she appeared ghostlike at his side, and handed him a joint. "I've had my eye on you," she said.

"You have?" he said.

"Are you surprised?"

"A little."

She smiled, remote and amused, the way you'd smile at a child. "Outsiders interest me."

"What do you mean?"

"In Cerulean Cliffs, you're either a rich artist, or you're just plain rich."

Ben thought of the financier who'd torched herself on her lawn, staggering about in screaming agony until she collapsed and the flames consumed her.

"You don't seem to be either," Veronica Glass said.

"I'm a poet," he said.

"But not a successful one."

"I make a living. That's more than most poets can say."

"But is it a good living? Does anyone know your name?"

"It offers me a certain freedom."

The freedom to write mediocre verse, he thought.

"Is that enough?" she said, "I mean for you," and of course it wasn't. He coveted the trappings of fame: the *New Yorker* profile, the Oscars on Stan's mantel, the trophy wives. In the night, as Lois slept at his side, he thought of Stan, stout and hairy, running his thick fingers down MacKenzie's long body.

He couldn't say these things to Veronica Glass, couldn't say them to anyone at all if you got to the heart of the matter, so he settled for, "It's what I have."

And then the lights blinked twice. Veronica Glass—that was how Ben thought of her—laughed and pinched off the joint. She handed it to him as the novelist announced that there would be an hour of readings—twenty minutes of her novel in progress (so much for the steam-kettle theory, Ben thought), followed by a young woman much admired for her jewel-like short stories, and a poet last of all. The poet, when he took the mike looked the part. He had a head of dark hair that swept back to his collarbones in perfectly sculpted waves, a voice that rang out across the crowd, a National Book Award. He was twenty-seven.

The lights came up.

"Do you envy him?" Veronica Glass asked.

"A little."

"Poetry makes nothing happen," she said.

"Does mutilation?"

"L'art pour l'art."

"Art moves me," he said.

And again she asked, "Is that enough?"

"Tell me," he said, "Where do you get the subjects for your art?"

"They volunteer. I have more volunteers than I can possibly use." She gave him an appraising look. "Are you interested?"

Before he could answer, he saw Lois across the room.

"Is that your wife?"

"Yes."

"What does she do?"

She was an accountant in the unruined age he did not say. He did not say that she read good books—books that moved her and said something true about the world—and that she loved him and forgave him his trespasses, which were many, and that that was enough. He merely smiled at her through the thump of music, the crush on the dance floor, the smell of sweat in the air. Veronica Glass lifted a hand to her in some kind of ambiguous greeting, but she was gone before Lois could wend her way to them through the crowd.

"That was Veronica Glass, the mutilation artist," he said. "You've read about her."

"I know who it was," she said.

Ben wanted to ask her to dance but they were too old for the bass pounding from the speakers; they'd lost their way. Sometime in the deepest trench of the night, a cry arose from the master bathroom. The music died. They all trooped up to look at the novelist. She was dead in the blood-splashed tub, naked, her arms flung out, slit from wrist to elbow as neatly as a pair of whitened gills. Her sagging breasts seemed deflated somehow, empty of life. Her pale face was at peace.

MacKenzie laughed hysterically, her knuckles to her mouth, her eyes bright with an almost sexual excitement. Cecy began to cry and Lois took her into her arms and hurried her home. Ben lingered as the party wound down. He watched the sun rise with Stan and MacKenzie. Afterward, they looked out over the wretched ruin that had already begun to engulf the writer's grounds. It crept toward them, turning the soil to ash. Flowers withered to dust. The guest-house sagged. They descended to the beach and walked home.

Cecy was sleeping. Lois had waited up.

Stan and MacKenzie went off to their bedroom. Ben and Lois heard MacKenzie cry out after a time. They wandered outside and sat on the edge of the verandah, legs dangling. Ben dug out the crumpled joint and lit it, and they looked out over the sea and smoked it together. Ben spoke of Veronica Glass, and Lois held a finger to his lips.

"I don't want to hear about her, okay?" she said.

They went into their dim bedroom. The sun cast narrow bars of light through the blinds as they made love. When Ben finished he thought of Veronica Glass; when he slept, he dreamed of her.

He dreamed of her awake and sleeping both. One more party, two, another passing encounter. She didn't always show up. He asked Stan about her. "She lives six houses down," Stan said, gesturing. "Crazy bitch."

"Crazy?"

"The things she does. You call that art?"

The last picture Stan had worked on had been a slasher flick. The usual: a bunch of kids at some summer camp, screwing and smoking dope; a crazed killer; various implements of destruction, the more imaginative the better. The virtuous survived. There would be no Oscars for this formulaic trash, Ben reminded him. And didn't it trade upon our worst impulses?

"It trades upon imagination," Stan said. "There's a difference between special effects and the genuine item."

He was right, of course, demonstrably so, yet—

Maybe not, Ben thought. Maybe special effects were worse. People thrilled to the mayhem on screen; they identified with the killers, turned them into folk heroes. No one thrilled to the work of Veronica Glass. Horror and fascination, sure—how could you do such things to a human being, and why? What had she said? *I have more volunteers than I could possibly use*. And worse yet: *Are you interested?*

And he was. The whole phenomenon interested him.

Beauty is truth, truth beauty, Keats had said.

Was there some terrible beauty here? Or worse yet, some terrible truth?

Or maybe Veronica had been right. How had she put it? L'art pour l'art.

Art for art's sake.

Perhaps it was these questions that led Ben to stray down the beach one day toward her house. Perhaps it was the woman herself—that blonde hair, those high cheekbones. Perhaps it was chance. (It was not chance.) Yet that's what he told himself as he mounted the stair to her house—a house like every other house along the cliff side: gray-stained shingles and acres of windows that threw back the afternoon light, blinding him, and suddenly he didn't know what he was doing there, what was his intent?

Ben started to turn away—might have done so had a voice not hailed him from the verandah. "The poet takes courage," she called, and now he saw her, leaning toward him, elbows on the railing. "Come up."

He crossed the lawn, climbed a set of winding stairs. She had turned to greet him, her back to the railing, clad in a sheer white dress. She held a clear glass with a lime wedge floating among the ice, and she laughed when she saw him. She brushed her lips first against one cheek and then another; they were moist and cool from the drink.

"So we meet by daylight, Ben Devine."

"How did you know my name?"

"It's no great mystery, is it? You're a guest of Stan Miles—and MacKenzie, of course. Dear, poor MacKenzie, and that lost child of hers. Who doesn't know you, those of us who remain, a weed sprung up among the roses?"

"Is that how you think of me, a weed?"

"Is that how you think of yourself?"

How was he to answer that question? How indeed did he perceive himself among the glittering multitude of Cerulean Cliffs? Stan had said they would fit right in—he and Lois—but did they? Ben had his doubts.

He opted for silence.

If Veronica—and when had that shift occurred exactly, when had she come to be Veronica in his mind?—expected an answer she did not say. Nor did she ask him if he wanted a drink. She simply put one together for him at a bar tucked discreetly into the shadows. He brought it to his lips: the tickle of tonic, the woodsy bite of juniper and lime. At first he thought that she didn't care about his response to her question, but then—

"Do you think the poet that read the other night—the one with the beautiful hair—was any better than you are?"

"He has the National Book Award to prove it."

"Is that the measure of success?"

"So it would seem. Here in Cerulean Cliffs anyway."

"What do you believe, Ben?"

"What's an artist without an audience?"

"I have an audience. They mostly despise me, but they can't look away. I have a raft of awards. Does that make me an artist?"

"I don't know. I don't know what you are."

"And yet you're drawn to me."

"Am I?"

"You show up at my home without invitation."

"It was you who spoke to me first."

Ben turned and rested his elbows on the railing. He finished his drink and studied the horizon. Ruin had crept still closer, ashen and gray, enveloping the sea. For some reason, tears sprang to his eyes. For the first time in months, he found himself wanting to write, to set down lines in tribute to the lost world—yet even this aspiration exceeded his meager talent, and he grieved that, too: that the poems in his mind slipped through his fingers like rain. He grieved the hollowness at the heart of the enterprise. Nothing lasted. Not marble, nor the gilded monuments of princes, shall outlive this powerful rhyme. Except that the rhyme too came to ruin in the end.

Veronica handed him another drink.

"It won't be much longer now, will it?" she said.

"No."

"What spectacular suicide have you devised?"

"None. I suppose I'll see it through."

"Perhaps suicide too is an art."

"That's the premise of your work, isn't it?"

"L'art pour l'art."

"Do you believe that?"

"I don't know. I suppose there is truth in what I do. The truth of ruin and death."

"You sound like Vinnizi."

"Is that what he told you? Poor Vinnizi. He was a fool. He made films about gunfights and car chases, that's all. The most artistic thing he ever did was hurl himself over that cliff." She paused. "Have you seen my work?"

"Photographs."

"Then you have not seen it."

"I'm not sure I want to."

Yet he did. In some secret chamber of his heart he yearned for nothing more, and when she turned away from him and started into the house, Ben followed, all too aware of the lines of her body beneath her dress. She turned to smile at him.

The door swung shut at his back. The air smelled of lavender. A whisper of air-conditioning caressed his skin. The floor plan was open, airy, the sparse furniture upholstered in white leather, and he was struck suddenly by the similarity to Stan's house—the similarity to all the ruined houses he had fled in the light of dawn. Only here and there stood white pedestals, and on the pedestals—Ben felt his stomach clench—Veronica Glass's art. A woman's arm, severed at the shoulder and bent at the elbow, segmented into thin discs laid in order, an inch between, as though the wounds had never been inflicted, the hand alone still whole, palm up, like Vinizzi's, in supplication. The flesh had been preserved somehow, encased in a thin clear coat of silicone; he could see the white bone, the pinkish muscle, the neatly sundered nexus of artery and vein. A detail from the *New Yorker* profile came to him: how she strapped her subjects down and worked her way up to the final amputation, sans anesthesia, applying the first thin layer of silicone at every cut to keep the volunteer from bleeding out. A collaboration, she called her work, and the horror of it came to him afresh: in the leg flayed and tacked open from hip to toe to reveal the long muscles within; the severed penis, quartered from head to scrotum, and pinned back like a terrible flower; and, dear God, the ultimate volunteer, the shaven head mounted on a waist-high pedestal, a once-handsome man, lips sewn shut with heavy black cord, small spikes driven into his eyes.

The room seemed suddenly appalling.

Ben flung himself away and staggered outside to the verandah. Downing his drink, he stared out at the sea and the encroaching ruin, and saw for himself the absurdity of Vinnizi's claim that all along he'd been making films about the end of everything. This was ruin and horror, this the art of final things. Then she touched his shoulder and Ben turned and she pressed her lips to his and dear God, his cock was like a spike he was so hard—

Ben thrust her away and stumbled down the spiral stair to the lawn. When he turned at the cliff side to look back, she was still there, standing against the railing, watching him. Her sheer dress blew back in some vagary of the wind, exposing her body so that he could see the weight of her breasts and the dark triangle of her sex. Another jolt of desire convulsed him and once again he turned away. He clambered down the stair to the beach, tore off his clothes and waded into the ocean, but no matter how long he scrubbed himself in the clear water that had not yet succumbed to ruin, he could not wash himself clean.

He told Stan of it; he told Lois.

His cigarette trembled as he described it. He drank off two glasses of scotch as he spoke and poured another. The bottle chattered against the rim of the glass. He had known the nature of her work, had seen the photos, had read the profile. Yet nothing had prepared him for the way its cold reality shook him. What had Dickinson written? I like a look of agony because I know it's true. And had any poet in his ken written a poem so true as Veronica Glass's work—so icy that it shivered him, so fiery that it burned? Was this not art, and did not his own work—the work of any poet or novelist, sculptor or composer—pale in comparison?

Ruin closed inexorably upon them. The parties became ever more frenetic. Suicides came in clusters now. One night, flying on heroin and prime, Gabrielle Abbruzzese slit her own throat at the stroke of midnight. The vast house rang with her otherworldly sonic landscapes, and she twirled as she died, her white ball gown blooming around her. Blood sprayed the revelers. Finally she collapsed, one leg folding under her like a broken doll's. Someone else seized the blade from her still warm hand, and then another, and another until the floor was littered with corpses. Ben and Lois watched from the gallery above. Looking up from the slaughter, Ben locked gazes with Veronica Glass, on the other side of the great circular balcony. She gave him an enigmatic smile and vanished into the crowd. The revel continued until dawn. Dancers twirled among the bloody corpses until ruin withered the privet and shattered the lawn; they made their escape as the land burned black behind them.

So passed the nights. The days passed in a haze of sun and sleep and alcohol. One boozy afternoon, Ben found himself alone with MacKenzie, watching Cecy in the yard. He made MacKenzie a vodka tonic and slumped beside her in her Adirondack chair.

"Have you given up poetry?" she asked.

"Yes," he said, and he thought of his impulse to set down some record of the dying world in lines, knowing how useless it was, how it too would come to ruin, and no one would survive to read it. He admired her body. She wore a bikini, and he could not help imagining the tan lines as Stan stripped it away and carried her off to bed.

"Why bother?" he said. "Who will survive to read it?"

"Perhaps the value of it is in the doing of the thing itself."

"Is it? Then why did you give up acting?"

"I was never really an actor," she said. "I'm not delusional."

She had been the star of a popular sitcom before her single disastrous attempt to break into film, the fading action star, the failed movie.

"I never really made it," she said. "Or if I did, I never was up to the challenge of real acting. I posed for the camera. The money didn't matter, not as a measure of artistry anyway. I was a poseur."

"That's more than I ever achieved. I was a poseur, too."

MacKenzie looked at him for the first time, really looked at him, and he saw a bright intelligence in her eyes, a self-knowledge that he had not known was there. It had been there all along, of course, but he'd been too blind to see it.

"I never read your poetry," she said.

"Who did?"

They laughed, and he felt that desire for her quicken within him.

Cecy cried out on the lawn. Her ball had plunged over the cliff. Ben retrieved it. When he returned, MacKenzie had moved to a towel. She lay on her stomach. She had undone the back of her bikini top, and he could see the swell of her breast.

"Why do you let Cecy attend the parties?" he said.

"I'm not a bad parent," she told him. "Her father—he was a bad parent."

"But you didn't answer the question."

She propped herself on her elbows, and he could see her entire breast in profile, the areola of one brown nipple. She looked at him, and he wrenched his gaze away. He met her eyes.

"I will not hide the truth from her."

"And in ruin is truth?"

"You know there is."

She lay back down, and he looked out to the sea, and even that was not eternal. "Do you want another drink?" he said.

"I'm positively parched," she said. So he made them drinks, and they drank until his face grew not unpleasantly numb and they watched Cecilia in the splendor of the grass.

Stan joined them as the shadows grew long and fell across the yard. Then Lois. The four of them drank in companionable silence through the afternoon. MacKenzie said again, "I'm not a bad parent. She has to face it the same as we do."

Lois nodded. "Perhaps you're right."

At the party that night—a sculptor's—Ben spoke with Veronica Glass.

"Are you ready yet?" she asked.

"I will never be ready."

"We'll see," she said, and drifted off into the crowd. Afterwards he sought out Lois, and they watched together as the sculptor put a sawed-off shotgun in his mouth and blew out the back of his head. A spray of blood and brain and bone adorned the wall behind him; if you stared at it long enough, you could discern a meaning that was not there.

They walked home at dawn.

Stan drifted ahead along the rocky white beach with Lois and Cecilia. Ben and MacKenzie fell back.

"Let's swim," she said.

"The water's icy," Ben said, but she slipped out of her clothes all the same. With a twinge in his breast, he watched the muscular flex of her ass as she ran into the water. She swam far out to the edge of ruin—he feared for her—before she flipped like a seal and returned. When she emerged from the foaming breakers, crystalline bubbles clung to her pubic hair. Her brown nipples were erect. She leaned into him.

"I'm so cold," she said. She turned her face to his and they kissed for a long time. He broke away at last and they walked home along the beach. By the time they reached the house and MacKenzie had showered and Cecilia had been seen safely to bed, Stan had laid out lines of cocaine on the kitchen table. The drug blasted out the cobwebs in Ben's brain. He felt a bright light pervade him, energy and clarity and a sense of absolute invulnerability. Somewhere in the conversation that followed, Stan proposed a change of partners.

"Yes, let's," Lois said, and that cool longing for MacKenzie possessed Ben. Then he thought of Veronica Glass, and he said, "I don't think I can do that, Stan." They went off to bed soon after. Lois had never seemed so desirable or his stamina so prolonged, and when he made love to her in their bright morning bedroom, he made love to her alone.

One by one, the Christmas lights along the coastline blinked out. The revelers dwindled, the parties became more intimate. Ben spoke with the poet, and they agreed that poetry was a dead art. Yet Ben was flattered when he learned that the younger man had read his work.

"You're just being kind," he said.

"No," the poet—his name was Rosenthal—said, reeling off the titles of Ben's three books. They had been published by university presses—small university presses, at that—but Rosenthal, who had been published by Little, Brown before Little, Brown decayed into rubble and his editor was ruined, quoted back a line or two of Ben's. Ben forgave him the National Book Award and his perfect hair, as well. It was all ruined now anyway, meaningless. Maybe it always had been.

That's what Rosenthal said anyway, and whether he meant it or not, it was true: as meaningless as Stan's Oscars or the dead novelist's Pulitzer or any other prize or accolade.

"And do you still write?"

"Every day," Rosenthal said.

Ben thought of Veronica Glass's dictum: art for art's sake. He proposed the tautology, knowing as he did so that even she did not believe it—that her's was the aesthetic of ruination and destruction and final things.

Rosenthal looked at him askance. "I write the truth as I see and understand it."

"And will you continue to write?"

"To the very end," Rosenthal said.

But the end was closer than he perhaps thought: the very next night, he and five others slipped into the black waves and under a full moon swam out to the ruin and ruin took them. As they pulled themselves onto the surface of the dead water, where the moldering fish had blackened into nothing, they became burned effigies of themselves, ashen. Over the next day or so the wind would disintegrate them too into nothing.

That was the night Ben saw Lois slip away into a spare bedroom with the frontman of the slam band, and whether she did it for revenge or out of despair or for some reason beyond his knowing, he could not say—only that he too had had his infidelities, and his was not to judge.

"And what will you do now that she has betrayed you?" Veronica Glass said at his shoulder. "Are you ready?"

"She has not betrayed me," he said. He said, "I am not ready, nor will I ever be."

They leaned against the bar, sipping scotch. She slipped him a handful of prime and they smoked a joint together, and the party degenerated into strobic flashes of wanton frenzy: he stumbled into an unlocked bathroom and saw MacKenzie going down on the architect who'd designed the Sony tower in Tokyo, long since ruined. He shot up with Stan in the kitchen. He found himself alone with Veronica on the verandah, looking out at the ruined ocean.

"Did you ever want a family?" he said.

She said, "Hostages to fortune," and he tried to explain that Bacon had meant something entirely different than what she was trying to say.

"No, that's what I mean exactly," she told him, and then he was lying on his back in the grass with Cecy, pointing out the constellations that ruin had not yet devoured. A great wave of grief swept over him, grief for her and grief for all lost things, and as he watched Rosenthal and his companions swim out to meet their ruin, he grieved for them, as well.

Afterwards, Ben threw up on the beach. Someone lay a cool hand upon his neck. He looked up and it was MacKenzie. No, it was Veronica Glass. No, it was Lois. He scraped sand over his vomit, staggered into the icy waves, and fell to his knees, lifting cupped handfuls of water to rinse his mouth until it felt clean and salty. He did not remember coming home, but Lois was in bed beside him when awareness returned. He whispered her awake. They wandered out into the vast glassed-in rooms, in search of drinks and cigarettes.

Stan and MacKenzie still slept.

Ben mixed gimlets and they sat out in the Adirondack chairs, their eyes closed, nursing their hangovers. Their lives had by then become an endless round of revelry and recovery, midnight suicides and daylight drinks on the verandah, grilled steaks, liquor and iced beer in the long afternoons, sex, drugs. Cecilia joined them for a while and then wandered off to the other end of the verandah to play some game of her own invention. She had the virtues and the vices of the only child—she was both intensely independent, playing solo games of her own devising, and profoundly dependent. She had been too early inducted into the mysteries of adult life and she had not yet the emotional maturity to understand them. She was prone to tantrums, and for inexplicable reasons, Ben alone had the ability to soothe her.

But today she was calm.

Ben turned his face to the sunlight. He held a sip of gimlet in his mouth and wondered when he'd last been completely sober—or when Lois had last been sober, for that matter. She'd gradually slipped into the world he lived in on the road, whether out of despair or some other more complex reasons of her own, he did not know. And regardless of what he'd said to Veronica, he did feel in some degree betrayed. But his feelings were more complicated than that. He felt too a renewed sense of physical desire for her. If she did not possess the beauty of MacKenzie—or Veronica Glass's aura of sexual intensity—she possessed the virtue of familiarity: he knew how to please her; she knew how to please him. Yes, and love, love most of all.

He reached out for her.

"Did you ever want children?" he asked.

She squeezed his hand. "It's sweet of you to ask. I used to, but—"

"But I wasn't the best candidate for fatherhood."

"No, you weren't. But you're a good man, Ben. I always believed that. I knew it, but it's a little late now, don't you think?"

"Stan and I were talking about it, that day we walked inland."

"And what did you see?"

"Ruin," he said. "Ruin and devastation."

"Yes. And any child we'd had, she would be ruined by now." Lois looked the length of the verandah. Cecy pushed along a miniature truck. She sang softly to herself. "That sweet child will be ruined soon enough. And think of the things she has seen."

"Sometimes— sometimes I think she's more equipped to see them than we are. It's part of her reality, that's all. She barely knows the world before."

"Do you think we're the last ones, Ben?"

"Does it matter? Someone somewhere will be. It's only a matter of time."

"And nothing will survive."

"Nothing."

"No, I think I'm glad we've been childless. We are sufficient unto ourselves. We always have been."

Ben heaved himself to his feet, went to the bar, and made them fresh drinks.

He stood at the rail and lit a cigarette. He recalled MacKenzie running naked into the moon-washed water and felt once again a surge of desire. The flesh forever betrayed you. He felt headachy and regretful and even now he could recall the shape of her body in almost pornographic detail. Yes, and Lois, too, slipping into the empty bedroom with the tattooed frontman of the slam band—Roadkill, that had been its name, and it too was ruined. And her hand upon his neck.

"Last night—"

"I'm sorry, Ben."

"No. I wanted you to know that I'm not jealous. I want to be. I should be. But the rules seem to have changed somehow."

He drew on the cigarette, sipped his drink.

"Yes, the rules have changed," she said. "There's a kind of terrible freedom to it, isn't there?"

"Your hand upon my neck. It felt so cool." He turned to look at her. "How did I make it home?"

"Stan and I practically carried you."

"And the stairs?"

"The stairs, my love, were an absolute bitch."

He laughed humorlessly.

"I remember opening a bathroom door to see MacKenzie—"

"You needn't bother. Last night became something of an orgy, I'm afraid."

"New rules," he said.

"Or perhaps no rules at all."

No rules at all. And what did that mean but ruin?

He thought of Rosenthal, writing every day, imposing a discipline of his own upon the world until even that collapsed into despair. Was not his own resistance of MacKenzie—or of Veronica Glass—a kind of discipline, a kind of personal rule, newly instituted. Maybe that was all you had in the end: the autonomy of the individual will.

"No," he said, "I have my rules still. Maybe for the first time I have them."

He ground out his cigarette in MacKenzie's ashtray.

"Is that why you wouldn't trade spouses with Stan the other night?"

"I don't know, I haven't thought it through. It just seemed wrong, that's all."

"Surely you want MacKenzie. I saw you kissing her."

He laughed. "I've wanted MacKenzie since the day I met her."

"Then why not take the opportunity? I wouldn't have minded."

"Maybe that's it. You wouldn't have minded. There was a time you would have."

She stood and came to him and cupped his face in both hands. She gazed into his eyes, and for the first time in years, he noticed how deeply green hers were, and kind.

"What a sweet man you've become, Ben Devine."

"I only love you," he said.

"And I you," she said. She said, "I'm sorry about last night. I didn't know."

"Didn't know what?" Stan said, pushing his way out onto the verandah. MacKenzie followed.

"What a capacity for drink you had, you old fool," Lois said with a sparkling laugh.

Stan dropped into a chair with a thud. He groaned and pressed a beer to his forehead. "Bullshit," he said. "You've known that as long as you've known me." He shot them a glance and shook his head. "Lovebirds, you."

"Lovebirds are entirely monogamous," MacKenzie said from the bar.

"Then you are no lovebird."

"Nor you, my dear."

"Nor any of us," said Lois, "except for Ben, monogamous in ruin."

"What's wrong with you, Ben?" Stan said.

Ben said, "I've always been monogamous in my heart."

"Your heart's not where it matters," Stan said.

"It's the only place that matters," Lois said. They were silent after that. Wind came in off the water. The last gulls screamed, and the red sun dropped behind the roofline of the great house. "Come play with me, Mommy," Cecy called from the grass. MacKenzie went down. They played a complex game involving the shrunken soccer ball. Ben could never decipher the rules, if there were any, but their laughter lifted into the air like birdsong, and that was enough. Waves washed the rocky shore; the sound of them was music. Stan broke out a joint and the three of them shared it as the summer day drew toward dusk. The air tasted sweeter then, and the beauty of all things grew sharper and more clear in its transience.

"So what shall we do tonight?" MacKenzie said when she joined them.

"Tonight Veronica Glass is our hostess," Stan said.

Carpe diem, thought Ben. He wondered what beautiful and grotesque death Veronica Glass had concocted for herself, and he took Lois's hand and held it tight. There was so little time left to seize.

As they climbed to Veronica Glass's cliff-side home that evening, they could hear the steady thump of music. The great windows pulsed with light and shadow. Wheeling scalpels of purple and red carved the dark. Reluctantly, Ben followed the others inside. He blundered through the crowd in revulsion, trying not to see the white pedestals with their grisly human freight. But he could not avoid them: colored lasers slashed the dance floor, and each bloodless piece had been illuminated by a blaze of clear light that exposed every detail in stunning clarity—every white knob of bone and gristle, every tendon, every severed artery, root-like and blue. The supplicating hand might have been begging him for mercy, the amputated head might have been his own.

Yet Ben felt something else as well, an almost sexual arousal that he could neither deny nor sate. He stumbled into the kitchen with Stan, where they snorted lines of coke and heroin that had been laid out on the counter-top. He poured himself a slug of eighteen-year-old

Macallan and drank it off like water; he smoked a flash-laced joint with a short, heavyset woman he had not seen before, a memory sculptor whose work had gone for millions before ruin took it all. Back in the enormous glassed-in atrium, he looked for Lois—for Stan or MacKenzie or even Cecy—but they'd all disappeared into the mob. He opened a door in search of the toilet, to find himself in a dim bedroom. Two couples—no three—writhed inside, on the bed, on the floor, against the wall. Someone—was it Stan?—held out an inviting hand. Ben reeled away instead, stumbled blindly through the orgiastic throng, and slammed outside.

He staggered down to the yard and stood cliff side, looking at the ocean.

Veronica Glass said, "It's quite the party, isn't it?"

"It's that all right. What madness have you prepared for tonight?"

"You started this, Ben," she said. "We chanced to meet on Vinnizi's lawn, nothing more. You're the one that wanted to talk about my work. You're the one that showed up uninvited at my door."

The wheeling lasers painted her face in shifting arcs of green and red. They illuminated the sheer material of her dress, exposing the shadows of her hips and breasts. Against his will, he found himself aroused all over again, by her or by her work, he could not say for sure. Probably both, and as if to deny this truth about himself—and what else was art to do if it didn't strip away our masks and expose us raw and naked to the world?—as if to deny this truth, he took a step toward her.

"It's anatomy, nothing more," he said. "It's cruelty."

"The world is a cruel place," she said. "Perhaps you've noticed."

An image of the sectioned arm possessed him, its imploring hand lifted like Vinizzi's hand. An image of the flayed leg, the head on its pedestal, its mouth sewn shut against a scream. An image, most of all, of the ruined and dying world.

His hand lashed out against his will. The blow rocked her. She wiped blood from her lip and held it up for him to see. "You prove my thesis," she said. And turning, "You could have had me, Ben. You saw the truth and you could have possessed it. It was within your grasp. Beauty is truth, truth beauty. Isn't that what you believe? Let me show you the beauty that lies at the heart of ugliness. Let me show you the heart of ruin. Let me show you truth."

She didn't wait to see if he would follow. But he did, helpless not to. Up the stairs. Across the verandah. Into the great glassed-in room. She touched a switch. The music died. The lasers ceased to sculpt the dark. The lights came up.

"It's time," she announced to the silent crowd.

She led them murmuring through a cleverly disguised door, and down a broad stairway. A cold amphitheater lay at the bottom. Enormous flatpanel screens had been mounted overhead, at an angle facing the audience. On the floor below them, gently sloping toward a central drain, Veronica had readied the tools of her trade: an x-shaped surgical table, upholstered in black; bone saws and scalpels and anatomical needles for pinning back flesh; rolls of clear silicon.

Even as Veronica began to speak, Ben knew with a sick certainty what she planned to do. "The body is my canvas," she said, "the scalpel my brush." Her audience mesmerized looked on. "I sculpt the living human flesh in ways that unveil to the unseeing eye both our fragility and our strength, our capacity for love and our capacity for cruelty. As ruin closes in upon us, let my art unfold on the canvas of your flesh: the glorious art of death—prolonged, painful, beautiful to behold."

She paused.

"I have a friend"—and here she fixed Ben, in the third row from the bottom, with her gaze—"I have a friend who equates beauty with truth, who believes that art serves something other than its own ends. I did not always countenance this, but my friend convinced me otherwise. For there is beauty in pain and in our capacity, our courage, to bear it. There is beauty in death, and in that beauty lies a truth, as well—the truth of the ruin that every day engulfs us, that has awaited us from the moment we came screaming from the womb, when we were hurled into a world indifferent to our suffering. In these, the last days of Cerulean Cliffs, we have seen our little assays in the art of death. I propose that you transcend these small attempts. We are all artists here. I challenge you to pass from this world as you have lived in it, to make your death itself your final masterpiece."

She paused.

Silence fell over the amphitheater, an undersea silence fathoms deep, the silence of breath suspended, of heartbeats held in abeyance. Ben scanned the crowd, searching for Lois—for Stan and MacKenzie, for Cecy—Cecy who had been born into a world of ruin and death. There. There. There and there. He feared for them every one, but he feared for Cecy most of all.

Someone stirred and coughed. A chorus of murmurs echoed in the chamber. A man shifted, braced his hands upon his armrests, and subsided into his seat. Veronica Glass stood silent and unmoved. Another moment passed, and then, because Cerulean Cliffs had long since plunged into desperation and despair, and most of all perhaps because ruination and devastation would soon overwhelm them every one, a woman—lean and hungry and mad—stood abruptly and said, "I will stand your challenge."

She walked down to the arena floor. Her heels rang hollow in the silence. When she reached Veronica Glass, they exchanged words too quiet to make out, like the wings of moths whispering in the corners of the room. The woman disrobed, letting her clothes fall untended around her feet. Her flesh was blue and pale in the chill air, her breasts flat, her shanks thin and flaccid. Silent tears coursed down her narrow face as she turned to face them. Veronica strapped her to the table, winching the bands cruelly tight: at wrist and elbow, ankle and knee; across her shoulders and the mound of her sex. Her head she harnessed in a mask of leather straps, fastened snugly under the headrest.

"What you do here, you do of your own will," Veronica said.

"Yes."

"And once begun, you resolve not to turn back."

"Yes," the woman said. "I want to die."

The screens lit up with an image of the woman strapped to the table. Veronica turned to face the audience. She donned gloves and goggles, a white leather apron—and began. Using a scalpel, she drew a thin bead of blood between the woman's breasts, from sternum to pubis, and then, with a delicate intersecting X, she pulled back each quarter of flesh—there was an agonizing tearing sound—to unveil the pink musculature beneath. The woman arched her back, moaning, and Cecy—Cecy who had known nothing but ruin in her short life—Cecy screamed.

Ben, startled from a kind of entranced horror, held Veronica Glass's gaze for a moment. What he saw there was madness and in the madness something worse: a kind of truth. And then he tore himself away. Lurching to his feet, he shoved his way through the seated masses to scoop Cecy up. He clutched her against his breast, soothing her into a snarl of hiccupping sobs. Together, his arms aching, they stumbled to the aisle.

"You have to walk now," he said, setting her on her feet. "You have to walk." Cecy took his hand and together they began to climb the steps of the arena.

There was a rustle of movement in the stands. Ben looked around.

MacKenzie, weeping, had begun to make her way to join them, Lois too, and Stan.

They were almost to the cliff side when the screaming began.

So ended the last suicide party at Cerulean Cliffs—or at least the last such party attended by Ben and his companions. Over the next few days they gradually shifted back to a diurnal schedule. Stan dug up an old bicycle pump to inflate Cecy's soccer ball, and they spent most afternoons on the lawn, playing her incomprehensible games. There was no more talk of trading partners. Their drinking and drug use dwindled: a beer or two after dinner, the occasional joint as twilight lengthened its blue shadows over the grass.

Late one morning, Ben and Stan made another pilgrimage inland. They traded off carrying a small cooler and when they reached the edge of the devastation—they didn't have far to go—they stretched out against the trunk of a fallen tree and drank beer. Ruin had made deep inroads into the driveway by then. The weeds on the shoulders of the rutted lane had crumbled, and the gravel had melted into slag. Scorched-looking trees had turned into charred spikes, shedding their denuded branches in slow streamers of dust. Ben finished his beer and pitched his bottle out onto the baked and fractured earth. Ruin took it. It blackened and cracked as if he'd hurled it into a fire and began to dissolve into ash.

"It won't be long now," Stan said.

"It will be long enough," Ben said, twisting open a fresh beer.

They toasted one another in silence, and walked home along the winding sun-dappled road under trees that would not see another autumn. Ben and Lois made slow, languorous love when he got back, and as he drowsed afterward, Ben found himself thinking of Veronica Glass and whether she had fallen to ruin at last. And he found himself thinking too of the poet, Rosenthal, who'd chosen ruin over discipline in the end, who'd surrendered up his art to death. *I write the truth as I see it,* he'd said, or something like that, and if there was no ultimate truth here in the twilight of all things—or if there never had been—there were at least small truths: small moments worthy of preservation in rhyme, even if it too would fall to ruin, and soon: Cecy's cries of joy and the sound of breakers on a dying beach and the gentle touch of another human's skin. Art for art's sake, after all.

"Maybe I've been wasting my time," he told Lois.

"Of course, you have," she said, and that afternoon he sat at a sunlit table in the kitchen, licked the tip of his pencil, and began.

No story is ever written in isolation, but I was especially fortunate in those who helped me find the straight path this time around. Nathan Ballingrud read and commented on drafts of almost every piece you'll find here. His judgment and advice through more than two decades of steady friendship have rarely been off the mark. Durant Haire and Jack Slay, Jr. also read and offered valuable feedback on most of the pieces here.

Robert Canipe and Christopher Rowe helped me track down a couple of endings that had gone astray, and my colleague Julie Voss blazed the trail out of a particularly thorny patch of plot that I'd wandered into. I am also indebted to the rotating cast of the annual Sycamore Hill Writing Workshop, which reviewed three of these pieces, and especially to its director, Richard Butner, who let me come out and play with the big kids. A special thanks goes to Neil Clarke, Ellen Datlow, Gordon Van Gelder, and Sheila Williams for keen editorial insights, and to Mark Teppo, who gave this book a home.

Most of these stories were written in the last three years at what constitutes blazing speed, for me. They came after a long spell in the dark--half a decade and more--when there were no stories to be had. Many, many people, friends, family, and strangers alike, helped me find the words again. I could not name them all if I tried, and there is anyway not enough space, so I will not try. If you are among them and you hold this book in your hands, you know.

It would be remiss of me, however, not to single out the three people without whom this book would never have been written at all. Jay Synn showed me the way back to the light. My wife and daughter were waiting on the other side. Laughter and love. Patience and resolve. This book is for Jean and Carson. Together, we keep the faith.

Dale Bailey lives in North Carolina with his family, and has published three novels, *The Fallen*, *House of Bones*, and *Sleeping Policemen* (with Jack Slay, Jr.). His short fiction, previously collected in *The Resurrection Man's Legacy & Other Stories*, has been a three-time finalist for the International Horror Guild Award, a two-time finalist for the Nebula Award, and a finalist for the Shirley Jackson Award and the Bram Stoker Award. His International Horror Guild Award-winning novelette "Death and Suffrage" was adapted by director Joe Dante as part of Showtime Television's anthology series, *Masters of Horror*.

"The End of the World as We Know It," The Bluehole," "Eating at the End-of-the-World Café," and "Lightning Jack's Last Ride" originally appeared in *The Magazine of Fantasy and Science Fiction* in 2004, 2013, 2010, and 2015, respectively. "The Creature Recants" originally appeared in *Clarkesworld Magazine* in 2013. "Mating Habits of the Late Cretaceous" and "Troop 9" originally appeared in *Asimov's Science Fiction* in 2012 and 2014, respectively. "A Rumor of Angels" and "The End of the End of Everything" both originally appeared at *Tor.com* in 2013 and 2014, respectively.